Buttermilk Book Publishing
Myrtle Beach, South Carolina
Copyright T. Allen Winn 2023
All Rights Reserved
This book is the product of the author's imagination.
Characters, the story and places are merely fiction.

Typecast Times New Roman
ISBN 979-8-9873669-2-9

AF504863

T. Allen Winn's

Absent on Arrival

1

We so looked forward to this vacation. She and I deserved it. This had been a tough year, career wise and a particular strain on our marriage. We indeed had some fences to mend to get our marriage back on track. Ten days away from it all, both of us had agreed to set business aside and avoid any related phone calls that might lure us back into the corporate web. I parked the car while my beloved retrieved an owner's luggage cart, accessing the cart storage room with our condo key. We had owned the condo for nearly seven years but rarely took advantage of it ourselves. It had proved to be decent rental property.

The first available parking place I could find had been on Level Six, four levels above where they kept the carts and the last parking level. I had dropped Mira off then decided to search for a parking spot. The hotel had ten floors. I felt a little guilty for Mira taking on this chore, but she had volunteered. I called her to let her know which level I had parked. Funny, she didn't answer. Sometimes cell phone reception wasn't the greatest inside these high rises and even poorer given the mountain location. I decided to wait by the SUV, figuring I might miss her if I tried to head her off at the pass. I began unloading the luggage and way too much other stuff we had brought. It looked more like we had planned to hibernate for a month. Oh well, most of this stuff should fit on the cart and what remained we should be able to carry.

Everything was now assembled on the garage floor, yet my dear Mira had not arrived. Of course, she hadn't dumb-ass I mumbled to myself; she doesn't know which level I am parked. Now I was in a pickle for my stupidity. I couldn't leave all this stuff unattended to go look for her and I couldn't see the elevators from here. This was lame even by my standards. I decided to at least walk over to the downward ramp. I could possibly see the elevators from there and keep my eye on our stuff. My footfalls echoed as I approached. Not a creature was stirring, even though the parking lot appeared close to maximum occupancy. It was not too unusual for our mountain resort this time of year. Many people ventured in the fall to the Great Smokey Mountains to take in the seasonal changes and the leaves vibrant colors. We had been lucky the condo had not been booked yet.

I ventured down the ramp, hopefully to glimpse the elevators. One thing for sure, no one could go up to the next level without passing by me. The elevators were located on the lower tier of every parking level, so I should be able to see anyone who might cross to my side of our parking spot. I could now see the breezeway to the elevators but not the actual elevators. Still, no one was out and about. I glanced at my watch. It was only quarter past eleven. Surely everyone hadn't called it a night. I tried her cell phone a second time. This time I reached her, or I thought I had. It was her voice mail. Well at least we had a signal.

"Hey babe, it's me. I'm on Level Six, just to the left of the ramp. Everything is unloaded. I'm presently near the bottom of the ramp. Take the elevator and I'll meet you here." Maybe she had gotten another call. We had an agreement. If she had, it better be social and not business.

Five more minutes elapsed. Was she playing games with me? She knows I'm not a patient man, especially not after a seven-hour drive to the middle of the boonies. Seclusion, it didn't get any deeper into the mountains than this; one two lane road in, nearly an hour drive through these hair pin turns, all for the price of privacy. It wasn't an all-inclusive. It had most of the amenities one would want without having to venture to the nearest town one hundred miles away to replenish supplies. You better have what you needed before you arrived. It was much too cumbersome to drive back out if you didn't.

Enough of this, I decided on plan B. I returned to the SUV, gathered what I could carry and lugged it to the bottom of the ramp. It required four more trips before I had accumulated everything in one spot. I locked the vehicle and rejoined the masses, still waiting for Mira and the luggage cart. Almost twenty minutes, where the hell was she? She could have pushed the cart up four levels by now. Plan C, I made the necessary trips to assemble our belongings next to the elevators. Our condo was the only one on the tenth floor. It was a luxurious penthouse suite. Possibly she had gone there before getting a luggage cart. It had been a long trip. Maybe she had required a bathroom break first. Knowing Mira, she probably started checking out every nook and cranny in the condo and had just allowed time to slip up on her.

There was nothing to do but load everything on the elevator and head up. We didn't need to check in since we owned the suite. There were two elevators, so it wouldn't be like I was hogging everything. One thing for sure, when I did get everything loaded, no one would be riding up with me. All the floor space would be taken. For the third time I moved the odds and ends, now more than ever convinced we had brought way too much stuff. To reach the penthouse required using the keypad on the panel and a unique pass code. This changed routinely but we had received the new one via email just a few days ago. I keyed it in, and the doors closed. The digital display indicated I ascended toward my destination. The door whooshed open to a foyer entryway. Another keypad adjacent to the suite's door required a second code. This was like maximum security to access. I keyed in the second code and entered.

"Mira, I'm home and I could use some help with this elevator full of our stuff." No answer. I called out a second time, entering and looking about, no signs of Mira. I heard that whooshing noise and whirled around to see the elevator door closing. I stood in disbelief watching the digital display take my hard work to the basement floor. After protecting it with my life it was now gone. I hoped it didn't fall prey to scavengers. As soon as it reached the lowest level, I keyed in the code on a pad located on the outside of the elevator, signaling its return. Almost immediately it did just that. I waited patiently for its arrival, hoping no one had hitched a ride for the return trip. The door opened.

"What the…?" The elevator was empty. No way, I knew how long it had taken to place everything inside. No one could have unloaded it this quickly. Maybe there had been several accomplices. Still, it had returned almost immediately.

Mira was going to kill me if I didn't locate our belongings. I yelled one more time, no answer. I entered the elevator and pressed the basement button. Down I plunged. I had never been to the basement before. Supposedly, it was the hub of life for the resort, out of sight and out of mind. Maybe some of the worker bees had unloaded our belongings, unsure what to do with them. That had to be it. In three more floors I should have my answer. Ground zero, the door whooshed open to sheer darkness. Immediately my senses were bombarded with a dank, musky, coolness. It reminded me more of a cavern than a basement. Why was it so dark? Even more disturbing, it was too deathly quiet. I could see maybe eight feet into the cavity illuminated by the elevator's interior lights. I peeked outside. It didn't improve my ability to see what might be out there.

"Did anyone out there unload my luggage? I'm Jay Myers. We just arrived. The elevator closed before I could unload our stuff." There had been no answer, no lights, nothing.

I strained to breach the darkness but to no avail. Was this some sort of sick joke? I'd have somebody's ass if they were *dicking* around with me. "Hey, come on, it's late. I appreciate a well orchestrated prank, but I'm in no mood for this foolishness tonight. We can keep it between us. I'll not report the incident to your superiors. What do you say?"

Not a peep, the outer region remained quiet and dark. What now, I wondered, still standing quite impatiently in the doorway? Obviously, I was getting nowhere. I pressed the Lobby Button, deciding to kick it up to those in charge. I had given them their chance. They had blown it royally. "Have it your way." The doors closed.

Jay watched the floors counting off until the bell sounded, he had reached the lobby. He exited left, heading to the desk, now puffed up like big old bullfrog. Jay resembled a bullfrog more than he would ever want to admit, more toad in appearance, than frog though. His head rested squarely on his shoulders, little sign of a neck. He was five feet, ten inches tall, big boned, but still nearly eighty pounds overweight. Jay didn't have a huge belly overhanging his belt line. Instead, he was more evenly proportioned, barrel chest, sort of a shorter version of *Tony Soprano* in the wise guy *Soprano* HBO series. He wasn't in bad shape for a forty-five-year-old who despised any exercise and had a chronic smoking problem. He had promised

Mira he would curb his nicotine habit. He had brought only a few cigars along and no cigarettes this trip.

Jay rubbed his hands through his comb over. Mira had tried to encourage him to just accept his balding condition and have his hair cut to do away with it. Jay wasn't quite ready to stare reality in the eyes. His nose looked too small for his face, causing his rosy, red cheeks to stand out as his predominant facial feature. He did have what Mira called, Elvis lips. Nothing else about him was a takeoff on the *King*. Jay counted his blessings often, to have someone like Mira as a wife. He wondered what she ever saw in him, but they had been together for nearly twenty years. She would be turning the big four-o this year, five years younger than him. It would be interesting to see how she handled that transformation, thought Jay.

Jay, now standing at the desk, searched for the night manager. No one was in sight. The lobby was void of human activity. In previous stays there had always been the usual hustle and bustle, even at this hour. He formed his lips into sort of a pout, completed another visual sweep, but still, not a creature was stirring. He could see the entranceway to the lounge but heard no music or buzz from the patrons. This was Friday for heaven's sake. That place should be jumping about now. He searched the desk, but it was void of a bell to ring. Come to think of it, he had never seen one, but there was always somebody manning it, so there had never been a need. Jay eyed the office doorway.

"Hello, is anyone back there?"

He paused and asked a second time, no response. Jay strolled to the opposite end of the desk and peered though the doorway. He knocked on the granite counter and hailed another call. This was just too odd. Possibly there had been some sort of emergency, he thought. That might explain the lights out in the basement. Surely, they would not leave the lobby desk unattended. He retrieved his cell phone and tried reaching Mira again. It went straight to voicemail. Taking a deep breath, he meandered in the direction of the lounge. All remained deathly silent. A chill ran down his spine. Something just wasn't right. Where were all the people? This was like one of those movie flicks where the entire population disappeared, except for a handful of survivors of course. Was he one of the lucky ones, he wondered? He certainly hoped so.

Jay cautiously stepped through the double doors of the lounge. No bartender manned the bar. No patrons occupied a single table. The small stage at the far end hosted an array of band equipment, minus the musicians. A banner boasted the band's name, *Afternoon Delight*, indicating they would be appearing nightly 10 P.M. until 2 A.M. Jay glanced at his watch, 12:07. They could be on break. That didn't explain the empty lounge. Surely everyone didn't go on break elsewhere. He needed a drink and was tempted to help himself but resisted the urge. He did decide to use the facilities and drain the snake. As everywhere else he had ventured thus far, the men's john was empty too.

Looking in the mirror as he washed his hands, Jay struck up a conversation with the man staring back at him. "Think, Jay. Where is everyone? Maybe there was some sort of emergency. That's it. Hey, it could have been a fire drill. Nobody does fire drills at midnight, get real. Besides, where is the alarm? Shouldn't there be a sounding alarm? Okay, this is a dream and I'm asleep in the car and Mira is driving. No, Mira hates to drive at night. It messes with her contacts. Who says it is night? If I'm dreaming, it could be anytime." Jay splashed water on his face and rubbed it around the back of his neck. "Just let me wake up, please."

2

Jay stood at the front desk a second time. Same as before, no one was around. This was just too spooky for a resort, apparently with near full occupancy based on the parking garage. He stepped through the opening and into the adjoining office. It looked normal. Several desks with computers, a coffee station, phones, all the stuff you would expect to see, except, absent of staff. Jay decided to roll the dice. He fingered one of the phones, examining the various buttons and their markings. One was labeled PA system. He was going to go out on a limb and try paging someone, anyone, to report to the front desk. What could they do to him? They were the ones displaying poor customer service, not him.

Here goes, "May I have your attention?" His voice echoed in the lobby. "Please report to the front desk. I need help, here." He waited for nearly thirty seconds. No one showed, nor did any of the phones ring. Time for something a little riskier, "Attention, someone is at the front desk stealing you blind. You better get here quickly." Jay almost regretted that stupid page the time it spewed from his mouth. He needed assistance, not an arrest. He received sort of a reprieve. No one responded. He retrieved his cell phone to try Mira again. Battery was down to the last bar; signal was strong though. He brought up recent calls dialed and selected the previous attempt to contact Mira. As before, it went directly to her voice mail.

"Hey babe, it's me again. Call me when you get this. I'm down in the lobby. You may have just heard me over the paging system. Something weird is going on here. I haven't seen a single soul, yet. What about you?" His phone beeped, indicating the battery was shot. Seconds later it went dead. Fear ran through his veins. Mira was among the missing too. Whatever had happened to everyone else might have happened to her. His breathing became labored. He fought off a panic attack. Jay eyed another room adjacent to the office. Entering it he realized it was walled with various monitors. This is where the security guard should be posted, watching the activities around the resort.

Each monitor was labeled with a location and each view changed providing various scenes from the floors, lobby, lounge, parking garage, the pools, and exteriors of the building. One thing remained consistent. No people were in any of the rotating views. Upon further examination he could freeze the view from any camera location if he so desired. One caught him by storm. He saw headlights of a vehicle approaching the oval drive out front. Too late to pause it on that camera, so he had to wait until it sequenced back trough. He pressed the pause button to view at that specific location when it did. Four people emerged from a sedan, two men and two women. He almost shouted out loud, his excitement at seeing actual human beings.

Jay rushed out of the office and into the lobby. He headed to the front entrance. The two couples were just entering the lobby. One of the men took a defensive position as he approached. It was then that Jay realized he must look like a wild man, arms flailing and a deranged grin on his face. He slowed his pace and mustered up a greeting. "Man, am I glad to see you folks."

The man relaxed his posture. "Are you the official welcome wagon?"

"I'm as close to one as you will receive."

"Bobby, what's with this guy," asked one of the women. "He's a little too weird for my taste."

"Yeah fellow, what's your story?"

"Sorry, I didn't mean to scare you folks. My name is Jay Myers. I just arrived about an hour ago."

"Congratulations for arriving safely," spoke the second man. "So, what's up with the meet and greet routine?"

"You're probably going to think I'm crazy."

"Way ahead of you, we're already leaning in that direction," said Bobby.

"Then what I'm about to tell you isn't going to paint a better picture."

"Bobby, I don't like this guy," said one of the ladies.

"Please, just bear with me. Like I said, I've been here just over an hour. My wife and I arrived, and while I searched for a parking spot, I dropped Mira off to retrieve a luggage cart. That was the last time I saw her. She hasn't answered her cell phone."

"Look buddy. We really don't want to get involved with you and your wife's marital problems," said the second man.

"Just hear me out. I haven't been able to find anyone. The place is like…I don't know…deserted. I was watching the security cameras when I saw your car arriving."

"Whoa, you were watching us on the resort's cameras. What sort of pervert are you," asked Bobby.

"You've got the wrong idea. I only took liberty to go into the office when no one was manning the front desk. The lounge was empty too. I didn't see a living soul on any of the monitors, zilch, all levels, and all locations. We're it."

"You're trying to tell us that this place is unoccupied this time of year. No way, this joint is always booked when the leaves change colors."

"I didn't say it wasn't booked. The parking garage is jam-packed full of automobiles. I had a tough time finding a parking space. What I'm trying to tell you is I can't find anybody, including any of the resort staff. My wife, Mira is missing too."

"Is this some sort of Halloween prank, buddy? Trick or Treat, we give. Now please step out of the way so we can get checked in, how about it?"

"Good luck, suit yourself. You let me know how that goes for you. You don't mind if I tag along, do you?"

"It's a free country," said the other guy, "Just mind your own business and everything will be fine."

Jay nodded and decided to have a seat in one of the lobby chairs close to the front desk. He watched and he waited. In less than five minutes the two guys had reached their boiling point, cattle prodded along by the ladies who were ready to check in and call it a night. Jay sat patiently. Finally, the one called Bobby walked over and boisterously asked, "What in the hell is going on here?'

"You tell me, wise guy. I'm staying out of your way as requested."

"I get it. I get it. Okay, so what do you think has happened?"

"That's just it. I have no clue. You've seen the same thing I've been seeing. Everyone has vanished."

"Get real, how about it. A resort full of people doesn't just up and disappear."

"Okay, smart guy, you tell me where the hell they are. I haven't conducted a room by room search, but maybe we should."

"Maybe we should just call security."

"Security isn't manning the cameras. If they were making any rounds, surely, they should be back by now. That doesn't explain the lobby and lounge being deserted. This is Friday night. This place should be hoping with activity. There's supposed to be a band playing in the lounge. Guess what, the band is missing in action too."

"Maybe we should try this again, Jay. I'm Bobby McAlister. The redhead over there is my wife, Marge. That's Dean and Chrissie Waldrop. Chrissie is Marge's sister. This is our first time up here. We're from Wilson, North Carolina. Dean and Chrissie live in Greensboro. We picked them up on our way here. So, what gives?"

"Like I've told you, I have no idea. We own a suite but haven't used it in about three years. We use it for rental property, and it is booked more times than not. We were lucky to block it out for us during the leaf changing season. It's eerie. I don't like it. Something is up. It just doesn't seem like a natural phenomenon to me. Listen to me. I sound like one of those investigators on *A&E*, the ones that investigate paranormal activity or hunt for Bigfoot."

"What do we do now?" asked Jay.

"I'm open for suggestions. Like I said, I've been snooping about and have come up empty."

"Maybe we should see how many people have checked in this place for starters. Shouldn't they have a guess sign-in ledger," suggested Dean.

"I don't think they use them anymore. Everything is done on computer," replied Jay.

"Then why don't we check out the computer. It's not like someone is going to bust us for doing it," suggested Bobby.

"I think most require a password, but I suppose it wouldn't hurt to take a look," added Jay.

"Maybe we should call 911 instead," suggested Dean.

"The nearest town is too far away. I wouldn't expect them to have 911 services here," responded Jay. "What the hell give it a try?"

"My phone is dead. Battery must be shot," said Dean.

"Mine just expired before you folks arrived."

"I should have a full charge. I had mine on recharge in the car before we arrived," added Bobby, retrieving his from the belt clip. "Odd, mine is dead too. Charger must have some sort of shortage in it. Hey, girls, check yours."

"Mine will not even come on," replied Chrissie.

"Same here," said Marge, "And I know mine had a full charge. I just texted Tabitha Prince just minutes before we arrived. Come to think of it, she never texted me back though."

Dean picked up the phone from the lobby desk. There was no dial tone. He pressed various buttons. Nothing happened. Remembering Jay, having said he used the page system, he pressed that button and spoke into the phone. Nothing happened. The computer screen nearest him was black. He checked two others, same condition.

"I say let's get the hell out of here," announced Bobby.

"I can't leave. Mira is missing."

"Tell you what," said Bobby, "Once we get back to civilization, we'll tell the local police. We wish you well, man."

The four exited the lobby. Jay again found himself alone and still confused. He mentally mapped out his next move. He decided it was time to knock on a few room doors. There were none on this floor, so he headed toward the elevator. Halfway there he heard footfalls. He turned to see the two couples had returned. The expressions on their faces told him there was trouble afoot.

"Our car won't start," stated Bobby. "The battery is deader than hell, just like our cell phones. What's going on up here?"

Jay shrugged. None of it made any sense. Something had impacted the batteries. What would suck the life out of all these batteries? Without thinking he pressed the elevator button. Nothing happened. The digital display above the door was not working. The elevator had powered down. He tried two other elevators, same scenario. The phones, computers and now the elevator were out. Luckily, the lights were still burning. He should never have thought that thought. The lobby was suddenly launched into complete darkness.

"What's going on," screamed Chrissie.

"Just hold onto my arm. I'm right here," replied Marge.

"We're here too," chimed in Dean and Bobby, simultaneously.

"Keep talking. I'll come to you," shouted Jay, flicking on his butane lighter.

Soon the five huddled together in the pitch blackness, uncertain what to do next. Other than heavy breathing, all remained quiet for almost a minute. Jay broke the silence.

"No emergency lights either, but then again, they would operate on battery back-up. Whatever is happening here is eating up any power sources."

"Speaking of eating up," added Dean, "What happened to all the people? Would they have been considered power sources?"

"I hope not," answered Bobby. "We could be next."

"Next for what," whined Chrissie

"One thing for sure, we can't just huddle here forever like a bunch of scared sheep," said Jay, the lighter offering the only light.

"What do you have in mind?" asked Dean.

"Bobby, we should go outside. I'm sure the light must be better out there."

"You're right, Dean. I can make out the doorway."

The gals remained silent and followed the lead of their husbands. Moving as one, they maneuvered toward the lobby's entrance doors, baby steps to keep from tripping over any furniture. Jay, lighter held out front, reached the doors first and announced they would not open. Of course, they wouldn't because they were automatic and required electricity. Jay fingered the closure. He could not pry it open. It held like a vice. What now, he wondered. "The door won't open guys."

"Then we find something to break the glass," announced Bobby. "Hold tight. I'll fumble around and see if I can find anything that might work."

They could hear Bobby's footfalls on the tile floor as he moved about. Twice he must have bumped into a piece of furniture, and then, all was silent. Jay cocked his head, trying to pick up movement, but could not zero in on any. Chrissie flinched, gripping

Dean's right arm. Marge clung to his left. Jay remained less than a pace from them, holding up the lighter but he couldn't breach the blackness more than a couple of feet in any direction.

"Damn it, Bobby, you better not be trying to spook us. This isn't funny. Please stop it." Marge begged again for Bobby to stop his foolishness, but he did not acknowledge her pleas.

Jay, holding his hand behind his lighter, walked in the direction where he had last heard Bobby. The others moved in unison. Marge called out again, as did Dean. Bobby was nowhere to be found. He was gone. There had been not a peep out of him or any sounds of a scuffle. Poof, he was just gone.

"We've got to find him," whimpered Marge.

"Now you know how I feel. Mira deserves the same attention."

Music broke the silence. It was coming from the lounge, as was a glimmer of light.

"Bobby, that isn't funny," yelled Marge. "You're really pissing me off."

With some rejuvenated pep in their steps, the four quickly entered the lounge. In a corner, near the bar the jukebox cranked out a familiar country tune, *Prop me up by the jukebox when I die.*" There was no other light in the lounge and there was no Bobby McAlister laughing his ass off.

"On the tables, the mini lanterns, gather everyone you can while we have the jukebox light to see by," barked Jay.

Most of the tables had tiny oil lamps used for ambiance. Odd, thought Jay, these should have already been burning. Never look a gift horse in the mouth. They had accumulated eleven on a table near the center of the room. Dean had located two flashlights behind the bar. Of course, neither of them worked. Battery operated; they were spent like everything else. He attempted flipping on several light switches. But no go; only the jukebox receptacle apparently worked.

"Save your lighter. I found a basket of matches," said Dean, "and two one-gallon jugs of fuel for the lanterns." He had also poured a shot of tequila, downed it and a second one, before asking if anyone else wanted one. He had no takers. This situation called for clear heads. Dean didn't seem to see it that way. He brought his glass and bottle of tequila with him. Chrissie frowned at his decision.

"Here's the way I see it after giving it careful consideration. We can wait it out here. We should have plenty of fuel to at least light up this place until dawn. Then we can try to find a way out and see if we can reach the main road on foot. Surely some passing car will come along. Or, we can utilize our lanterns and begin searching for Mira and Bobby, or anyone else we can find."

Dean downed a shot. "Hey Jay, you do realize hoofing it out of here is no easy task. This place must be thirty miles back into this mountainside off the main roadway."

"Thirty-seven, to be exact," replied Jay.

"Pardon my crudeness, Jay, but you look in no shape to make that journey. Hell, none of us are probably up for it. Chrissie would come the closest to doing it. She does walk about four miles daily."

"Honey, I've never done anywhere close to thirty-seven miles."

"What about bicycles? This place must have some bikes," said Marge.

"I think I have seen bikers here unless the people brought their own. Come daylight, we might be able to find a few," said Jay. "Before you say it, Dean; no, I'm not really built for biking, either. Someone should stay here in case others show up. I'll volunteer for that duty. Besides, I want to find Mira."

"I need to potty," announced Chrissie.

"I'll go with you," said Marge.

"I say we all go. We've seen what happens, otherwise," recommended Jay.

"Girls need their privacy," said Chrissie.

"Then we'll stand outside, but you're not venturing off alone," warned Jay.

"She's my wife. You can't talk to her like that."

"I'm just trying to keep it real, Dean. We don't need any more Houdini acts."

"Okay, I get it. We go inside with you girls. You'll have your privacy inside the stalls. I could take a whiz too come to think of it. Don't look at me like that, Chrissie. You girls always travel in herds to the john, so Jay and I are now honorary members of your little posse."

"It just makes sense that we stick together given the circumstances," added Jay.

"Well, come on girls," motioned Chrissie, tugging a lethargic Marge along. Her sis wasn't doing so well, tittering on the verge of shock after Bobby vanished.

The jukebox abruptly stopped with its lights going out, plug pulled, so to speak. Each of the stranded vacationers carried a table lantern, more than enough illumination to guide their way. Jay thought how foolish he had been venturing around by himself, but then again, anywhere he would have been he would have been there alone. There had been no blackout then. Maybe whatever lurked out there had required recharging during that time. Whatever lurked out there, those thoughts filling his brain suddenly jarred him. Something lurking in the darkness sounded like the evil creatures from horror movies.

Power outages were one thing, people going poof put an entirely different slant on this. He mentally estimated head counts. If this place were near full occupancy, and if he figured on a minimum two people per vehicle, one hundred fifty rooms then there could be upwards of three hundred people missing, not counting resort staff. No, three or four hundred people didn't just vanish into thin air. If they did, Mira was one of them, as was Bobby McAlister. Somehow, assigning real names and faces to this scared the living begibbies out of him.

Jay stood in the bathroom. He propped it open with his body while Dean stood guard just outside the stall doors. He didn't know these folks well enough to invade that much on their privacy. Keeping them in plain sight served his purpose. Dean glanced in his direction every couple of seconds as if expecting him not to be there. One flush then a second indicated the girls had peed or whatever they needed to do. Once they stepped out Dean stepped into a stall. The sounds of him letting loose echoed in the bathroom. The girls washed up and soon they were back in the lounge.

Dinging sounds followed by whooshing drew their attention to the lobby. Without saying a word all four stormed the elevators. One of the three elevator doors stood open. The digital display above the door was now working. They hesitated, unable to see inside from their angle. Marge suddenly broke into a sprint shouting Bobby's name, entering it as if expecting the reunion with her hubby. The door immediately whooshed shut behind her. The others quickly closed the distance. They were too late to prevent her departure, but watched as the elevator floor display indicated it was descending. Jay cringed, realizing it had stopped at the basement.

"The stairs," yelled Dean, already pushing on the door, and entering the stairwell. Chrissie followed.

"You don't want to go down there," yelled Jay, but then he too followed. Staying here alone was no longer a viable option. At least they had the lanterns, he reminded himself.

Jay, keeping the two others in sight, descended the flights quickly. Dean pushed the door open and plunged through the basement level. Before Chrissie could follow, the door slammed shut. She shouldered it without thinking but it didn't budge. Jay arrived and gave it a try too. It held firm as if welded shut. Both fell backwards, stumbling until they piled one on top of the other, landing on the bottom steps. The scream was blood curdling and seemed to go on forever. It belonged to Dean Waldrop.

3

Chrissie sat in Jay's lap, his arms holding her tightly. Finally, the scream stopped. Jay wasn't necessarily convinced that was a good thing, not for Dean. Chrissie regained her senses and managed to break Jay's grip and stand. She turned to face him; fear shown on her face.

"I've never heard Dean scream like that before," she said. "He doesn't scream that loud, even during sex, and believe me, I've often had to stuff my panties in his mouth when we were at my parent's house." She wasn't sure why she had said that to a total stranger. She really wasn't sure why she had said it at all. That scream hadn't sounded anything like he had enjoyed what was happening.

The basement, Jay almost said. Something evil resided in the basement. That previous smell jolted his memory. A resort's basement shouldn't smell like what he had smelled during his luggage hunt. It wasn't foul, nor smelled like decay, as you would expect in a horror flick, but still, it was odd. The thought struck him like a bolt of lightning. They were being picked off one at a time and only two of them remained. Is this how it happened to the others, he wondered. Hundreds had been taken one by one to nourish some unseen hunger. Get these thoughts out of your head, he told himself. This isn't a slasher-movie. This was worse than that. It was real and it was happening to him.

Chrissie turned to him for answers. "What's happening to us, Jay?"

"I don't know. I wish I did. Mira and I came here to try to mend some fences. Nothing serious like infidelity or abusive behavior, we had just grown apart, like I'm sure many couples do after twenty or so years together. The spice was sort of gone, oh hum, taking one another for granted and so forth. We thought this might be the fix." Jay wondered why in the hell he had also aired his dirty laundry to a stranger.

"What do you think attacked Dean?"

"Attack sounds a little harsh, but I can't argue the point. I don't have a clue what happened to him. We better figure out something or we're going to be next on the menu." He regretted saying that as soon as it had left his lips. Talk such as this wasn't helping their cause. Who was he kidding? They were in the grips of a ticking time bomb here. "Let's head back topside. I don't like being down here."

"But what about, Dean, we can't just leave without him."

"We can't help him. You heard what I heard. We can only help ourselves until we can solve this mystery."

"But…"

"We've got to go, Chrissie. I feel your pain. Mira is out there somewhere too, as is your sister and brother-in-law. We can't fight this thing until we understand what we are fighting." Fight this thing, thought Jay, I'm not sure if I even want to know what this thing really is, and I'm not so sure we can lick it if we live long enough to find out.

Oddly when they returned to the lobby all the lights were back on. This was getting weirder by the minute. The thought crossed Jay's mind. IT had just fed, whatever the hell IT was, so maybe it didn't need to tap into the power right now. He instinctively retrieved his cell phone. The display was active, but how can a battery recharge itself? He asked Chrissie to check hers. It too appeared to be operating now. Unfortunately, neither had a single signal bar. What use were the phones to them. Jay rushed to the lobby check-in counter. The phones were back up, as was the computers.

Jay stared at one of the computer screens. As figured, it required a login and password to access the system. He had the odd feeling that someone or something was toying with them, tossing out life preservers and then yanking them away. That required intelligence, didn't it, not some blood thirsty primal monster. Focus, he told himself. Seize the opportunity, seek out weapons, other survival tools and devise a defensive strategy. It was way too early to go on offense. It hit him. If the electricity had been restored, then the automatic doors should open. He grabbed Chrissie by the hand and sprinted in that direction. She never questioned, just followed him blindly, what other choice did she have.

Jay approached the zone of what should have been the electronic eye that would active the doors. Nothing happened. Whatever they were up against had the knowledge and ability to control everything independently. This was just another example, along with their cell phones. This had gone from a feeding frenzy to the beast messing with them cat and mouse style, playing with its prey until once again hungry, then IT would pounce. This wasn't the only door in this joint. All of them would not be operated electronically. Emergency exits typically just had the push bar for easy escape. Jay scanned the perimeter and spotted a red EXIT light. Chrissie saw it too, even though Jay had not divulged his assumptions. She took the lead this time.

Chrissie slammed into the door bar with full body force and careened off it like a ping pong ball hitting a paddle. She fell flat on her ass. Jay helped her to her feet. His worst fears, IT could not only control electronic components, IT could also manipulate mechanical contraptions. This upped the ante significantly. What on God's earth could do this? Nothing could do this, nothing that he could think of, so maybe it wasn't from this world. Of course, it's not from this world, he told himself. This is beyond man's capability. What does this leave? It either had to be paranormal activity or of alien origin. He was not an expert on either of the scenarios. Possibly Chrissie was, but he doubted it. Regardless, they were screwed royalty.

"By any chance do you know anything about paranormal behavior?"

"You think ghosts are doing this."

"Do you have a better explanation? I'm open to all scenarios."

"I read a lot and yes, paranormal suspense thrillers are one of my favorite genres."

Jay eyed the female standing before him, maybe a little more in detail for the first time. After all, she was his only ally right now. She was petite, possibly in the five-foot, four range, no more than hundred ten pounds or so. She had short cropped blondish hair, her appearance almost reminding him of *Tinker Bell*. Her stature didn't match her voice. She had a deeper, raspier voice than one would expect for a lady so tiny. Maybe it was a smoker's voice. She wore a low-cut blouse that exposed truly little cleavage. She wasn't too wide at the hips. Downside, she would not be an asset in a fair fight. Who said they would be doing battle and if they did, it would be fair?

"Reading paranormal novels are like spending the night in the Holliday Inn Express. I don't think it will qualify you as an expert in the field. What about UFO's, alien encounters?"

"Ditto, but that doesn't make me an expert on that topic either, right. You failed to mention Sasquatch, Werewolves or Vampires, so should I assume you discounting them?"

"Okay, smart mouth, you tell me what you think is happening. I know I'm reaching, but this is not like anything I have ever encountered. What about you?"

"All I know is everyone I came here with has vanished. I'm scared. I'm more scared than I have ever been in my life. I want to find Dean, my sister and Bobby, just like you want to find your wife. I don't want me or you to be the next ones. I do agree something supernatural or beyond our scope of explanation is doing this. You've already tossed out things I haven't taken time to consider. Here's one more. Could it be one of those top-secret governmental projects? Maybe we're guinea pigs for some sort of new secret weapon."

"We'll add that to our list. One thing is certain. Sooner or later, someone is going to try to reach the resort, and if enough people report outages, they'll send somebody up here to investigate. Plus, this place requires deliveries to operate. Trucks should be arriving routinely." But will we be alive by the time either one of those scenarios fall in place, thought Jay, or just among the others missing, an unsolved mystery.

"I don't want to die."

Jay pulled Chrissie close and held her. It just seemed to be the right thing to do. She didn't resist him comforting her. Why would she? There was nothing sexual implied. Sex was the furthest thing from Jay's mind right now. They were each other's lifelines, plain and simple. Ironically thought Jay, they must have resembled *Beauty and the Beast*. The lights blinked, reminding both they should waste no more time, and take advantage of the power being on before darkness stuck again. They could cover more ground separately, but both agreed splitting up would only offer an open invitation, ringing the dinner meal, so to speak.

First, they gathered all their lanterns and fuel, placing it on the lobby's check-in counter. They had chosen it as their central command center. From there they ventured out, short excursions, always taking lanterns just in case the power wigged out. Although food was the furthest thing from their minds, they took time to gather snacks and water from the lounge. They did this for the long haul if a long haul was in their future. Jay doubted the premise. From the lounge they had also gathered an assortment of cutlery, several knifes offering them some semblance of weaponry. Jay again doubted the knives would fend off what waited out there for them. Chrissie had retrieved a couple of brass candle holders from the mantle of a huge fireplace in the lobby. The candles had been removed, leaving the long holders as mini bats.

Jay had rummaged through all the drawers and files looking for anything that resembled a login and password. He had found neither. Everyone had a personalized code, but he had hoped he would find a master list, or maybe someone's scribbling on a pad or sticky note. He often wrote down his new password until he was sure he could remember it. In a game room they had found a couple of pool tables. Cue sticks made better weapons than those candelabras. They gathered up all of them. Jay used a knife to whittle and sharpen the ends. Nearly forty-five minutes had passed, and the lights remained on. Amazing, thought Jay. Could their adversary have moved on, returned to where it had emerged? One could only hope, but he doubted it.

Jay almost chuckled out loud as he and Chrissie passed in front of a huge mirror. He and she looked nothing like *Conan and the Princess Warrior*. There was nothing intimidating about them. A flutter in the pit of his stomach told him they had not a chance in hell of getting out of this. Who were they fooling? What were they supposed to do, just roll over and take it? No, they would go down swinging, if whatever were out there would allow them to take a complimentary swing or two. He refrained from yelling out a challenge. Better to leave well enough along. He might get what he asked for, and he wasn't ready for that quite yet, if ever.

They avoided the elevators. Jay considered them death traps, a one-way ticket to the basement. He was convinced that whatever they were dealing with had set up camp in that dungeon like environment. There was something significant to that thought pattern. Possibly their adversary shied away from the light. Excluding Mira, the other three had been taken in the darkness. Maybe Mira had been too. Jay really didn't want to think about her in that way, but he had to face facts. He probably was never going to see her again. Hundreds of folks were missing. She wasn't even a blip on the radar screen to whatever was responsible.

Two restaurants, another bar, a spa, a gym, and an indoor pool were one floor above them. Jay contemplated if they should venture up the stairs and scope it out but wasn't sure he wanted to leave the ground floor. The basement experience had soured him on venturing off too far. Of course, he had visited the penthouse, but that had been by elevator. That too had taken him to the basement and possibly a close call. He glanced at his watch. It had stopped earlier but was now ticking away. Jay reset it, trying to account for the estimated lost time. It should be around two, daylight still hours away. Somehow, he drew comfort, thinking the sunshine would chase away the demons. A gambler would never play the odds that they would bask in the morning's rays. He stared at the stairway, teetering on the brink of a meltdown.

"Are you thinking about going back down to that basement?"

Jay jumped, startled by her voice. "Not in this lifetime. I was thinking about going up though. If nothing else, it would put another floor between us and the basement." Right, like it did those other hundreds of people any good, thought Jay. Then again, maybe others were holed up in their rooms, barricaded and fending for themselves. They could be asleep and unaware of what had transpired. Think about it, he told himself; just because none were on this floor, didn't mean everyone was dead or missing. The floors above them would be where most of the people would be, in bed, possibly safe and sound. Those who had been enjoying the nightlife might have been the only ones taken so far. That made perfectly good sense, didn't it?

"Do you think there are others alive above us?"

"What do we really have to go on, only what we've witnessed and experienced on this floor? I made an awfully bad assumption that everyone was either dead or had vanished. What if his thing dwells in the basement and has limitations on how far it can go? Or maybe it is gradually working its way up floor by floor. It fills its belly and rests, and then hunts again once the hunger pains return."

"You're now making it sound more like a beast, rather than a ghost or little green men."

"We must keep all the options on the table. I'm just saying there are too many unknowns to be certain what we are dealing with here."

"But a beast couldn't do everything we've witnessed, could it?"

Jay shrugged. "I'm not insinuating it is a beast of our world, something like a lion or tiger. No, this is way beyond anything man has every experienced, at least, this man. Let's face the facts. There has never been, on record, a paranormal or supernatural occurrence that compares to this, unless you know something I don't. I'm not talking about those fiction novels you read. I'm talking documented and published accounts."

"I guess not. I would prefer not being the discoverer of the first. I suppose it is too late for that, isn't it?"

"We can rule out any known encounters of the third kind too, unless you count and believe the Roswell cover-up back in the forties."

"You're confusing me, Jay. First you blame this on paranormal or alien activity, and then you discount them. What's left?"

"I'm confused enough for both of us, Chrissie. I'm just a babbling fool right now. It keeps me from going entirely insane by getting it off my chest. Don't take everything I say with a grain of salt. This resort is secluded. Maybe we're some sort of guinea pig for something larger to come. I still think going up is the answer."

"Do we go up to the next floor or not?"

"You have a say. What do you want to do?"

"I think if there is a chance of finding others alive, we should."

"Okay, let's go gather our provisions and remainder of our little arsenal and do just that. It beats waiting for something to find us."

4

The Big Blue Resort was nestled in a secluded section of the Great Smoky Mountains, southwest of Hazel Creek. Ten floors, seven with rooms, the resort could house around three hundred fifty people. The hotel staffed nearly fifty employees during peak seasons. Fall was prime time with the changing of the autumn leaves. One access road brought the visitors to the resort, indeed guaranteeing a secluded stay. Amenities such as horseback riding, bicycling, and walking trails offered what most visitors cherished. It amounted to the closest thing to an all inclusive in the shadows of the mountains, a rare jewel for most.

Mason Wells had been the resort's only manager for nearly thirty years. He was the perfect person for the job, cordial and hospitable, a divine southern gentleman, born and raised in Tennessee. Much of his regular staff had been with him from the beginning. You could not run them off with a stick. They appreciated Mason and could think of no other place they would prefer to work. No one had ever retired. Elijah Cowan was the elder, almost eighty-seven years old. He filled the position of resident concierge. Everyone dearly loved old Elijah and the stories he could tell.

Fran Woodward was over housekeeping. She settled for nothing short of perfection from her handpicked staff. She reminded everyone of Phyllis Diller, in appearance only. She spoke more like *Flo* from the *Alice* television series. She even had that saying, *'kiss my grits'* down pat. People weren't sure if she ever slept. She could be seen flitting about almost any hour of the day or night. A widower, prior to coming to work at the resort, Mason had always provided her with accommodations. This place was her home, and everyone was family.

Haskell 'Junior' Johnson was the grounds keeper. His little horde of worker bees maintained an immaculate landscape. Tourists joked that no pinecone ever touched the ground. Haskell and his team must snag them in mitts or nets before they ever reached the surface from the towering longleaf pines. Haskell beamed with delight, when hearing the friendly jabs, never denying the possibility.

29

Dexter Parnell was head cook and bottle washer, as he called himself. He was an extraordinary chef. Any hotel or restaurant would have paid a king's ransom to have him as their resident head chef. Dexter was too laid back for city life, even though he had grown up in Cleveland, Ohio. With nearly twenty-seven years of southern living under his belt, he had perfected the ultimate good ole boy accent.

Then there was Joseph Ironhorse, facilities manager, the maintenance head honcho. Injun Joe didn't take anything off anyone. He ran his maintenance department like a Navy ship. Mid-thirties rode hard and put up wet, he looked more like a man in his fifties. His skin was weathered like leather but make no mistake, he could do the work of three young bucks. He raised the bar and expected those who worked for him to challenge him by raising it too. A series of generators were in place to completely operate the resort in case of power outages. They would kick in the instant the main power was disrupted. Injun Joe prided himself on this system, his brainchild. No other resort in the region had the capability to sustain in the event of an ice storm or any other types of blackouts. Tourist would never sense the switch over. It was that smooth and seamless.

Thursday, just one day ago, the matriarchs of Big Blue Resort met something they could have never fathomed or rationally described. Folklore and fantasy could not have prepared them for what crept from the shadows of the mountains. The resort's thirty-year reputation snuffed out and potentially transformed into something so sinister, it could be lost forever. One question remained for those yet to discover the power; could it be stopped, or at least restricted to the mountain wilderness? One thing for sure, time was on no one's side.

5

Jay and Christie had found several backpacks in the office, courtesy of the lost and found department. Everything useful they could carry was stored inside. Defying logic, the power remained on, something Jay was very leery of, sensing a set-up down the road. Their primitive weapons seemed no match for their potential opponent, but they had to play the hand they had been dealt. He had no aces up his sleeves. Without uttering a word, they ascended the two flights of stairs taking them to the next floor. The door opened with ease. That alone worried Jay, too much of a welcome mat, given their previous encounters. Was the spider welcoming them into its web? If so, his hunch about the basement was badly skewed.

A vast room lay in front of them, just as he had remembered. The restaurants were located, each in opposite directions, anchoring the floor. The pool, gym and spa were directly across the room from the elevators, marked clearly as such. He had never used any of them. Jay was more of a grazer. The restaurants served his needs. His appetite suddenly roared to life. Big man required more nourishment than most. It took large quantities of calorie intake to maintain his manly figure. His stomach let out a long rumbling growl as if sensing its surroundings.

"Are you hungry?"

"Not really," replied Christie.

"My mom always said, eat before you get hungry. She forced us to take pee breaks when we stopped during trips, whether we had to go or not. Clean underwear was never a choice but a way of life. Let's see if we can rustle up something. We wouldn't want to face what might lurk ahead on an empty stomach and in a weakened state, would we?"

"I take it you're hungry. I heard you stomach."

"A cow wouldn't be safe right now. We can stop in the Bear Bottom Bar afterwards for a beer or glass of wine."

"You're serious, aren't you?"

"Every man, or gal, deserves a last meal. Sorry, I didn't mean it to come out that way."

"By the way, you excluded zombies."

"Why would I want to eat a zombie?"

"No, I mean zombies are large on the apocalypse world ending list. Most zombies prefer the cloak of darkness to do their dirty deeds. That might be why the abductions are happening when the power is off."

"Do zombies have the ability to control electrical and mechanical devices at will?"

"Could be Alien Zombies, a new breed never encountered," she quipped.

"On your reading genre list, I assume."

"They're hot right now, nudging out vampires and werewolves. Have you never watched the *Walking Dead* on *A&E*?"

"I'm not the *A&E* type. I'm more the *Food Network*, or have you not noticed?"

Christie laughed. It sounded wonderful to hear laughter, thought Jay. Mira had a lovely laugh. Hers was not put on, not too shrill or filled with snorts, but instead, just perfectly girlie. His heart panged for her. Damn it, why had they not parked the car first and then retrieved the luggage cart together? No, they would have never done that. Well hell, he could have been the one to go for the cart instead. No, she hated parking the SUV in such close quarters. It would have gotten him and then eventually her. The pecking order hardly mattered now. What about their son, Jason? He would never know what happened to his parents. Jay slid deeper into his little pity party.

"Jay, which restaurant do you want to try? Either is fine with me."

"I always liked Clingman's. They have the best porterhouse steaks. Did you know it was named after the Clingman Dome, the highest point in the Smokey Mountains?"

"You do realize there will be no one there to cook this signature porterhouse, don't you?"

"Hey, I can cook a mean steak, too."

She began tearing up. So much for the sound of laughter, thought Jay.

"Are you a vegetarian," he asked, trying to keep lightened the mood.

"Dean cooked wonderful steaks. He called himself 'The Grill Master'. He said the key to a successful steak was in the marinating. He had some concoction he called his special little secret, often saying he was going to patent and sell it, make us millionaires."

"I miss Mira, too. If possible, we will find them, I promise." Just keep saying the right thing, Jay, and try to believe, he told himself.

Sniffling, Chrissie just nodded, before wiping her nose with the bottom of her blouse. She exposed her pierced naval. Jay had never seen a pierced naval up close and personal. He turned three shades of red when he realized Chrissie had caught him staring. She smiled and pulled down her blouse. Jay whirled and headed toward The Clingman. He really needed to stop by The Bear Bottom and down a stiff drink, but he fought back the urge to quench his thirst and settle his nerves.

The double doors leading into the restaurant were closed. Jay tried them and found they were locked. Of course, they were locked, he thought. They always lock them up after hours. You can't just have anyone wondering inside them. "Stand back," he warned Chrissie. He stepped into the batter's box, gripping the sharpened end of one the pool cue sticks and swung as if going for the long ball. The glass shattered. He jabbed out the remaining glass from the frame and reached inside and unlocked the door.

At first glance nothing appeared out of place. All the tables were set for tomorrow's seating. The Clingman was spick and span, ready for the next horde of customers. Jay grabbed a menu from the reception area. Fingering down it he found what he had been looking for, the Blue Ridge Porterhouse, a mountain of a meal. If it were still on the menu, he could find it in the freezer. He motioned to Chrissie that they would head to the kitchen. She followed Jay like a little puppy dog, intent on not allowing him out of her sight.

The kitchen was in pristine shape. Nothing appeared to be out of place or the worst for wear. Whatever they were up against didn't just merely destroy the surrounding environment. It had purpose but did not go at it with reckless abandon. Jay eyed what he had been looking for along the back wall, two sets of huge stainless-steel doors leading to a walk-in cooler-freezer combo. Those porterhouse steaks would be in the freezer side. His mouth lathered up just thinking about one, offering his spent brain to temporarily forget about their dilemma.

He opened the door and stepped inside, but then immediately retreated, shoving Chrissie backward. By the look on her face, she didn't exactly appreciate the aggressive push. The panicked look on Jay's face indicated it had purpose and had been intended to shield her from something inside the freezer. Jay remained silent for a few seconds, almost hyperventilating. He leaned over, placing his hands on his knees, his breathing quite labored.

Chrissie spoke first. "What's in there, Jay?"

Still wild eyed, it took Jay a few more precious seconds to compose himself and return his breathing to normal. "It's a woman."

Chrissie almost pushed by him, but Jay grabbed her firmly by the arm. "Don't," he muttered. "She's frozen like a popsicle."

"Dead?"

"Most certainly best I could tell."

"Do you think she become trapped inside?"

"Not possible. These babies are built with safety in mind to prevent anyone from becoming trapped. You can always open them from the inside."

"How did this happen, then?"

Jay rubbed his chin, and then the back of what little neck he had nervously before speaking. "She was afraid to come out. This must be the only explanation."

"She froze to death because she refused to leave the freezer. That makes no sense at all."

"Sure, it does. Think about it. She feared what was out here worse than freezing to death."

"She had to know she would die if she stayed inside, but out here she might have stood a chance."

"Maybe, maybe not, we don't know what she may have seen or experienced before holing up in this freezer. Possibly this was her best-case scenario."

"How can committing suicide be the best case, Jay?"

"I don't have that answerer, but she had a valid explanation for doing what she did."

"Are you telling me we might be better off doing the same thing?"

"You know as much as I do. The lady went inside for a reason. It appears obvious to me that she thought it safer to remain here. If anything, it sets the tone for what we might be up against. I'm not trying to scare you, but it is what it is."

"I've been terrified from the moment Bobby vanished. I wish we would have never come to this gosh awful place. It wasn't my idea. Marge found it online and thought it would be a wonderful experience to see the fall colors. She invited me and Dean, insisted it would be the perfect getaway. We were just supposed to be here for the weekend." Chrissie then thought about her missing sister. "I'm not saying it was Marge's fault. She couldn't have foreseen any of this was going to happen, God bless her soul, wherever she is. What do we do about that lady in the freezer?"

"We do nothing. What can we do? She's preserved where she is, perfect for the coroner."

"What about your porterhouse?"

 "Lost my appetite, and that's not something I make a habit of, but since we're here, we may as well check what's behind door number two."

Chrissie waved him on, standing back to allow him access. Jay cautiously opened the refrigerator's door. He jumped back immediately, pool cue in assault position. Chrissie instinctively pointed her cue stick toward the door, ready to impel whatever might exit the cooler.

"Whoa," yelled the person inside, teeth chattering.

"Come on out," advised Jay.

"Not a chance, you come inside and close the door, quickly please."

Jay looked over at Chrissie, unsure whether this was a smart move, but given what he had witnessed in the freezer, he stepped inside. Chrissie followed. The gent immediately pulled the door closed. He blew heat into his hands and rubbed them together. The three stood in a stare down.

Jay finally asked, "Just who the hell are you?'

"I was about to ask you the same thing. I work here. I'm the chief cook and bottle washer. My name is Dexter Parnell, resort chef. Your turn."

"Jay Myers and this is Chrissie Waldrop. We're lodgers of your wonderful resort. What the hell is happening here?"

"Is it gone?"

Jay shrugged. "Is what gone?"

"I'm not sure."

"What the hell is that supposed to mean, you're not sure?"

"It means just what I said."

"What made you hide in the cooler? By the way, did you know there was a dead woman in the freezer?"

 "What did she look like?"

"Frozen," answered Jay.

"I mean a description."

"I didn't look too closely, but I can say she looked like a black woman, and she was larger than Chrissie, a little heavier."

"Ah cripes, it must be Twyla Edwards. She's my pastry chef. Did you see anyone else?"

Jay shook his head no.

Dexter took a deep breath and then asked, "How long have you been here?"

"My wife and I arrived before midnight, and Chrissie and her folks a short time after."

"Where are the others then?"

"We hope you can shed some light on that little mystery," said Jay.

"I'm not sure what you want from me."

Chrissie took charge. "We arrived here with reservations Friday through Sunday. My husband, my sister and brother-in-law have been abducted at your elite resort. Jay's wife is missing too. You're the first unfrozen person we've seen since meeting Jay when we first arrived. Why are you hiding in the refrigerator?"

"You've seen no one then?"

 "Do you have frost in your ears? Tell us what you do know."

Go Chrissie, thought Jay. "Do we really need to stay in here?"

"Do whatever the hell you want but I'm not going back out there."

Jay looked the chef up and down. He was about his height, maybe fifty pounds lighter, and he could be in his fifties, maybe early sixties. He was never good at guessing age. Dexter was very fair skinned, but that might be misleading, given how long he had been hiding in the frig. His hair was graying on the sides, and he wore it in a ponytail. The chef's face was pitted, possibly from bad acme as a kid. He was dressed in chef style shirt and trousers, both white. Something had terrified him into doing this. Jay figured he might have pulled the same maneuver, if faced with whatever was responsible for what was going on here.

"Let's try this again, Chef Parnell. We're in this together but it would help us to know what we are up against.

"I told you I don't know."

"Okay, so what prompted you to hide in here?"

Dexter inhaled, taking a deep breath, and then exiled a frosty reminder. "Did you say this was Friday?"

"Well actually it is in the wee hours of Saturday morning, now," replied Jay.

"And you have seen no one? The resort should have been near full capacity."

"We haven't explored any of the other floors; only this one and the lobby, a brief visit to the basement. I did go to our penthouse when we first arrived."

"You've been to the basement?"

"Twice," said Jay. "Well, I've been twice, sort of."

"And you made it back?"

"Both times, but I recognize where you're going with this. Dean, Chrissie's husband, and her sister disappeared in that basement, so what gives?"

Dexter sat down on stacked boxes of vegetables. Tears began rolling down his cheeks. He was a broken man. Jay figured he probably wasn't the same guy a couple days ago. Hiding in a cooler for longer than a day would do this to anyone, especially if what were outside drove him in here.

Chef Dexter Parnell had used his pass key to access the Clingman. None of his staff had yet arrived but should be within the next thirty minutes. He completed a brief inspection of the dining room before heading to the kitchen. Perfection hinged on the guests' first impressions. That began in the dining room. He engaged the kitchen's lights, scanned the perimeter, and beamed with delight. His staff oozed of the perfection expected. He would put them up against anyone. Hearing footsteps, he turned to eye Twyla Edwards, his pastry chef. "You're early."

"Couldn't sleep for some reason this morning, felt uneasy and on edge," smiled Twyla, her smooth ebony complexion almost glistening under the florescent lights. "It's a curse. My great, great grandmother was a Haitian princess, said to have the power. What trickled down to me amounts to no more than occasional premonitions and a once in a blue moon fifteen-dollar lottery win, some legacy."

"I'll have coffee going in a second and will add my secret ingredient to knock the edge off the morning stress. You're not officially on the clock yet. Allow Doctor Parnell to cure your ailments before we're off and running."

"Sounds wonderful, Dexter, I do indeed enjoy your special little recipe."

"Mere mint and lemon with a twist of cinnamon, but it has worked many a miracle."

"Ah, so this morning you have chosen to expose your secrets to a mere mortal."

"I'm in a good mood, but don't get too comfortable, the circus begins soon enough."

Twyla leaned against the bar, watching Dexter doing his thing. Persistent, the ominous feeling had a strangle hold on her, almost suffocating her. This was unlike anything she had ever experienced. She surveyed the room, feeling a presence, someone watching her. Perhaps an intruder had slipped in through the unlocked door. She shrugged it off, thinking a guest would show their face, ready for breakfast to possibly offset a terrible hangover. No, she sensed the uninvited, wasn't sure how to interpret her feelings. When Dexter returned with the coffee, she shared these feelings with him, something she would have never normally done. Nothing about this felt normal.

"Do you not feel it?"

Dexter took a deep breath and closed his eyes, not mocking her, but instead trying to grasp what might be in the air. Yes, he felt something. The air was energized, his skin feeling prickly, a hint of static electricity blended with a burned smell. Was it his imagination or just the power of suggestion? He wasn't sure but it was all around him. He opened his eyes and made direct contact with those belonging to Twyla. He saw fear, no terror in her brown eyes. It jolted him like a bolt of lightning, as if they had an uncanny connection. She blinked, feeling it too.

His phone rang and vibrated on his belt. The display indicated Mason Wells was up and at it, too. "Yes Mason, to what do I owe the pleasure at this hour?"

"I couldn't sleep, maybe weekend jitters," replied Mason.

"It seems to be contagious this morning."

"I just wanted to confirm we are sold out. Every room is booked through Sunday."

"Anticipated, we're on top of it, Mason, not to worry."

"There was never a doubt from me. I just wanted to say…" The phone went dead.

Dexter looked at the display on his, but it was blank. How could that be? It had been on charge last night, just like every other night and it had shown a full charge. He had not used it until now. Possibly the battery had gone bad and no longer holding a charge. He retrieved a house phone, same thing, no dial tone. "Twyla, let me borrow your cell phone, please."

She handed it to him. Dexter held it up to her asking if she had charged hers. She said it had a full charge when she had left her room. All the staff stayed on site during the peak season, long hours and too far to commute. Dexter glanced at his watch. It had stopped and so had Twyla's. Before Dexter could mutter a word, the power shut down. The kitchen became pitch black. What had happened to the generators, wondered Dexter. The system was such that the generators were programmed to engage immediately, a mere blink, if any break would be noticed. Nothing had happened.

Twyla screamed. Dexter could hear her running to the opposite end of the kitchen. He started to yell but his voice froze in his throat. Despair, what an unusual feeling to have right now, thought Dexter. His world was replaced with total emptiness. He had never felt so alone. His skin burned. Someone, no something reached out to him, and not in a good way. Dexter struggled to breath. His brain urged him to flee but run where? Nowhere felt safe. Danger was all around him, but it seemed preoccupied, not focused just on him. This was an odd feeling. Finally, Dexter willed his feet to move. None too soon, his ears were ringing, and he felt the weight of a semi parked on his chest. Was he having a heart attack?

With an uncanny catlike sense, Dexter moved through the dining room, avoided tables or any other obstructions. He reached the refrigerator cooler and scampered inside. The sudden coolness soothed his burning skin and almost immediately he no longer endured the feelings he had just experienced outside. His breathing returned to normal. The weight had been lifted from his chest. He had no desire to venture outside the confines of the cooler. He could explain none of this. He was safe but safe from what? His world remained darker than any darkness thought possible.

"That's it," asked Jay.

"That's it," confirmed Dexter, embracing the warmth given off by the kerosene lanterns for the first-time shedding light on his world since entering the cooler.

"Just thinking, if the power was off most of your time in here, how come the lady froze in that freezer?"

"Simple, a freezer will maintain cold temperatures, providing you keep the doors closed. That's why they recommend during prolonged power outages to keep the doors closed as much as possible."

"It's still hard to fathom why she would stay inside and freeze to death."

"I do and don't understand why she did it," said Dexter.

Jay looked at Dexter. Had the man gone crazy? "I don't follow that statement at all."

"I do," spoke up Chrissie. "It's like you said earlier, Jay. Something out there scared her more. You felt it too, didn't you Mister Parnell? You felt it in the basement, Jay. We've all felt something."

"Why didn't, whatever this thing is, breech the cooler and freezer," asked Jay.

"They're airtight," replied Dexter.

"Maybe, and they're both cold."

"Or maybe it wasn't hungry," added Chrissie. "Think about all the other guests here. It could have been preoccupied. You, choosing the cooler instead of the freezer, saved your life, Mister Parnell."

"While we have plenty of food here," stated Jay, "We can't stay inside forever."

"Why not," said Dexter. "We can wait it out until we are rescued."

"For one, we won't even know if anyone arrives if we remain in here. Besides, how long do you think it will take for someone to check inside? This would not be on my top ten places to search if I were looking for the guests. What if this whatever it is gets the rescuers, then what?"

"You're just a darn ray of sunshine," spouted Dexter. "I was much better off in here alone. Why don't you leave, go slay the dragon if you feel so compelled? I am no hero. I for one prefer to remain on this side of the turf."

"We call that above dirt where I come from," added Jay. "Trust me, I have no death wish on my agenda, either."

"But yet you think you can do battle out there with sharpened cue sticks," smiled Dexter.

"You did tell me there were originally six of you, didn't you? Sheer numbers mean nothing, either. If it did, we wouldn't have hundreds of people missing now would we, son?"

"How do you know they're missing? You've been cowering in here the whole time. You're a member of the staff, upper management at that, so why aren't you out there being a leader?"

"I'm the chef. I'm not a security or even a combat officer. Something tells me I could be *General George Patton* and it wouldn't really matter."

Chrissie was tiring if their bickering. "Let's take a timeout. Squabbling among ourselves is pointless. Did anything eventful happen leading up to this anomaly? What I mean to ask is did you or any of the staff, or guests experience something unexplainable in the last few days?"

"Nothing was reported."

"No odd ongoing activity has been mentioned in any of local newspapers or television," inquired Jay.

"Like unidentified flying objects," chimed in Chrissie.

"You're trying to blame this on UFO's and little green men."

"She's just throwing everything on the table, Mister Parnell."

"Dexter, just call me Dexter."

"Dexter, debate is over. I say let's take it to a vote, stay in here or venture outside."

"Take all the votes you'd like, young man. This is no longer a democracy. It's every man or lady for themselves. I stay put, end of story."

"Let me get this straight. You didn't see a thing, but you felt all hot and tingly, are fearful the boogeyman is out there waiting to get you, and you are willing to camp out in here indefinitely, just to avoid contact."

"I'm willing to sit it out to remain alive."

"Nothing has gotten us, and we've been scoping out the resort," added Jay.

"Tell that to those you said you have lost."

"Suit yourself, Dexter. We're going to find a way out of here," he then paused and looked over at Chrissie to make sure she was on board.

"I do want to find Bobby, Marge, and Dean, but I must concede he does make a good argument. He has survived by staying in here for whatever the reason."

"Amen, lassie, I'm not quite ready to go belly up just yet."

"Aren't you the least bit curious what has happened to other resort staff and the guests?"

"Twyla is dead. Your family is missing. You haven't seen a single soul. That's good enough for me. Send the rescue rangers here if you make it out safely."

"Can you at least point us to a way out of here," asked Jay.

"The lobby and basement levels, doors and windows on both," Dexter replied. "But what makes you think this thing will allow you to escape? So far, it has countered your every attempt."

"Good luck, Dexter," said Jay, turning to exit the cooler. He pressed the lever, but the door didn't bulge. "A little help here, what's the trick to opening the door?"

"No trick, just press down on the lever and push the door open."

Jay tried again. Nothing happened. Dexter tried. The door didn't move. They both pushed, but nothing. Chrissie even joined in, but no dice.

"Our enemy knows we're in here," whispered Dexter. "It must have followed you two. Thanks a lot."

"That absurd," scoffed Jay, thinking he was probably right.

"What do we do now?" asked Chrissie.

The door eased open, untouched with them now at the mercy of whatever waited outside.

7

Mason Wells, the resort manager stood in the doorway. He held a revolver, aiming it directly at Jay's chest. Jay flinched, expecting the stranger to fire first, ask questions later. He should have recognized him, but they had visited the resort so infrequently he hadn't taken the time to get to know the staff.

"It's all right, Mason," spoke up Dexter, stepping into view. "He's one of the guests."

Mason dropped the weapon to his side. Fran Woodward stepped from behind the door. "Well butter them up and add cheese, kiss my damn grits, you're alive, Dexter," she said.

"I am. How did you two avoid the situation?"

"We were holed up in the safe, Mason, Kipper Cox, Troy King and me," responded Fran.

"And what prompted you to hide in the safe," asked Jay, "and why weren't the guests warned of the dangers?"

Mason just stared at him, dumbfounded, in some sort of funky daze.

"Mason, where are Kipper and Troy?" asked Dexter.

The resort manager didn't answer, seemingly drifting in and out of shock. Fran finally spoke up, "We waited as long as we could. Kipper suffers from claustrophobia. We didn't know. She just freaked out, bless her heart. We had no choice. We opened the safe's door. She ran outside into the pitch blackness. We never saw her again. She didn't even make a peep, just vanished into thin air, I reckon."

"What about Troy, where is he. He was a strapping young lad, played football at UNC-Asheville," stated Dexter.

"We wandered around outside for a few minutes looking for Kipper. Mason had a flashlight and the pistol. Troy thought he saw movement. You know you can't tell that boy anything. He acts first, pays the piper later. He stumbled over half the lobby furniture, Mason holding the light in that direction the best he could. Troy was right there and then he wasn't. It was like whoosh, and he was gone. He didn't yell or make nary a sound. We thought maybe the big ole boy had stumbled and fell. We went over to where we had last seen him."

"And," encouraged Chrissie, needing to hear this, after what had happened to Bobby.

"And like I said, he wasn't there, not on the floor, not behind the furniture, nowhere," finished Fran. "I don't reckon I have ever seen nothing like that in all my born days, except on TV with one of those magicians. We had this peculiar feeling. We both felt it, like something was around us, trying to get to us. It's hard to explain but it was sure there. Mason whipped that flashlight around like one of those laser swords in *Star Wars,* but we didn't see a thing. I could hardly breathe. It was like invisible hands were trying to choke the life out of me and rip me apart at the same time."

"What did you do then, Fran?" asked Dexter.

"Mason said we better get back in the safe, so we headed back in that direction. It wasn't easy though. Every step took all the energy we could muster. It was like the air was so thick you feel it. You've seen those people on the Weather Channel trying to walk against or stand in hurricane force winds. That's the way it felt, except there was no wind, not even a breeze. Behind us was this ferocious pulling. We were being sort of pushed and pulled at the same time, if that makes any sense at all. It was like somebody didn't want us to get back in that safe and had this real hankering for us to go somewhere else."

"You never made it back to the safe," inquired Chrissie.

"Mason began whipping that flashlight around again. At times it would let up a tad. What I mean to say, is whatever tugged at us sort of stopped and started back. I don't know. It was like the flashlight cut through the heaviness like a razor-sharp knife. Maybe it was one of those force fields you see in the movies."

"I knew it," interrupted Jay. "IT fears the light."

"It, just what the hell are you talking about, Mister?"

"Never mind, just finish your story."

"Story,' snapped Fran, "You think I'm making this up, don't you? Let me tell you one thing; Fran Woodward doesn't make up stuff. I tell it like it is. You can kiss more than my grits if you're calling me a liar."

"I'm not calling you a liar and I'll keep my mouth shut. Please continue."

Fran crossed her arms and gave Jay, *The Look*. Mason remained silent and motionless. Dexter had managed to force him to take a seat in a chair nearest the cooler door. He had also disarmed Mason and placed the firearm on an end table within reach if he needed it. He had lodged another crate in the cooler's doorway, afraid it might close. Everything Fran was saying just reinforced why they should all stay in the cooler for protection against whatever lurked in the resort.

"Like I was trying to say, we got ourselves caught between a rock and hard place, out there in that lobby with all this crazy foolishness going on, and not knowing exactly what we should be doing. Mason was pointing that gun every which way, but how do you shoot somebody who won't show their face? Now, I'm not one to promote shooting anybody, but let me tell you the truth, if you mess with me, you're going to get hurt. Well, I didn't have the gun, but I would have sure told Mason to fire away if we had to do it."

"We get it. What happened next?" asked Jay, growing impatient with the prolonged tale?

"Hold your horses, sport. I'm getting there. The light flickered back on. I never could figure why we were ever in the dark in the first place. We have those fancy, expensive generators that are supposed to kick in if we lose power. Injun Joe must be falling down on the job."

"Injun Joe," questioned Jay.

"He's the facilities manager, Joseph Ironhorse," clarified Dexter. "Joe oversees maintenance and the resort's infrastructure. He's about as sharp as they come. I wouldn't go blaming any of this on him, Fran."

"I'm not throwing rocks at anybody. Lord knows I'm not perfect. I'm just saying those generators didn't come on and do what they're supposed to do, or how we've been told the way it's supposed to work."

"Is it okay to say you made it back to the safe and stayed there until now?" asked Jay.

"You can say anything you want to say, but that don't make it fact. You want to do this or do you want me to tell it. You decide? For the record, I don't appreciate all these interruptions. You're either interested in what I'm saying or you're not. I'm not just spitting in the wind."

"Fran, we're all on edge and rightfully so. Please don't take this personal. Tell us what happened, no more interruptions," said Chrissie, attempting to restore order.

The lights, without warning, shut down, catching everyone off guard. Dexter screamed at the top of his lungs for everyone to get inside the cooler. The pressure closed in on them swiftly. Fran switched on the flashlight and whipped it in the direction of Mason, less than three feet away. He was gone. Jay grabbed her by the arm, jerking her toward the cooler. Dexter closed the door once the others made it safely inside. He had forgotten to retrieve the gun, not that it would protect them from the unseen. Chrissie lit several extra lanterns just for good measure. There was no such thing as too much light right now, the more the better.

Dexter took in the scene. He had inherited three new roommates. While he appreciated the company, he selfishly considered how this would impact his long-term survival. Three more people equated three more mouths to feed. While there was no shortage of food inside the cooler right now, it did cut into his supplies. Worst still, the quarters were too cramped for four. Personnel hygiene would be a major factor if they were trapped for an extended stay. He wasn't sure about the oxygen level with three extra breathers. The door could be opened periodically to replenish it, as bad as he hated opening it for any intervals. He had been doing just fine alone; now this.

Jay studied his cohorts too. Who should be the leader? Two ranking resort staff members were among them. Did that mean one of them deserved the position? Fran was a piece of work, outspoken and head strong, but he cringed at turning over the leadership role to her. Dexter was totally out of the question. He offered no solutions except for staying here. Chrissie, no, count her out too. He was back at square one, him, and he didn't cherish being responsible for the others' safety. What this really called for was a clear head, not so much a leader or hero. He justified his role in that matter. Jay held firm to his belief, the most important thing, find a way out of this madhouse. Let the professionals solve the mystery. What were the odds of them surviving, he wondered? If hundreds had already been taken, just what chance did they really have? Taken, but taken where, if taken at all? Possibly taken was the wrong term.

No debating it, people were vanishing, but their fate was yet to be determined. Had they been consumed or just whisked away? He thought about Mira and hoped they were just being held somewhere, but where? Some vacation thought Jay. We were supposed to reconnect, bond, and work through our issues. These weren't exactly the issues he had envisioned. Why hadn't they just stayed home? This had been a mutual decision to come, so there was no value in blaming anyone.

Chrissie just wanted to find her husband, sister and brother-in-law and go home. She was no longer interested in explanations. She prayed for their safety and a safe return of her loved ones. This nightmare couldn't go on forever, could it? Chrissie assessed her fellow survivors and their predicament. She wasn't sure if predicament adequately described their dilemma. She tried to think of anything she or the others could have done differently to prevent this from happening, but what could they have done? No one could have envisioned this, whatever this was, and Jay had made every attempt to warn them upon their arrival. They had thought he was just some sort of lunatic. She silently recited The Lord's Prayer and asked God to get them out of this.

Fran, hands on hips, locked eyes with her secret lover, Dexter. She was tempted to go over and give him a big ole hug. She certainly needed one. In their present situation there really wasn't any value in keeping their relationship secret, was there? Mason was missing, probably dead, and given their current circumstances, workplace ethics probably no longer applied. Well, calling what they had a relationship was stretching things too. Until now it had been more like each of them using one another to scratch an occasional itch. Up until now, Fran had not actually realized the magnitude of her loneliness. Live the moment as if it will be your last, right? If ever there was a case for that premise, this had to be it.

A mishmash of four unlikely cohorts now hunkered down in a giant refrigerator, possibly the sole survivors of apocalyptic proportions. Surely if four folks like them could survive, there must be others out there, thought Fran. She recalled one of her favorite movies of all time, *The Poseidon Adventure*. She remembered how the character played by *Gene Hackman* had been tossed into the leadership role to lead them to the bottom of the ship which was then the top of the overturned ship. She saw this Jay feller in that role of the good reverend. As much as she dearly treasured Dexter, he was *Ernest Borgnine's* character, *Detective Lieutenant Mike Rogo*, opposed to doing the right thing. She envisioned herself as *Rogo's* wife, played by *Stella Stevenson*. Chrissie had to be *Nonnie Parry*, played by *Carol Lynley*. Yep, she had it all figured out, just one big blockbuster movie, hell on earth.

Caught up in her fantasy, Fran blurted out, "Maybe we're supposed to climb up to escape, instead of go down." Those folks in the movie did just that, but then again, the ship had been turned upside down by a giant rogue wave.

"What's that supposed to mean," asked Jay.

"In the *Poseidon Adventure* they climbed up, not down, where the dangers waited on them. I liked the original one, not the remake."

"Lady, you're a piece of work."

Chrissie butted in. "Think about it, Jay. This might make some sense."

"Excuse my ignorance but we're not on a ship upside down."

"No, but you keep saying the light might be our friend. We know we don't want to venture into the basement, and we've had nothing but bad experiences in the lobby. Whatever this is, it can control the resort's power at will. On the roof, it can't. We'd be in the sunlight."

"Only if we time it right and arrive during the daytime hours," added Jay.

"You mind if I butt in," inquired Dexter. "So, you make it to the roof and it's the middle of the day, then what? Where do you go from there? The roof isn't exactly the first place a rescuer would look, unless you were caught in a biblical flood or maybe a towering inferno."

It was Chrissie's turn to get short with Dexter. "It sure beats hiding in this icebox."

"I'm with you Hon. I say it's time we took charge and kicked butt along the way."

"Fran, listen to yourself. You're the head of housekeeping, not a Navy Seal. We need to stay here, wait for those who will eventually come."

"Oh, *Rogo* of little faith, what did I ever see in you, Dexter, other than a good lay?"

Neither Jay nor Chrissie took note of the little romantic twist. It meant nothing to them. They could have been husband and wife for all they knew. Dexter, on the other hand, could not believe Fran had spoken so candidly in front of complete strangers. Fran caught his reaction and poured more lovey-dovey stuff on for good measure, milking the embarrassing moment with Dexter. She called him her midnight fantasy closet lover. It then clicked with Chrissie that this was a first-time open confession transpiring. Jay just shrugged it off, uninterested in their affair, or whatever the hell it was supposed to be. Sexual conquests were the furthest thing from his mind.

Jay suddenly noticed. "Where's that gun the hotel manger had?"

Dexter dropped his head and then confessed it was on the table outside. Everything had happened so fast, there was no time to think things through properly. Guns weren't really Dexter's bag. Sure, he could fire one and wasn't a bad shot, he just didn't own a weapon. Jay was no better. He didn't own any guns, either. He had only fired a BB gun a couple of times and a pellet rifle once. His childhood friend Pat Norris had owned both. On the other hand, Fran possessed a concealed weapon permit. She had a 9x19 mm Walther P99, German semi-automatic pistol, but unfortunately it was back in her room. Given the circumstances, Fran almost felt naked without it.

"Dexter, did you ever attempt to leave after it became daylight?"

"I told you. I haven't budged an inch from this spot since Thursday. Why would I?"

"It will be dawn in about four hours, but I'm not sure how dark the interior is without lighting," added Jay. "We still have our lanterns and now the flashlight. I think we should try for the roof."

"Be my guest," chuckled Dexter, "but you already are, aren't you?"

The cooler motor came on, startling everyone. "Power is back on," announced Fran.

"That means we have lights again outside, doesn't it? We should probably try now, shouldn't we?" suggested Chrissie.

"Unless it's a trap," warned Dexter. "We're dealing with a supreme intelligence. Our advisory might be tossing out bait, I'm telling you. Damn fools, all of you, if you take it."

"Damn fools, all of us, if we just sit here and wait, and hope someone comes for us," responded Jay.

"Now would be a good time to get that gun," suggested Fran. "I'm a cracker jack shot."

Dexter laughed at her comment. "Do you really think an arsenal of weapons will do you any good against this thing? At best, you'd be firing away at shadows. Have any of you seen your target? Of course, you haven't. Staying in here is our best chance. We have provisions. Plus, nothing has bothered me in here." Go, please just go, thought Dexter. I don't need any of you waiting this out with me. Damn fools, you're just going to get yourselves killed.

"You're so wise. Why haven't you switched on the lights when the electricity was up and running?" asked Jay?

"The switch is on the plate out there," pointed Dexter.

"Sorry, that would have meant you would have had to open the door, my bad," answered Jay, shaking his head in disgust. "Tell you what; we'll flip it on when we leave."

"You're just too damn kind, son."

"Why don't you boys can it? All this feuding and fighting is senseless. Dexter, you should know better. You represent the integrity of this resort and should be more willing to step up to the plate, not cower in the corner. I really expected more out of you. You're not the man I thought you were."

"Fran, we're off the clock, don't you get it? It's us now. We can't be held responsible for something of this magnitude. This is going above and beyond. I'm not sticking my neck on the line for anybody."

"Not even me, apparently," she fumed.

Dexter just dropped his head and said nothing. Fran understood it loud and clear. Screw him, she thought, and then recalled, she already had. He could run a mean kitchen and his staff both admired and feared him. They should see him now.

"Open the door. I'm going for the gun," stated Fran.

"Hold on," replied Jay. "We'll do this together. Once we're out we head for the nearest stairwell."

"Can you at least leave me one of those lanterns," asked Dexter. "After all, they are resort property."

"I thought you were off the clock and in this only for yourself," smarted Jay.

"Please."

"Sorry, we'll need them. Remember, you're safe in here."

Chrissie almost spoke up, but given the circumstances, she decided to stay out of it. She was feeling a bit claustrophobic and had never suffered from it before. What waited outside terrified her even more, but she, like the others, was ready to take her chances. If it were God's will, she would survive this. She said another quick prayer and prepared mentally for the journey to the roof. She whispered I love you, Dean.

8

Jay Myers, a simple man, a no standout in the crowd sort of person, had now assumed the leadership role in the most terrifying situation of his life. He didn't embrace this self-appointed assignment with vigor. He accepted it as a matter of fact, lesser of the evils, no one else up for the task. He had no real plan, just making it to the roof in one piece for starters. He wasn't even one hundred percent sure this was the soundest decision. Dexter had been dead on, how do you fight an enemy if you have no idea what it is, and how it does what it has done so far? Jay wondered would they find more people along the way, just like Fran had indicated in her movie reference. If they did, possibly there would be a person among them more qualified to take charge and lead than him. He could only hope.

Before opening the door, Jay assessed his cohorts. Fran was certainly a fire ball, full of piss and vinegar, but she wasn't exactly a spring chicken. While he had no doubt, she would fight tooth and claw to the bitter end, if it came to it, he wasn't sure that gained them any advantage in the big scheme of things. She had already stated how she had almost been overtaken by this phenomenon. She was fair game like the rest of them, gun totter or not. He hoped the possession of light offered them a chance and would be somewhat of a deterrent. Again, this was anyone's guess given the uncertainty.

One thing struck him odd, though, and it had to do with the flashlight. Everything power driven had been impacted, even the batteries in the cell phones, so why not the flashlight? If the flashlight had been indeed the equivalents of a weapon, why hadn't the enemy simply snuffed it out too? Jay saw this as a key fact. He just couldn't decipher the significance, but it must be significant just the same. He'd take any advantage tossed their way. Darkness did seem to be when this entity was at its most powerful. He couldn't imagine a something as a simple flashlight being the slayer of the dragon though. Light gave them hope so why question its value and power for now.

Chrissie was a little spitfire. Like Fran, he was confident she would take on anything full throttle now that she had shaken the initial shock of losing loved ones from her system. She was beyond the pity party and mourning cycle. He felt confident she could be counted on to kick ass if the opportunity presented itself. Jay thought, who am I fooling, we're pathetic at best. Dexter was probably right. We have no clue what's out there and the powers it possesses. One thing for sure, this thing seems to have the ability to think. Worst still, it has an appetite and humans are apparently on the menu. This was the perfect horror movie scenario, a handful of survivors battling the unknown while being systematically picked off. The fat gullible non hero type rarely lasted extremely far into the credits. He didn't like his chances.

Jay took one last opportunity and asked Dexter if he would reconsider coming along with them. Dexter held firm to his strategy, staying inside the cooler and waiting for help. He wished them good luck or maybe just good riddance. Jay sensed he really didn't care for them being in his cooler. It was now or never. Jay opened the door, lanterns extended, and Fran aiming the flashlight. Nothing leapt at them. It looked normal, well lit and a typical kitchen environment, minus the hustle and bustle of cooks and wait staff. They had barely cleared the doorway when Dexter snatched the door closed. As promised, Jay did flip on the light switch to the cooler. Providing the power remained on, his little hiding place would be illuminated.

As one, the three inched their way forward. Fran spotted the pistol still on the table where Dexter had placed it. Their adversary had no use for guns, so it appeared. She broke from the others and retrieved it, balancing it in her palm, measuring its weight and feeling the power she now possessed. There was no sign of Mason Wells or any evidence of foul play. Although the lights were on and they could conserve the fuel and their lanterns, they dared not extinguish them, fearful it could change at any moment. History pointed out that this thing struck quickly and without warning. Jay doubted they would have a chance to relight them if it so chose. Fran did switch off her flashlight to conserve the battery. She pointed to the door near the elevator, the stairwell.

"We could use the elevator while we have power," she said.

Jay shook his head, no. "We'd be at its mercy in there. My gut tells me it would whisk us away to the basement. Trust me, you don't want to end up down there. Are the rest of the levels. rooms for the guests?"

"For the most part, but only after the next floor. Every other floor does have a supply room, linen, and such. We use them for quicker service, restocking and so forth."

"What's on the next floor?"

"It's our quarters; the staff, those who stay here fulltime and others who reside here in the peak season. It's a hell of drive out of here if you must do it daily, so it works better for us and the resort if we stay. Hey, we could stop by my room and retrieve my Walther P99. I have plenty rounds of ammo for it. I can hand over this pea shooter to one of you."

"I suppose we may as well since we're heading in that direction," Jay replied.

Who gets that other gun, Chrissie, or me, pondered Jay? It was a far stretch from a BB or pellet gun. He paused at the door to the stairwell. He sure hoped they were making a wise decision and there was some merit in this daylight assumption. He took one last look toward the kitchen. He wasn't sure what he had expected to see. Jay gripped the doorknob and cautiously pulled the door open. The lights remained on. The stairwell was well lit. Jay couldn't help but look at the descending stairs first, almost as if expecting demons to rush up them from the bowels of hell. They didn't. If not for what he had already experienced all would have seemed normal. It was far from normal though. Jay sensed it would only get worse before it got better, if better was even in the cards.

"We'll never get to that roof moving like a pack of snails," spoke up Fran. "Haven't you ever heard it's harder to hit a moving target? Hell, we could be swatted in a single lick the speed we're moving."

They were at least in the stairwell. Jay with his hand on the rail and one foot on the first step looked upward hoping for the best. He stood frozen. Fear had consumed him. The lights flickered. Jay blinked, hoping it was him instead. It wasn't. The lights blinked a second time. The thought rushed through Jay's brain; was it encouraging him to get a move on? What if going up was what the beast really wanted? Questioning his decision, he stood his ground.

Fran saw his dismay and took charge. She brushed past him, flashlight in one head, finger on the button, and gun ready to fire in her other. Chrissie nudged Jay but he just couldn't muster the courage to take that next step. Sweat beaded on his forehead. He could feel it running down his neck and spine. Chrissie touched his hand. Jay jerked it away. He couldn't focus on what he had led the others to believe was the only choice, some leader. The stairwell lights blinked off. Jay momentarily stared at his lantern. Fran had already clicked on her flashlight. The lights came back on. Jay's gaze shifted to Fran holding the flashlight. Why had it not gone out too? He removed his hand from the rail and retrieved his cell phone. It was still dead. Both operated by battery. Why the phone and not the flashlight? There had to be a method to this madness. Solving it might be crucial to them making it.

"You two better get your butts in gear if we plan to make it to that roof in my lifetime," yelled Fran.

"Jay, please, we do need to go," encouraged Chrissie.

Jay sucked in air as if he had just surfaced from the bottom of the pool gasping for that first breath after staying under too long. He remembered as a kid how he and his pals used to hold their noses and then duck to the bottom of the swimming pool in those *see how long one could hold their breath* contests. He never won any of them. Billy Compton always did. Jay said Billy must have gills instead of lungs.

Chrissie looked into his eyes and asked, "Jay, are you okay?"

Of course, I'm not okay, thought Jay. What kind of stupid question is that? I've lost my wife. Crazy crap is happening, people vanishing, the power coming on and off, something controlling us like a demented puppeteer, why in the hell would you think something is wrong with me? He turned and looked into Chrissie's eyes. He saw compassion, but deeper he registered her fear. She was part of this madhouse too. He didn't have the market cornered. Jay expelled his breath loudly, realizing he was holding it as if submerged. Billy Compton would have been proud of his feat.

"Let's go," he finally replied, forcing his feet in motion and up the steps.

Fran was waiting for them at the doorway to her floor. She had clicked off the flashlight. "My digs are on the opposite end of the hallway. You want to wait here or come with me?"

"We better stick together," answered Jay.

"Then you damn well better do a better job than you have been doing." Fran quickened her pace, throwing caution to the wind with one mission, getting her gun. Jay and Chrissie trailed her by nearly twenty feet. Jay began knocking on doors as they passed. Chrissie joined in, knocking on doors on her side of the hallway. Fran, unfazed, just pushed onward. The lights remained on, no more flickering.

Midway down the hallway, Jay and Chrissie stopped dead in their tracks, hearing the latches of a door being unbolted behind them. Fran was too far ahead to hear it. Jay wheeled, snatched one of his sharpened cue sticks from his homemade shoulder harness and readied to do battle. Chrissie followed suit with a cue stick too. Jay tried to determine which door but couldn't be sure. He held his ground, not eager to confront whatever this might be. More sounds, and this time he zeroed in on a door, two doors back. He backed against the wall, the same side as the door. Chrissie hunkered down behind him. Could this be the demon or was it another trick?

Fran had turned to witness their odd behavior. She placed her flashlight on the floor and double gripped the pistol. She eased in their direction. Neither of them looked back at her, both focused on something behind. She scanned the length of the hallway, but she could not zoom in on what had captured their attention. Suddenly, a bright light shown against the opposite wall from where the two had paused to stand their ground. It reminded Fran of a hunter spotlighting deer. It was that bright. A figure stepped into the hallway, temporarily blinding those in the hallway with the brilliant light.

"Shut that off you damn fool, Injun," barked Fran. The light went dark. Jay and Chrissie both blinked, attempting to readjust.

A second figure stepped into the hallway behind the first. Fran set her gun's safety and dropped her arm, then picked up her flashlight. "You boys are a sight for sore yes. Folks, this here is Injun Joe and that there is Junior Johnson."

Jay nodded, acknowledging the introduction. Chrissie mustered up a half smile. Fran quickly closed the distance and patted them on their backs.

The one called Injun Joe extended his hand to Jay. "I'm Joseph Ironhorse. I work here. I'm in charge of the facilities. This is Haskell Johnson. He maintains the grounds."

"I'm Jay and this is Chrissie."

"Call me Junior and he doesn't like to be called Injun Joe." Junior chuckled, adding, "That's why we call him that. We love getting under his red skin. Fran, do you have any idea what's been happening?"

Fran replied, "More important, how'd you two make it this far, holed up in your room?"

9

Joe thought about Fran's question and recalled his friendship with Haskell Johnson before speaking. He and Junior were roommates, had been for years. Mason gave them one of the larger suites located on this floor. Some thought they were too close, possibly companions, but there wasn't a gay bone in either of their bodies. Their kinship had evolved quickly and unexpectedly, given their diverse backgrounds and cultures. Joseph Ironside was a blueblood Navaho. Haskell was a third-generation hillbilly. Typically, the two didn't mesh well in this territory. Neither of them was the typical type.

Most folks thought Joe was a Cherokee given the locale here in the Smokey Mountains near the Cherokee Indian Reservation. Joe didn't deny or defend his heritage. Sometimes it was just easier to allow them to think he was a Cherokee rather than explain the difference in being a Navajo. Joe had met Haskell at a flea market in Sevierville, Tennessee. Haskell had a booth selling used power tools. Joe had been in the market for a portable generator and Haskell had a slightly used one on display. After a lengthy discussion, Haskell had divulged he had fallen on hard times. His landscaping business had gone belly up after losing his wife to cancer and the expenses incurred in her doctor's care and hospital bills. The flea market was a means of survival.

Joe mentioned to Haskell that the resort needed some help maintaining the grounds and had been searching for experienced help. He gave Haskell a card and a contact name. A month later Haskell had interviewed and had been hired as an assistant. Eighteen months later he was running the show as the senior groundskeeper. Through many after-hours drinking binges, the two had become unlikely friends. It came with an expensive price tag for Haskell 'Junior,' Johnson. Joe forever regretted his role in this.

Haskell's family hated Indians, any Indians and didn't partially approve of his choice of friends. His relationship became very strained with his dad because of it, and to this day he had truly little to do with Haskell. There had always been a feud between his hillbilly family and friends with the Cherokee tribe. Joe being a Navajo instead of a Cherokee meant little to the matriarchs of the Johnson family. It had started generations ago when Haskell's great, great grandfather had entrusted an old Indian to sell his moonshine to tribe members. The Feds finally caught wind of the firewater reaching the reservation and after a lengthy investigation, nailed the Indian for peddling the goods. In return for a lighter sentence, the Indian had thrown Haskell's relative under the bus, leading the Feds to the still. Old man Haskell received a lengthy prison sentence and died while in the federal pen. This had prompted a bloody feud, some said worse that the Hatfield's and McCoy's.

During the most recent resurrection of the feud, threats were numerous, most directed at Joe, but Haskell had received a couple of close calls as well. Joe lived at the resort. That minimized his contact with the outside world. As time passed the attackers focused their attention on Haskell, who rented a house in town. Sadly, many of these threats came from his kinfolk. Most were distance kin, not caring how abusive they became, joined in by the local drunks and bullies. Large quantities of booze were usually involved prompting bolder and more abusive attempts. Haskell reached his final straw when they set his house on fire. He barely escaped but lost all his personal belongings. The local sheriff, blood kin, didn't pursue the culprits.

Joe suggested he move to the resort. Feeling much of the blame, he negotiated the larger suite with Mason. It was the only one available at the time for the hired hands. That arrangement had worked and remained in place to this very day. While none of Haskell's kinfolk ever forgot about his bond with Injun Joe, the attacks became less frequent because of him staying at the resort. Now they were like an old married couple, set in their ways, knowing what to expect of one another. It was the perfect relationship, without the sexual or marital hitch, an odd couple indeed.

"Damn, Joe, are you going to act like a wart on a frog, or are you going to answer me," asked Fran.

"It's like this," Haskell jumped in, "Joe was up as always, way before the first light of dawn, making his normal racket, causing me to stuff my head underneath my pillow. Even with my door closed I swear he can make more ruckus than a renegade bull in a china shop. I think he does it on purpose because he knows I can sleep later than him."

"You hog the bathroom like a beauty queen," fired back Joe.

"Ladies," interrupted Fran, "Stifle it and just get to the point."

"Like Junior said, I was up at my normal time, trying hard not to wake *Sleeping Beauty*. I had just gotten out of the shower and dressed when something didn't feel right."

"Here we go with that 'like only an Indian can sense things,' nonsense," piped in Junior.

Joe gave Junior the *go to hell* look, before continuing. "The pressure in the room was different. I have my scuba diving certification and it felt like it does when you're on a deep dive, a crushing feeling."

"Were the lights still on," asked Jay.

"At that point they were. The tugging began. It was literally as if I was being pulled toward the bathroom window by some unseen force. I had to really focus to resist it and hold my footing. The pressure behind my eyes was incredible, almost as if they wanted to pop out of their sockets. The air felt charged. That's when the lights went out. You know me. I always have my Torch strapped in the holster to my side."

"Torch," commented Chrissie, envisioning a long fire burning stick.

"Torch, the world's most powerful flashlight," clarified Joe.

"Joe has a flashlight fetish if you ask me," added Junior. "He must have fifty of them in here, all shapes and sizes, brand names. It's scary. It reminds me of a woman with her assortment of battery-operated toys, not that I would know anything about that. He suffers from a serious medical problem if you ask me."

"The feeling diminished considerably after I switched on the Torch. It almost returned to normal."

"Not from my room it didn't. My alarm sounded. I have one of those clocks that flash the time on the ceiling. It's like a bright flashing neon sign. It illuminates the entire room. That combined with an alarm sounding like a runaway freight train is the only thing that wakes me up, except for Joe's loud bumping and banging about."

"But I thought the power was off," stated Jay.

"Battery backup, my salvation and for the record, I locate the clock away from the bed. Those snooze buttons are the kiss of death."

Battery, thought Jay, here we go again. There is something significant about the battery.

"Hell's bells, that still doesn't explain what prompted you to stay in your room,' said Fran.

"What makes you think we stayed in our room? I'm facilities manager. It's my job to make sure this place runs like a fine oiled machine."

"I had forgotten I had set my clock so early," added Junior. "I was expecting delivery of a new bush hog and still had to ready the old one for pick-up. Service guy had told me he would be here by six on his way to another job. With the power off I dressed and went down with Joe."

"What struck me as odd, the emergency generators didn't kick in," said Joe. "I've tested and retested this fail safe and it has never malfunctioned."

"We couldn't use the elevators, so we headed to the stairs. Joe gave me an extra Torch. We headed down the hallway together. Odd, no emergency lights were on either."

"That was very disturbing," added Joe. "The emergency generators didn't kick in, nor did the emergency lights kick on. Like I mentioned, the system had been tested numerous times. It always worked flawlessly."

"Joe prides himself with that sort of crap," said Junior.

"We reached the stairs and started down," continued Joe. "That suffocating feeling was stronger than ever in the confined space of the stairwell. The shadows were alive, shape shifting, something my people understand. I asked Junior did he feel it.

"Indian mumbo jumbo, I told Joe. Just fix the power outage like you're paid to do."

"You never felt anything," asked Jay.

"Hold your horses, we're getting there," said Junior.

"We descended directly to the basement first," said Joe. "That's where the generators and power grid are located."

Jay cringed at the mere mention of the basement. To him, that was where the root of this evil resided. The basement, both Marge and Dean had vanished in that basement, along with his luggage. On pins and needles, he almost held his breath waiting to hear what these two survivors had found down there. He hoped any discoveries would help define what was happening.

"Stupid me, I went along with Joe, figuring I could lend him a hand if he needed it. Man, I should have stuck to my business and headed to the utility building outside. Then I wouldn't be trapped in here like a rat on a sinking ship."

"I'm glad you came with me," admitted Joe. "If you hadn't, you would have never believed it."

"Hell, I would have been better off in the long run, not knowing."

"Fellers, this isn't a damn suspense novel," butted in Fran. "Can't you give us the short version and spare us the side talk? I need to go get my gun and I could really empty this old bladder too."

Joe rolled his eyes. "We reached the access door to the basement at the bottom of the stairwell. I placed my hand on the door's bar about ready to push. That's when the sensations overwhelmed my Indian intuition. It jolted me like poking my finger in a light bulb socket. For the first time I was terrified. My brain was bombarded with wild imagines. I backed away from that door."

"He practically knocked me on my can with his back pedaling."

"What kind of images," pressed Jay

Joe frowned, strained to put what he had seen into words. "Do any of you ever watch the Discovery Channel?"

"What's this now, a Nielsen headcount?" asked Fran.

"He's not jerking your chain," spoke up Junior.

"Just tell us what you think you saw," said Jay.

"One time on the Discovery Channel they had a segment on worm holes. The moderator displayed all these multi-dimensional portrayals of what one was supposed to look like. What I saw in my head was an inverted vortex, a worm hole, sort of, or that's the image that comes to mind. I didn't want to open that door."

Chrissie jumped into the conversation. "Did you open the door or not?"

"Stupid ass me, I pushed past him and opened that door, figuring ole Injun Joe here was just having one of his spiritual moments. He has them from time to time. Usually, I just humor him or give him crap. It depends on my mood and the audience at the time. This time I wasn't in the mood to play his silly games, so I opened the door. That was a bad mistake, an awfully bad mistake on my part. I learned a valuable lesson. Never take likely what you think is a load of Navaho bull."

"What did you see," questioned Chrissie.

"It's not what I saw. It's what I didn't see that let me know I wanted no part of that basement."

"What are you doing now, Junior, quoting nursery rhymes," snapped Fran.

"The mother of all vacuum cleaners was trying to suck me through that doorway," claimed Junior. "It was weird though because the air was not moving around me like it would have been from a vacuum's suction, yet I was being pulled. I do mean pulled with tremendous force. I was clinging to that doorframe with my hands and feet."

"I saw that Junior was in trouble and grabbed for him. I too could feel the vicious claws of the great spirits attempting to whisk us both away. Pressed close against Junior's back, creating a log jam, I managed to redirect my light. I wanted to witness what so desperately wanted our souls. We both fell backwards, Junior landing on top of me. He quickly kicked that door closed. I sensed the door breathing, moving outward then inward, much like an enraged animal. Prey had been stolen from its clutches. That's when I realized we were the intended prey."

"I told Joe, if he was waiting on me, he was backing up. We hauled ass back up those stairs. I wasn't sure what we had encountered but I didn't want to stick around and find out."

"The shadows closed in on us and nipped at our heels. The evil spirits clung to the darkness. It moved as did we. The spirit world beckoned us, lusted for our very essence. A worm hole should not possess intelligence, should it? Or does man not fully understand its power? With both Torches guiding our escape we pressed upward. Neither of us aimed our light behind us. I think we feared what we might see."

"I just wanted out and away from whatever was down there," stated a profoundly serious Haskell Junior Johnson.

"We opted to exit on the lobby floor, feeling an urgent need to report this to Mason and those on night duty. Like the other floors, the emergency lighting was not working. We quickened our speed and reached the front desk. No one was manning it. It was dark so we figured like us, they had taken flashlights and were scoping out the situation. We were wrong. We found no one."

"I yelled numerous times, but nobody answered. It was deathly quiet. I looked over at Joe. I have never seen him display such emotion. He was as scared as me. Let me tell you, there is nothing worse than being afraid of the dark. I have not experienced this fear since being a wee chap, knee high to a grasshopper. Terror, I'm telling you, sheer terror, and I had no real clue what terrified me so."

"The persistence, still lurking in the dark, reminded us that we had not yet reached a safety zone. Where could we find such a place that the evil spirits would not follow us? I did not have that answer. I sensed we must not stay there though. As much as I dreaded it, we headed back to the stairwell. I tried to convince myself that we were seeing no one because it was the middle of the night for the guests to be out and about."

"This joint is quite spooky with no lights," added Junior.

"Back in the stairwell I personally felt entrapped, the walls closing in on me. The spirits were still angry and out for blood. I sensed at first the danger still oozed from the basement floor, but then I was unsure. In the darkest realm of the stairs leading upward, I could feel something waiting for its opportunity to whisk us away."

"We had taken a quick look around, checking out both restaurants and the bar. All was undisturbed and deserted. I kept telling myself, it was all right, too early yet for anyone to be stirring. If they were asleep, they had no clue the power was out. Joe resembled a scout, looking and listening for any sign of danger. He did everything but place his ear to the floor and listen for footfalls."

"We mustered the strength and courage to again enter the stairwell. Nothing there had changed. Evil still lurked downwards and upwards. We chose upward, but I have no real explanation why, except that the worst of what we had encountered was down in the basement. It was the lesser of the two evils. The stronger pull was from below."

"We entered the first level where the guests reside. Joe insisted we knock on doors and evacuate everyone, so we did. We received no responses. After about the tenth door Joe opted to use his passkey and open a few. We peeked inside. Seven doors later we had found no one. How queer though, their luggage was still in tack. None of the rooms had been ransacked. Most beds were unmade, giving one the impression that those who had been sleeping had to go for a bathroom break or something. The bathrooms proved to be empty as well."

"My concerns inflated, I now feared something quite catastrophic had occurred. I tried my resort issued phone but was greeted by a dead battery. I always left it on charge before retiring for the night. It should have had a full charge. I had Junior check his phone, dead just like mine. Maybe Mason had already evacuated the guests, but how could that be, and for what reason. No alarms had sounded. Going door to door would have taken much longer than the time that had expired."

"We checked two more floors, countless rooms, forever that presence dogging us," said Junior.

"We found not a living soul or dead one," added Joe. "On the outer edges of our lighted sanctuary something hungered for its next meal, but not as strongly as before. Its hunger had been temporarily quenched, maybe by those now missing. I suggested we return to our suite. There I had plenty of battery powered light. For some reason I grew comfort in that thought. Darkness was our foe."

"We remained here until we heard you knocking on the door," stated Junior.

"Daybreak had given us hope. We had switched off our flashlights after drawing open the curtains. We were about to leave when I ran my hands along the door's surface. The spirits were there, waiting on the other side. While sunshine filed our oasis, darkness still owned the hallways on the other side."

"Joe told me that he feared opening the door as had been taught him during his fire fighter training when a raging fire lurks on the other side. Never open the door that feels hot to the touch. Once opened, what lies beyond the door would surely consume us as would a fueled fire. I no longer questioned his premonitions. We waited it out here until now."

Inside the suite, Fran, Chrissie, and Jay filled them in on their experiences. It substantiated Joe's beliefs. The underworld's spirits had somehow been released and were out for revenge on mankind, explained Joe Ironhorse. Five strong, none of them had an immediate plan in mind. All agreed their perils were of the worst magnitude. Jay hoped one of these fine gents would take the leadership reins.

How do you fight evil spirits, wondered Jay, if that was indeed their adversary? He thought about poor Dexter in the cooler. Jay didn't cherish being alone right now. Worm holes or black holes, were they in the mix? Something had taken Mira and countless other folks. Apparently, it wasn't finished yet. It had more hell to unleash. Would its boundaries be restricted to the resort? For all Jay really knew the entire world might have already been impacted. They had no way of knowing, cut off in this mountain wilderness. Could they be the only survivors, he questioned?

They finally exited the stairwell to the next floor, a replicate of the previous one. Moving methodically down the hallway they knocked on each door, gave a shout out to anyone who may be inside. They didn't take time to open any of the doors with the passkey this time. In less than ten minutes the small task force was again climbing the stairs. Jay began rethinking this strategy. Not only was this depressing, not locating any of the guests, it also was costing them precious time. Still, what if they didn't do it and someone was holed up waiting for the rescue wagon. Two floors later they entered the next hallway, déjà vu, all knowing the drill.

Jay knocked on the door, his side of the corridor, and thought he heard something. He pressed his ear to the door and then knocked a second time while the others watched patiently. Not a word was being uttered, except those being spoken by Jay. "Is there anyone in there?" Jay turned to the others. "I swear I heard something."

"Allow me," said Joe, inserting his passkey into the slot. The door was unlocked.

Jay eased the door inward. Both Fran and Junior assumed a firing position with their pistols. Chrissie held her cue stick up as if ready to toss a spear. Joe had clicked on his Torch, just in case. Jay called out again, no answer. The entryway looked like dozens of others they had already breached. Nothing seemed out of place. A quick scan of the king room with desk and loveseat revealed no sign of life. Joe motioned to the bathroom. Jay checked. The door was locked. This didn't mean it was occupied. Perhaps the occupant had locked it for privacy reasons before they had vanished.

Junior whipped out a pocketknife. He used it to pry between the door and door facing, gaining access. Jay slowly pushed the door open. The others stood on alert. The bathroom was empty. Jay nodded, signaling to the others that the shower curtain was drawn closed. Fran stood over his left shoulder, weapon pointed, the safety off. He snatched back the curtain, the hanging fasteners clicking loudly as he did. The bathroom erupted in a series of screams. It took Chrissie a nano-second to realize some of the screaming was coming from her. The other scream came from a young boy huddled in the shower, aiming a flashlight with a battery so weak the light bulb barely glowed. In his other hand he clutched a long strand of rope. It was an odd combination to say the least.

11

Jay eyed the small boy sympathizing with his precarious situation. "Son, it's okay, we're not going to harm you. We're the good guys."

The young lad, wild eyed, frantically looked at the bathroom full of invaders. He aimed his flashlight at them as if it was a *Star Trek Phaser*. The flashlight was in the image of one of the *Transformers*, an immensely popular merchandising toy given the success of the movie franchise. The kid could have been no more than seven or eight, given his size. He was fully clothed, jeans and a tee shirt with a *Transformer* plastered on the front.

Chrissie stepped forward and squatted by the tub. She smiled and reached over and touched the boy on the head. He flinched, jerked spasmodically, looking at her wildly and then shrank backwards. "Hi, my name is Chrissie Waldrop. What's yours?" He blinked nervously but did not respond. Chrissie climbed into the tub and sat at the opposite end. "We're here to help you dear. There is no reason to be afraid of us. That's Jay, Fran, Junior, and Joe. Did you know Joe was an actual Navaho Indian? Joe, along with Fran and Junior, work here at the resort. Jay and I are guests just like you."

The boy stared directly at Chrissie, still withdrawn, knees folded against his chest. He maintained his death grip on the flashlight and rope. The others watched as she tried to break through to the young boy, obviously suffering severe shock.

"Joe, hand me your flashlight, please." Joe did. Chrissie switched it on and set it between the boy and her in the tube. She pushed it towards him with her foot. "Joe says this is called a Torch, the world's most powerful flashlight. It's yours if you want it."

The boy shifted his gaze to the flashlight. In one fluid motion he discarded his and snatched up the Torch. He held it to his chest and then aimed it directly at Chrissie. At least this was a little progress thought Chrissie. Jay smiled. He realized this might be doing Chrissie some good too. The boy took a deep breath, appeared more at ease. They were making headway, slowly, but things like this took time. Without warning, the power shut off. If not for the Torch, the bathroom would have gone pitch black. The surrounding atmosphere transformed. The presence was upon them. They had dropped their guard and had gotten caught with their pants down. Junior stood just outside the bathroom door, fumbling with his own flashlight. Others did the same with flashlights provided them earlier. Precious seconds passed, but it seemed much longer.

"Whew, that was too close," muttered Fran.

What progress that Chrissie had made with the kid had been lost? Joe couldn't say he blamed the boy. This had to be even tougher for a young mind to comprehend. Obviously, his parents or any siblings had vanished. He had been saved by a toy flashlight. While maybe the boy didn't understand the significance of the light, he certainly knew lights fended off the boogeyman.

"We've dilly dallied long enough," spoke up Jay. "Don't we need to get a move on it if we're going to make it to that rooftop?"

"Haskell, take the point while we get this young lad out of the tub," barked Joe. Junior didn't answer.

Fran whipped around her flashlight. Junior was not behind her. She scanned the remainder of the room, no Haskell Johnson to be found. The room door was closed, and she had not heard him leave. The answer slammed her with vengeance. "IT GOT HIM."

"How is that possible?" asked Joe, "He was standing right there behind you."

Fran waved her gun about. "Hell, I know exactly where he was standing, but I'm telling you he's gone. Don't tell me you didn't feel it. The air around me changed like it was electrically charged. Something even tried to reel me in, I'm telling you."

"Not Haskell, please, no, not him," sighed Joe.

"Why are we still standing here?" asked Jay. "We should get to that roof. We can't help your friend. I'm sorry, but this is not our first rodeo. We all know what happened. This presence, evil spirit or whatever it is took him, just like Fran said."

Joe gave the order. "Lights remain on at all times. We can't take any more chances. The spirit takes advantage of our mistakes."

"You have no argument from me," replied Fran. "By the way, the gun is gone along with him. Do you suppose that means that bullets can harm this so-called spirit? Maybe that's why it snatched it too."

"Jay, please help Chrissie with that boy," suggested Joe.

"Are we finally heading to the roof then," asked Jay.

"How can we? If there's one survivor, there could be more. We must search the remaining floors."

"In case it hasn't registered with you, Joe, we're playing on its terms right now. Lights off, it's in its element. We are at its mercy," warned Jay.

Joe would hear none of it. "How does the creed go, no man left behind?"

"I'm not arguing that point with you, but we can't afford to lose more people."

"I don't think being here or any other place will have a bearing on that. We screwed up. We dropped our guard and now he's gone. We can't make that mistake again," added Chrissie.

"Just help her with that boy," Joe asked again, tone more like an order than a request this time.

"Junior, Jay, Joe," quipped Fran. "Do all the men in my life have names beginning with the letter 'J', and are all of you cursed to damnation?

"You left out Dexter," Joe reminded her.

"Ah, but his full name is Jason Dexter Parnell."

"How about calling me by first name, Franklin, then, not that I'm superstitious or anything," added Jay.

"Enough,' screamed Chrissie. "I'm tired of all of you making light of this situation. We're fighting for our lives, not to mention wondering what happened to our loved ones. This is no place for such nonsense."

"Point taken," answered Joe, as the lights came back on.

"We're being baited again," warned Jay.

"That's a fact, Hon, but ole Fran's not even offering a nibble, let me tell you. If it ever sinks its teeth in my hide, I'm going to leave a mighty bad taste in its mouth, gunpowder, and piss, and that you can take to the monster farm."

"Lights on everyone, let's move out," said Joe.

"And safety off, finger on the trigger," added Fran. "Bring it on if you got the balls to take on the likes of me, Mister Shadow Spirit."

"I wouldn't tempt fate if I were you," warned Jay.

"You're not me, so don't get your panties in a wad. You just help Chrissie coddle the little chap and leave the man stuff to me, Hon."

Chrissie still had not managed so much as a grunt from the little boy. The lights going out had been a major setback in her efforts. She could imagine what the poor kid must be going through, given what they had all experienced. Chrissie was a bit energized, having the boy to take care of. It served as the perfect distraction to their perilous predicament.

Jay was the one now about at the end of his rope. How much more of this he could possibly stand? How much can anyone be expected to endure? Like Fran had so eloquently put it; we're in one of those horror movies being picked off one at a time. This thing, whatever IT was, had a plan that included eliminating every human being. That was obvious. IT was tiding up, talking care of the stragglers now. It would certainly help if they knew what they were dealing with, but all they had to go on was its association with darkness. Did it really fear the light? Could the light somehow render it powerless? Did the darkness empower it or just conceal its existence? Neither Jay nor the others had those answers.

The stairwell seemed more forbidding than ever this time. Climbing the steps took all the energy Joe could muster. Haskell Junior Johnson being taken had impacted him more than he would ever admit to the others. The man was a true friend, his best friend and roommate. How could this be happening? Would the roof really be their salvation? A peculiar thought overwhelmed Joe. What if this entity was herding them to the roof? Maybe it had entered their minds and planted the seed. None of them could know the powers it might possess. His people believed in spirits, good and evil ones. Every spirit had a purpose, a place in their culture. Could this be the second coming, in Biblical terms, he wondered.

Joe Ironhorse considered himself somewhat of a religious man, and while he was no expert on the Bible, he did remember the *Book of Acts*. He recalled some of the signs. *The coming of Christ will be instantaneous and worldwide. For as the lightning comes from the east and flashes to the west, so also will the coming of the Son of Man be,* Matthew 24:27. These flashes of power on then off, could it be the sign? Instantaneous, it had been for the most part. Joe envisioned other so-called signs, Thessalonians 4:16, *in one single event, the saved who are alive at Christ's coming will be caught up together with the resurrected to meet the Lord in the air. Then we who are alive and remain shall be caught up together with them in the clouds to meet the Lord in the air. And thus, we shall always be with the Lord.* Could they be a handful of the saved ones? Maybe there were pockets like them around the world. Matthew 24:30 states *the coming of Christ will be visible to all. Then the sign of the Son of Man will appear in heaven, and then all the tribes of the earth will mourn, and they will see the Son of Man coming on the clouds of heaven with power and great glory.* This must be our purpose to reach the roof, he convinced himself. Where else can we bear witness to this, coming from the heavens above? Yes, that must be it.

"For the Lord Himself will descend from heaven with a shout, with the voice of the archangel, and with the trumpet of God. And the dead in Christ will rise first," Joe spoke loudly.

"Don't tell me we're pausing to have a revival," said Fran. "Have you been touched with a surge of the Holy Ghost, Bother Joe? Don't get me wrong, a little prayer certainly can't hurt our situation. You just sort of sprung it on us out of the blue."

Joe blinked and stared at Fran expressionless unaware of his emotional outburst. He didn't respond, which seemed odd to Fran. She let it slide but wondered if ole Injun Joe was losing it. To play it safe she brushed by him taking the lead. He mounted no opposition to the maneuver. A matter of fact, he allowed the rest to pass and sluggishly brought up the rear.

Fran embraced the adventure. She was Annie Oakley, gun totting and ready to take on the cattle rustlers. She had given the boys plenty of opportunities to lead. Now it was her turn to take charge. She lived for this moment and had always felt she was destined for a greater calling in life than just being the lady in charge of seeing rooms were cleaned. *Hell yeah, my time has arrived.* She almost yelled it out loud. She could feel its presence, on the fringes of their artificial light. It beckoned, an almost soothing invitation, luring her to come forth and partake of the forbidden fruit. She couldn't be so easily enticed. Relentless, the attack on her senses continued. She hadn't remembered these sensations during early encounters. Before it had only been a change in the air, then that unforgettable magnetic pull. Was it upping its game? It really didn't matter what sort of tricks it pulled. Fran stood her ground, not one to be deceived or manipulated. It was wasting its time on her. Some of the others might be low hanging fruit, easy pickings, but not her.

Fran nodded. One by one the others' brains were being turned to mush, for one reason or another. That's what it did. It softened you up first, tenderized you and then slapped you on the grill. Not me, she proclaimed mentally. Give it your best shot. I have no fears or phobias for you to use against me. My only flaw, I have needs like any red-blooded woman. I thought Dexter Parnell was the answer and could fulfill my womanly cravings. How stupid was that? You can do much better than that, old girl. He was just a mere steppingstone to get you by, nowhere close to a soul mate. *Hell, I don't need a man in my life at all, if comes right down to it. I've gotten by without one.* Who was she kidding?

"Damn you, Dexter," she whispered. "You screwed up everything." Being a spineless coward just doesn't do it for me. A woman like me requires a real man, like *John Wayne*. He was a man's man and woman's man to boot, rugged and rowdy. *Duke* appreciated a good woman. He didn't take foolishness off any of them. He liked a woman to be aggressive and then he would put her in her place. Dexter was more the *Pat Bertram* type, *Roy Rogers'* little dufus sidekick. She had been too blinded by the sex to have seen it. Too long between couplings had clouded her perception.

Jay tapped her on the shoulder. "Are we going up or are we going to check out this floor? I vote we keep moving."

"What makes you think this is a democracy, fat boy? Of course, we're going to look for survivors. That was our plan and we'll be sticking to it. There's your stairway to the stars. If you want to get a jump start, have at it." Jay fell back in line. "I thought so. Tell the others we're going in. Lock and load." She had always wanted to say that, even though she was the only one with a gun.

12

The search was much less enthusiastic. Injun Joe and Jay went through the motions, while Chrissie clung to her new life preserver, the little nameless boy. Only Fran remained literally gung-ho. They eventually completed a clean sweep, all rooms, no survivors detected. Injun Joe had remained lethargic, too out of character for the usually upbeat and resilient facilities manager. Fran felt she carried the weight of this little expedition on her shoulders. It was fine by her. She was a tough old bird, full of piss and vinegar, a kick ass persona, ask questions later, a regular *GI Jane.* Her world revolved around the television and movies. She could relate almost anything to either. She was in her finest roll, preparing for a performance worthy of an Academy Award.

The corridor remained lighted, but everyone as agreed, kept their lights on. Fran assessed that their morale was all but being flushed down the toilet. She had to somehow snap this bunch of losers out of their deep dark funk. Any encounter would surely guarantee causalities at this rate. They could dare afford losing another person. Fran figured they could offer up the boy as a sacrificial lamb if the time came. He was not contributing to their cause, only serving as a distraction, hampering them. Survival of the fittest, wasn't that how it was supposed to work. Hell, she could sacrifice any of them, if the truth be known. *Listen to yourself, Fran, are you just trying to save your neck? Damn right I am.*

Son of gun, it finally hit her. *You're working me, aren't you? You're planting these filthy little seeds in my head, cultivating a Fran to serve your needs. If you can't get to us, then you'll have one of us toss you your meals. I wonder how many of the others are being fed this crap. Mind control, why not? It's the oldest trick in the book. Zombie fry our brains and we are at your damn mercy. That's okay. I'll just change frequencies, block you out all together.* She fingered the trigger on her gun. *Just give me one clean shot and I'll take your ass out, that's all I'm asking.* "Hey fellers, we need to go on offense. It's about time we put our heads together and chew on what we think is doing this. I don't want to just cut and run."

Jay responded first, "We've done that already. We're clueless."

"Work with me, fat boy. Is it man or beast, spooks or demons, space aliens or beings from another dimension, our government or just some sort of natural phenomenon? Can it be killed or defused? Did it just happen to us or is this widespread? Why does it crave people, or maybe it's any kind of energy source that floats its boat?"

"What does it really matter," answered Chrissie. "We're no match for it, regardless. It's whisked away an entire resort. What makes you think we can do anything?"

"Your attitude really sucks, missy. Hell, why don't you switch off your light and then you and the little feller can just go hand and hand into the belly of the beast. Be done with it. You're either in or you're not."

"That's not a very nice thing to say."

"Little lady, nice people finish last. Snoozers are losers. Either you're with me or you are against me. I've got a million of them, but bottom line, we've got to pool our resources and figure out how we can beat it at its own game."

"You talk the big talk," spoke up Joe, seemingly snapping out of his stupor. "Fact is, this is God's will. He will decide the outcome. It is out of our hands."

"Come on, Joe. Where's your Indian spirit, your warrior spunk? Surely, you're not going to roll over and let it win. Even God expects us to stand up for what we believe."

"Winners, losers, it is but a game. The afterlife is what's most important to each of us. We must prepare for the second coming, for it has arrived."

"Tell me it ain't so, Joe. I always liked that line directed to *Shoeless Joe Jackson* in the Black Socks scandal. Come on Joe, we're not down for the count yet. Trust me when I say this, God is not pulling

the strings on this one. He wouldn't spoon feed us like this, It has got
to be the devil or in this case maybe old Satan's disciple. It's not His
way. Nope, this would have been over two days ago if He would
have been in charge. Don't you get it?"

"Quiet," warned Jay.

"That's the spirit, Jay. Step up to the plate,"

"Quiet, damn you, I heard something."

"What did it sound like," asked Fran.

"Please, just stifle it, okay. There it is again. Didn't you hear it?"

Fran cocked her head. "Damn straight I heard it, footfalls coming
from the stairs. I wouldn't be so quick to take the bait though. This
could be a trick to get us in the stairwell and then snap shut like a
Venus flytrap."

The footfalls grew louder, coming from below, and then faded away.
Whatever or whoever it had been, had passed their floor, heading
upwards. By the sound of it, who or whatever it was was in a hurry
to get to wherever they were going. Fran looked at the expressions
on the others' faces. All appeared concerned, except Injun Joe. He
didn't seem fazed one way or the other.

"Those were human footfalls," said Jay.

"That's what it would like you to think. Don't you get it? This thing
uses mind control. Look at us. It's using something different to get
the better of us. It's inside our heads, using our thoughts against us.
I've seen the plot millions of times in the movies. Think happy
thoughts. It'll grow tired and go someplace else. It probably feeds on
our fears."

"That might have been my Dean or maybe Bobby or Marge. One of them escaped." With that Chrissie jerked open the stairwell door and sprinted up the steps. The kid was left to fend for himself.

"We've got to go after her," said Jay.

"Hop to it, Lone Ranger, if that's what you think. My gut says it's a trap. There's no need all of us playing the fool."

"But up is where we want to go, right?"

"Yes," spoke up Joe. "In one single event, the saved who are alive at Christ's coming will be caught up together with the resurrected to meet the Lord in the air. We must go upward to the roof." With that Joe entered the door and disappeared too.

Fran looked around, shaking her head in disgust. "That leaves me, you, and the little tike. What do you want to do?"

Jay sucked in a deep breath and tried to breathe normally. "Do we really have a choice?"

"I guess not. Can you manage the little snot nose?"

"Don't call him that."

"Okay then, the little sprout is your responsibility. I'm not the best role model for him, plus, I'm not the motherly type. If you got him, let's go. I wish I hadn't stopped smoking."

Fran cautiously opened the door, shouldered it while scanning the interior with her flashlight as if it were some sort of death ray in the stairwell. Her gun remained on ready in her other hand. She was a lefty. She cocked her head and listened. She could hear someone above them climbing the stairs. The speed was slow and deliberate. It had to belong to Injun Joe. That gal had been in too much of a hurry. Fran hoped she had kept her flashlight on, because if she hadn't, they could kiss her butt goodbye too.

Fran pictured Mamma Bear, Papa Bear and Baby Bear climbing the two flights of stairs to reach the next landing. She kicked the door open, shining her light down the hallway. One thing she could say for ole Joe, he owned some mighty mean flashlights. The beam made it to the end of the corridor. No one was on this floor. Chrissie didn't have a passkey, but Joe did. Jay tapped her on the shoulder and motioned above. She heard it too, someone still climbing the steps. A whoosh of cool air indicated the roof had been breached by someone above them.

"Well, there's only one way to skin this cat," said Fran, closing the door and hitting the next set of stairs. Jay, the kid in tow, followed. Pulling the boat anchor boy along behind him and utilizing one of Joe's flashlights didn't leave Jay with a freehand for his cue stick. This didn't fret him too much because he didn't really think it would do him much good against the menace of darkness. A few brief moments passed when Fran came to an abrupt stop.

"We're here. Just what do we think is behind door number one? Ready or not, here we come, Mister Boogeyman or whatever the hell you are."

The door swung outward. The night's fresh air felt wonderful on their faces. Dawn was still a way off yet. Fran had visions of the world not as they know it, being exposed when daylight offered them the opportunity to assess the countryside. The three exited the door and now stood on the roof. It was a glorious, cloudless, star filled night. She walked over to the buildings edge and listened.

"You hear that," she whispered to Jay.

"I don't hear anything."

"That's just it. I don't either. Up here there are always sounds, frogs, owls, whippoorwills, insects, something. You know what this means, don't you? They've vanished too. It's not just isolated to the resort building. I'd rule out ghost and demons now. This is something bigger than that."

"We need to find Chrissie and Joe."

 "Where's the kid?"

Jay whipped around. The boy was gone. He had just turned his hand loose while peering over the roof's edge no more than ten seconds ago. He started to yell for him, but what would he yell. He didn't know the boy's name. Simply yelling would serve no purpose and it would probably just scare him.

"Are you kidding me? Some babysitter you turned out to be. One responsibility and you blew it. It seems to me that everyone around you tends to disappear. Are you our boogeyman?"

"Can it, Fran. He was just here. If I were really the boogeyman you'd be gone by now."

"Funny, lard ass, I know the routine. Like magic he's gone too. It looks like it's just me and you, now and I promise to keep an eye on you just the same."

Jay looked frantic. He had dropped his flashlight and was rubbing his hands over his face and through his hair. He began shaking his head back and forth wildly. The man had reached his limit. In just a few short hours, feeling more like days, he had lost his wife and had witnessed, or sort of witnessed, the disappearance of what, eight, nine people. He had lost count. He looked to the heavens for answers.

"Just take me and get it over with," he yelled at the top of lungs.

The pain on his cheek rattled his cage. He shook almost convulsively, trying to regain his composure. A deer in the headlights of an approaching vehicle had nothing on him. His breathing was out of sync. He was on the verge of hyperventilating when the pain overwhelmed his other cheek. He placed both hands to the sides of his face, resembling the *Home Alone* kid after he applied aftershave lotion to his face.

"You better snap out of before I have to swat you again."

"You hit me."

"Twice," confirmed Fran, displaying her open hand raising it like a cobra ready to strike again, if need be, to jolt him out of his meltdown.

Jay sucked in a deep breath. "I guess I'm supposed to thank you, but that hurt like hell, so excuse me for not. Does this mean you trust me again?"

"Hell no, and I'm not a needy gal either. I'm just not quite ready to tackle this alone." She raised her gun aiming it at Jay.

"I'm in. You don't have to shoot me to convince me."

"Are you looking for this?"

Jay turned to address the voice behind him. Fran lowered her gun. "Kiss my grits! Dexter, what the hell?"

Dexter Parnell was holding the boy in his arms. "By the way, if you're looking for that lady and Injun Joe, they went that away," he pointed toward the other side of the roof where the heat and cooling units obstructed their view. "I heard them behind me on the stairs and went into hiding. I hunkered down and stayed low. I just caught a glimpse of them when I finally had the guts to look."

Fran eyed him up and down. "What made you leave the damn frig?"

"After the lights stayed on for a while, I guess I came to my senses in the cold. I decided I didn't want to face whatever this is alone. I've never hauled ass up stairs like that before in my life."

Fran had selfishly wished he would have said he had done it for her. A girl can hope. Either way, it was still good to see Dexter. She had been hard on him before, so maybe she could make it up to him.

Normally it wasn't Fran's style to apologize or ask for forgiveness, but these weren't normal times.

"We need to find Chrissie and Joe," interrupted Jay.

Fran, arms crossed, said, "One thing's for sure, If they're not behind those units over yonder, they're not on this roof."

Chrissie Waldrop existed in nothingness. The darkness had captured her before she had reached the roof. In her haste to find Dean and the others she had clumsily banged her flashlight against the railing, the flashlight going out, launching her immediately into the blackness. The force, like a blanket, had closed around her, scooped her up and snatched her from the stairs. Her skin burned as if having been exposed to an electrical jolt. The heat and humidity were almost unbearable. Breathing was difficult. Moving was impossible. She wanted to scream and wasn't sure why she hadn't. Chrissie had never felt this desolate before. The sheer magnitude of darkness penetrated her soul. She feared she was in the bowels of hell, but she saw no pit of fire. Nevertheless, she waited for Satan to meet and greet her.

13

The rejuvenated band eased toward the other side of the rooftop, Fran leading. The boy clung to Dexter. Jay gladly relinquished his babysitting duties. Flashlights beamed like search beacons sweeping a prison yard. The team cautiously inched forward. The huge heating and cooling units obstructed their view. If someone would have shouted boo, they would have probably all have scampered for cover. Fran broke the silence, almost doing just that.

"Joe, Chrissie, are y'all behind them units? It's us. We're all right'cher on the roof."

The silence was deafening. No response could be a good thing, thought Fran. "Red rover, red rover, we're heading right over."

Nothing but Jay's nasally breathing broke the silence. His nose whistled every time he breathed in making him wish he had his trusty nasal spray. It was packed somewhere in the missing luggage. He thought about Mira and the others. They were probably all in the same place. Fran fingered the trigger, giving the large unit wide berth as she maneuvered to enable her to see the far side. The others huddled behind her, chicks shadowing a hen. Dexter wasn't surprised the ole gal had taken the lead. She was the same way in bed, come to think of, prompting a slight smile on his face.

Fran advanced until she could see around the first unit. Nobody was there. The others peeked around her to confirm her observation. She focused on the remaining unit, the only other place anyone could hide on the rooftop. She discarded her flashlight, instructing the others to keep theirs steadied at the unit's blind spot. She assumed the two-grip stance with her weapon, looking too much like a police detective. Fran so loved this role; one she had been destined to play. She sprung into action, leaping to position herself, catching the others by surprise.

91

"Well drop my drawers," she sighed. Injun Joe sat in the stereotyped Indian position, his back to them, hands held upward to the night's sky, flashlight resting by his side. "Joe, I sure hope you're asking the spirits for a helicopter or something to get us off this roof." He didn't flinch, nor did he answer.

She walked over to face him, her gun put away and now shinning the light directly in his face. He blinked and then said, "What can I do for you, Fran?"

"You really need to make up your mind if you're going with God on this or the great Indian spirits."

He smiled. "One God fits all."

"By any chance has the Man up above told you how we're going to get out of this mess?"

"Have you seen Chrissie," butted in Jay.

"She was not here when I arrived. Perhaps she is already one of the lucky ones," Joe eyed the heavens.

"Lucky my ass," snapped Jay. He then looked over at Fran. "We're up here, so now what?"

"We wait for sunrise," she replied. "Didn't we decide that light is our friend."

"Would someone like to fill me in," asked Dexter. "I thought I saw the girl with Joe."

"Injun Joe here has wigged out on us. He's been spouting the Lord is here, the second coming has arrived, salvation for all of us," smarted Fran. "As for what you thought you saw, beats me."

"I'm not sure you should joke about something like that," Dexter responded.

"Fine, join his little prayer meeting if you want."

Joe stood and without a word began walking toward the stairwell.

"Now what," demanded Fran. "Where in tarnation are you headed, Joe?"

"The basement is where we will find the answers."

"Oh, give me a break, you said the roof and here we are. Make up on cotton pick'in mind," fumed Fran.

"I'm not going to that basement again. I've made that perfectly clear," argued Jay. "That's where you said you and Haskell Johnson encountered that wormhole, remember. I'm not going back down those stairs."

"We won't have to use the stairs. We will take the elevator," replied Joe.

"Hey chief, or whatever you're posing to be right now, the elevator isn't working, no power. Even if it was, I'm not getting inside of another one and I'm certainly not going down there." Jay folded his arms, standing his ground.

Joe walked over to the elevator, ignoring their protests. Fran walked along side frantically waving her hands about and raving like a wild woman. The power rumbled to life. Joe pressed the button on the panel and the door opened. "Going down," he announced.

Fran stepped into the doorway, blocking him for entering. "This is crazy talk, Joe. It's a trap. It's latched onto your mind."

Jay added, "No one who has entered that elevator has ever been seen again."

"Joe, let's talk about this," pleaded Fran.

"You do wish to know the truth, don't you? We will find it down there."

"Restrain him guys," yelled Fran.

Dexter and Jay jumped Joe, ultimately becoming an entanglement of limbs, wrestling for position. Fran held her position, blocking the doorway. The little boy ran past them and into the elevator. Fran relinquished her spot to retrieve him. Suddenly Joe stumbled into the elevator, Dexter, and Jay clinging to him, resembling a couple of leeches. The trap had been sprung. The door whooshed shut. The elevator rumbled to life, descended toward the basement, almost feeling as if it were freefalling. Jay envisioned feeding time.

They released Joe and held onto the sides of elevator for dear life, expecting to die in a horrific crash. Fran clutched the boy and readied for the worst. The elevator slowed as it reached the basement level and settled normally to a stop. Now what, each thought, all except Joe. The doors opened. The basement was well illuminated this time. Joe quickly exited. The others exchanged glances, hesitant about following him. Jay pressed the roof access button. Nothing happened. He began pressing the other floor buttons like some prankster. Nothing happened. He pressed the button to close the door. Nothing happened. This thing had them where it had wanted them all along, thought Jay, in the basement served up on a silver platter. He struck one of those dumbfounded poses staring out the doorway. He had spotted his luggage neatly stacked less than ten feet away.

"Like it or not, it looks like this is where we get out," said Fran. "Keep your flashlights burning just in case this is an ambush."

Jay threw up his arms. "What would make you think anything else? Of course, it's a trap."

"I should have stayed put," sighed Dexter, grabbing the boy by the hand. "Come on kid, we're off to see the Wizard."

As soon as they disembarked the elevator door closed. The power remained on making them even more suspicious. Jay scanned the perimeter. It looked like a normal basement. There were no mad monsters or aliens with tentacles ready to pounce on them. There was a forklift for unloading delivery trucks, meaning there were truck bays somewhere. Stacks of boxes probably contained various goods needed to support the resort.

Fran clutched her pistol in her left, flashlight in her right. "Joe, we're in the basement like you wanted, so what's the great revelation?"

Joe looked at her, puzzled, lost, and perplexed by her question. "I thought we all agreed we were supposed to go to the roof. Why did we come to the basement?"

"I knew it. The monster uses brain control." And just like that the lights went back out. Flashlights zipped about like Star Wars laser swords. The four adults formed an outward circle, pressed back to back, the boy between Fran and Dexter.

"You feel that," asked Jay. The pressure and energy were all around them, charged and ready, just within the fringes of the shadows. "This isn't a wormhole. Wormholes don't exhibit intelligence."

"Maybe we can communicate with it," added Dexter.

"It's smart, all right," confirmed Joe. "We journeyed to the roof to embrace the morning sunshine. It used me to bring everyone here, as far away from the daylight as we could possibly be. We'll not see the light of day down here."

"There must be delivery doors," stated Jay.

"There is a truck door and ramp down here," said Dexter. "It's like an oversized garage door with a keypad and remote. You don't really think it's going to allow us to open it, do you?"

"Surely it can be manually operated, a contingency for when the power is out."

"Good thinking, Jay," said Fran.

"We should wait until we know it is daylight outside. Out there in the dark may be more dangerous than in here," spoke up Joe, sounding more like his old self.

Jay jerked to attention. "It's her. She's here."

"Chrissie is here," asked Fran.

"No, Mira, she's here I'm telling you."

"It's screwing with your mind. Fight it," warned Fran.

"Maybe she found a safe place to hide. You did, didn't you? So why couldn't she? Is there another cooler or something like that down here?"

"There is a root cellar of sorts. I suppose it's mostly airtight," answered Dexter.

"That's got to be it then. Think about it. You were safe in the walk-in refrigerator, as was Fran and the resort manager in the safe. Light played no factor but for some reason it couldn't breach those two places. That means it isn't just the light alone that keeps it at bay. There are other factors involved."

Dexter thought about that and asked, "Could it have been the cold?"

"The safe wasn't refrigerated," pointed out Jay. "It could have waited you out. That refrigerator would have thawed out sooner or later. Besides, each time it allowed the power to come on, so did the refrigeration system. No, it wasn't just the cold. It's the same thing with the flashlights. Why couldn't it control that power source? What does one have to with the other?"

Fran's light flickered and went out "There goes that theory."

"No, I don't think so," answered Joe. "We've just pushed the battery life. No flashlight is intended to remain on for extended periods."

"Then that means it's just a matter of time before the rest bite the dust," said Fran.

"I've still got a couple of the lanterns in my backpack and at least one container of fuel," said Jay. "Unfortunately, Chrissie had the remainder of them. Can we go check out the root cellar?"

"Couldn't hurt, especially if you're right," said Joe. "It could be our new safe room."

Joe led this time with Fran a half step behind him. Dexter and the boy followed, Jay bringing up the rear. Jay shivered, feeling that stalking presence reaching for him in the darkness not being penetrated by their light. Most children feared the dark. This was unfamiliar territory for an adult. He would occasionally peek back over his shoulder. He couldn't help it. He never saw anything but that didn't deter the process. This something that goes bump in the night was all too real.

"There it is" said Joe, aiming his flashlight at the door.

"It looks like a bank vault," commented Jay.

Joe nodded. "The original owners of the hotel installed it down here. It was used as a vault to store paintings, works of art and other valuable antiques. In the early years this place was a getaway for the rich and famous, exclusively. The hotel frequently sponsored art shows or showcased sculptures from those more cultural individuals of our society. The Biltmore Estate in Asheville was very proactive in this process. Eventually the hotel closed and remained closed for nearly twenty years, until the new owners purchased it and constructed the massive place of today. They began marketing it as an all-inclusive mountain experience, more affordable to the common folks. The vault became a dinosaur and now a root cellar. It was too expensive to have it removed, so the locking mechanism was deactivated, no longer needed to protect potatoes and such."

"There you have it," said Jay, "Connect the dots. It fits the profile of the others."

The door was closed, routine, pointed out Joe. The cluster of survivors stopped and cased it, almost resembling a gang of safe crackers. Dexter stepped forward and grabbed at the huge handle and pulled. The door opened effortlessly. Beams of light invaded the cavity. Shelving had been installed for organizing the goods. Food wouldn't be an issue if they had to remain here for a lengthy stay. Jay held his breath, hoping his intuition would pay off and Mira would be inside.

Dexter stepped inside first. Jay passed the others, the anticipation getting the best of him. The vault was much larger and deeper than he had envisioned. It had obviously been customized to accommodate enormous sculptures or other art of significant size. It reminded Jay of photographs he had seen of the early era bomb shelters. Most likely it had been retrofitted for the hotel.

No one uttered a word, each scoping out the joint. Fran shoved her gun in her waistband and snatched up an apple from a crate. She polished the Granny Smith on her blouse before taking a bite. Tangy juice exploded in her mouth. She wiped her mouth with the back of her hand and then offered a bite to the kid, but he didn't react to her gesture. Fran shrugged and took a second bite. The kid didn't know what he was missing.

Joe spotted a box marked apple juice. He ripped open the top and extracted one of those 'child sized' sippy containers with a straw. He opened the flap and inserted the attached straw. He then offered it to the boy. At first the boy shied away, but Joe pushed it toward him a second time, mimicking taking a drink through the straw. He took it and sucked the contents down so quickly Joe thought the container would concave in his little hands. He prepared another one and handed it to him. He sipped on this one, and for the first time, Joe saw a bit of a twinkle in his brown eyes. Joe gave one a try, not half bad.

Dexter opened a plastic one-pint container of blueberries and scooped out a handful popping them into his mouth. Typically, he would have advocated washing them first, but somehow that didn't seem too important given their current circumstances. Something moved in the back of the vault, his view obstructed by a wall of boxes stacked nearly head high. The others had heard the noise too. Fran placed her apple back in the crate and removed the weapon from her waistband, releasing the safety. Jay held up his modified cue stick like a javelin thrower. They closed in on the noise coming from the deepest point.

Converging on both sides of the stacks, two from each location, they pounced as one. Huddled behind a second fortress of crates and boxes were two heads and four sets of eyes peering from behind their makeshift barrier. Each had hands raised and crowbars readied to do battle. Dexter recognized them immediately, seasonal help. The man was in his twenties and the lady in her mid thirties. He didn't recall their names. They had started less than a week ago. Neither welcomed them with open arms, understandably so, unsure who or what they should trust given what they may have experienced in the basement. Fran pointing the gun at them didn't reconcile the situation.

"Stay calm," said Joe. "Everyone, please lower your weapons. We're all on the same side."

"I just want to go home," spoke up the young man, a tear rolling down his cheek.

The lady stood. "Why has it taken you so long to find us?"

Joe wasn't sure how to answer their questions. There wasn't an easy explanation. Troubles abound, they had all suffered, but he could understand the new hires concerns. He thought carefully before he spoke, "This has been a difficult situation for all of us. We do apologize for not getting to you sooner. We've been searching the entire facility, I assure you. What did you two experience in the basement? Excuse me, I should introduce myself first." Joe made the formal introductions.

"I'm Rhonda Robinson and he's Henry Wilder."

"Now, please tell us what you saw," said Joe.

"That's just it," replied Rhonda. "It isn't what we saw. It's what we didn't see that has us concerned if that makes any sense."

"It makes perfectly good sense," spoke up Dexter. "Tell us what you experienced."

Rhonda looked over at Henry as if to ask should we tell them. "We were stocking items in here. A truck had arrived late last night. Mister Pinckney asked if we could come in early and put things away. That would have been yesterday morning by all accounts." Dexter butted in telling the others that Jasper Pinckney was the supervisor for managing the stock.

"We've been here for over a day," added Henry.

"We arrived around three thirty. Mister Pinckney wanted us done by seven. Seth Ledbetter was here too. He's an older guy, been her forever he told us. He likes things put up a certain way."

Dexter told them that Seth worked for the original owners of the hotel and lived in a cabin not far from the resort. He was a bit of a recluse but was very dependable. Sometimes he could be odd and quirky, but he pulled the weight of several half his age. Seth is seventy-nine and a Hoss, Dexter told them. He motioned for Rhonda to continue.

"Seth enjoyed telling us tales of the mountains and living the good life off the land. He said you could find anything you needed to survive here."

"He could tell some whoppers," added Henry.

"Yesterday he was wound up tight, talking nonstop. Most of it we had already heard before. He tends to repeat himself a lot. I figured it has to do with his age, even though he certainly didn't act it. He told us he was worried."

"Worried, about what," asked Joe.

"This is where it gets sort of weird. Remember, what I'm about to tell you is his words, not ours. He asked us did we know why the hotel closed twenty years ago. Of course, we didn't. I'll try to tell you the best I can what he told us. Here goes."

In Seth Ledbetter's words,

That thing that happened, the original owners kept it hush-hush, had to back then. They couldn't afford bad publicity, not for the Smoky Mountain tourist trade, especially when the leaves are changing colors, big bucks to be made. This place was so far back in the middle of nowhere they really thought they could sweep it under the rug, and they succeeded for a long period. I've been living in these mountains for pert near fifty years. There's no place I'd rather be, even with the strange on goings. You learn to ignore them if they don't affect your life. The mountains are full of myths and folklore. Say what you want, but the tales must have some point of origin.

I suppose I had felt the change coming for a while even before it ever happened. My arthritis can predict more than just weather changes. Ole Author is pretty dependable if I do say so myself. I felt it brewing. Nope, it wasn't a storm, but it was coming just the same. It was on a Sunday night. I had finished with my hotel chores that morning and had the rest of the Sabbath off. I wasn't due back until about daybreak Monday morning. My old cabin is no more than three and half miles from here, way the crow flies. I got me a well marked trail over the holler and through a draw down by the creek. I always bring my kerosene lantern, day, or night. I never know when I must work late, and most times it's dark as pitch when I come in. It always pays to play it smart.

My dog, Oscar, flea bitten coon hound he is and old as Methuselah, worthless for hunting, but still a good company, wasn't acting quite right that Sunday night. Critters can sense stuff we can't. He whimpered nearly all night. I finally penned him up in my out shed so I could get some shut eye. Next morning after a breakfast of sopping gravy and biscuits I gathered up my stuff and headed to the hotel. It was around three in the morning, so my lantern lit the way. I allow extra time at night. I have even crossed paths with a black bear a time or two, but I'll save those stories for another time.

It was sometime after four when I was close enough to be able to see the hotel lights. Oddly I didn't see them though. It's always lit up no matter what time of night it is. Moon was at first quarter so light wasn't good. I couldn't even make out its silhouette against the night's sky, not until I got close. Before I did though I felt it. First, I noticed how deathly quiet it was. The thought came to me a bear might be in the area. Crickets and frogs don't stop their ruckus for a bear so I ruled it out. It was just too still for the mountains, no matter what the season. I sensed I was being watched too. My head felt like I had it shoved inside a bucket. The hairs on my arms tingled. I shivered. The pitch blackness was closing in on me almost suffocating like.

I finally reached the service entrance of the hotel. I have a key to the basement. I figured it must be some sort of power outage for it to be so dark. It was the off season, those few short weeks between the end of the summer crowd and the beginning of the color watchers. There hadn't been too many rooms taken over the weekend and all had been expected to check out Sunday morning. There was only about a dozen of the regular hotel staff. They would be beefing up that count in another week or two.

I yelled out after getting to the basement. Nary a soul answered me, but it was right early yet. Still, Vincent Holmes was usually up and about, stoking the coal furnace. It was right spooky, and I don't ever get spooked. I climbed the stairs to the lobby. Back then we didn't have an elevator. There wasn't but three floors. New owners expanded, using the old basement and foundation when they reopened to what you see here now.

The lobby was dark and empty. There wasn't a lantern or flashlight in site. That struck me as mighty peculiar. I rambled about for a while, but nobody was around. I've never had that to happen before, not a single time, I'm telling you. Worse still, that crazy feeling I was having, like someone was trying to reach out and snatch me right up. I didn't believe in the boogeyman, or at least I used not to be one to believe. I'm not sure anymore. I searched all the floors and never ran across a signal person.

I didn't want to burn up all my kerosene, so I found me a flashlight behind the lobby desk wondering all the while why the night attendant didn't have it with him. I blew out my lantern just before switching on the flashlight and in that one second it tried to get me. It was like something was trying to smoother me with a giant plastic bag. My skin was burning like I was caught in a grease fire. My thumb twitched enough to click on that flashlight, and it just went way. I looked myself over for burns but didn't see any signs. I set a match back to that ole lantern, figuring there was no such thing as too much light.

I went back down to the basement, snatched up my lunch bag and waited outside until daylight. The whole time, sitting there just waiting, I felt it all around me. Shortly after daylight, the lights came back on inside. I figured the co-op folks had fixed the problem. I mustered up the guts to look around inside a second time. I didn't find anybody that time either. The phones were working so I called the hotel owner over in Knoxville. He asked me to stay put, he would send somebody over.

Long story, short, nobody was ever found. They made me sign some papers to keep quiet and gave me a nice sum of money. They closed the hotel shortly after that. To this day I'm not sure what they told the folks of them what went missing. I stayed to myself but did come up here from time to time. I wanted to know what happened, but I never had that peculiar feeling again, not until this morning.

"Seth gave us his lantern and told us to light it and put it in the root cellar. He said if the lights go out, for us to get in here as fast as we could and close the door. He warned us to not open it until he or somebody came back for us. He rounded up a couple of flashlights and four candles, some matches. He was acting a little crazy to us.

A while later we were standing in the doorway waiting for Seth not more than ten feet away as he was pushing a cart full of goods in our direction. He refused to use the fork truck and neither Henry nor I were trained to use it yet.

"He was right there," added Henry. "I could almost reach out and touch him. The lights went out without warning. I heard Seth scream, 'get'. I saw Seth and then he was gone, right there, just in the edge of the shadows. I felt it. It was just like he described. I pushed Rhonda in here and closed the door behind me. "

"Here is where we have been ever since," said Rhonda. "We ran out of kerosene first, then eventually the candles burned down to nothing, and the batteries went dead after a while longer. We struck matches and burned some cardboard until we ran out of matches. We've been in the dark ever since. We didn't know if it was day or night outside. Our watches were not working. Seth told us whatever we did, to stay away from the dark. We've been waiting for somebody to come for us, all the while in the dark. Is it gone?"

"I'm afraid not," spoke up Fran. "The boogeyman is alive and well and wreaking havoc still."

"The boogeyman got my mommy and daddy and little sister," said the boy, his tiny voice catching them off guard.

14

Jay wished Chrissie could have been here to hear the boy's first words. He wasn't sure why he emphasized the importance of this event in his little pea brain, but he supposed he was reaching for anything at this point. He wondered if she and Mira were together, wherever this thing had taken them. He shivered, thinking maybe they hadn't necessarily been taken anywhere. Whatever they were up against could have simply consumed them. He shook off that premise. He had to hold on to the hope that all of those who had vanished would eventually be found alive and well. He must believe to survive.

"Son, can you tell us your name," asked Dexter.

"My name is Dwayne."

"How old are you, Dwayne?"

"I'm six, almost seven. Mommy and Daddy told me they were going to have a birthday party for me here. I think I'm seven now."

"Happy birthday, youngster," said Fran, rubbing him on the head. "What's your last name?"

"Dwayne Evans, I'm hungry."

Fran plucked another apple from the crate, wiped it on her blouse and then handed it to Dwayne. He tore into it this time. She, like the others, decided not to push the chap too hard about his parents and sister. What good would it do to stir things up for him? They knew the routine and the outcome all too well. Dwayne had been lucky to have had that toy flashlight in his possession at the time of the power outage.

Fran eyed the latest newcomers to their troupe. Henry, a light skinned black kid, was a little scrawny. He didn't look much like he could hold his own in fight, even if he fought dirty. He probably stood couple inches shy of six feet and couldn't have weighed more than a hundred twenty pounds soaking wet. Rhonda, on the other hand, was what Fran referred to as big boned. She was a healthy heifer, not fat but quite stout by comparison. She might be a spitfire when the time came. Her long black bangs irritated Fran though drooping too much in her eyes. She was always doing this little head flip to shift them back. Funny, she thought, gauging their warrior potential.

She was glad Joe had snapped out of it. Injun Joe possessed a wealth of knowledge about the resort and had a commonsense approach to situations, except for recently when the thing had taken control of his thoughts. And there was Dexter, after she had all but written off his sorry butt. He might not plug the hole left by Junior, but it was still good to have a friendly face among them. She at least had familiar comrades to spend her last hours if worst came to worst. That left the wild card, Jay, 'fat boy' as she had dubbed him. She had first been a bit impressed by his tenacity, but now she wasn't so taken by him at all. Well, she thought, maybe the thing had messed with his head too. She should probably give him the benefit of the doubt, cut him a break for now.

Her thoughts drifted to those friends and coworkers missing. Mason Wells had been the best boss she had ever had. He dissevered better. Hell, they all dissevered better than this fate. Her crew had been top notch. They were her family, sisters, and brothers so to speak. She had been close to every single one of them. Snap out of Fran, she scolded herself; no need to piss in your corn flakes. It's time to figure out how to lick this thing. It's not going to suck on these old bones without one hell of a fight, I guarantee you.

"Joe, what's the plan?"

"Fran, I wish I had one. Waiting it out to daylight still tops my list. Sadly, we're just drawing at straws on that, hoping the sunshine will chase away the evil spirits, so to speak."

"I hate to harp on the *end of the world* movies, but I wonder if everywhere is like this. I just have these bad images in my head that when darkness fell around the globe, this happened to every town, city, and country. I can't help it. My brain is screwed up like that."

"Don't beat yourself up, Fran. We must consider all the possible scenarios. We'll face that one when and if we get to it. I suggest we focus on our survival first. That's what we can control. I must have faith we do have some say so in this yet."

"I've listened to both of you, but neither of you are painting a rosy picture or tossing out an action plan," interrupted Jay.

"What about you, fat boy? You're up to your eyeballs in it too. Do you have the answers to our fate stashed away in that little brain of yours?"

"I didn't mean to come off condescending. I'll be the first to admit that I don't have a clue what's going on or what to do about it. I'm terrified at the consequences. We've been through a lifetime of hardships so far and it's not improving."

"I just want to go home," whined Henry.

"Son, haven't you been listening to this conversation," snapped Fran. "There might not be anything or anybody out there left. We could be it."

"Come on, Fran," pleaded Dexter. "The kid doesn't deserve that sort of talk."

Fran didn't honor that comment with an apology nor did she 'pretty up' her thoughts or talk for anybody. Instead, she threw her hands and walked away. It is what it is, she thought. You can paint her up all you want, but a whore is still a whore. That was a saying her daddy had used when refereeing to her mama. Daddy had run her mama off when she had been a little girl. He had caught her fooling around with Lenny Gibson, the grocery store owner. Fran had been five the last time she laid eyes on her mama. To this day she never knew whatever happened to her. Daddy had forbidden any talk about her from Fran or her brother and sister. Daddy died two years ago.

She suddenly wondered what had happened to Colton and Kendra and if her siblings were all right. She could only hope this didn't go beyond the mountains.

"Henry, we all wish we could escape this nightmare," added Joe. "For now, we must stick together and work through it. A wise tribal leader once said, 'live your life that the fear of death can never enter your heart'. If it is His will, we shall overcome this."

Spare me, thought Fran, but she kept her mouth uncharacteristically closed. Hope and change reminded her of that load of horse hockey the last president had been shoveling. That bunch of empty promises had hopefully ensured him being a one term wonder. If they could survive the hole that man had dug for America, then surely, they could dig their way out of this one. Maybe there's hope and change, if this thing got him too, not that it really mattered now. Still, he had screwed things up enough those first four years he was running the show. Look at me, she sighed, turning this mess into politics. Evil resurrects evil, I suppose.

"How long do you figure before daylight," asked Dexter.

"We're in the waning hours for sure," answered Joe.

Jay felt like he had already spent a week at the resort. This was supposed to have been his and Mira's self healing weekend. Maybe this was meant to be a sign to tell them just how hopeless their situation had been. Joe had mentioned 'His will'. Things work out for a reason. It was going to be a dice roll for them to have worked out their issues, but at least both had been willing to give it a shot. Perhaps Mira had been more optimistic than him. He had probably let things go too far for way too long to really think they had a prayer to undo their strained relationship. Sitting here now, it seemed obvious most of the blame had been his. Why hadn't he told her? No, he had made her think it was all her fault. He had been foolish and inconsiderate. If he found her, he would undo this and make it right. Easy to say now.

Rhonda Robinson wasn't sure where she fit in with these people now sharing the root cellar with her and Henry. She was certainly glad to see them but wasn't enamored by their stories of gloom and doom. Down on her luck, she had taken this job to help with the monthly bills. Her husband Bill had lost his job recently with a local construction company, cutbacks, and bad economy to blame. They had four children. She could proudly say they had never been on welfare or any other assisted government programs. Her husband had reluctantly recently filed for unemployment benefits. Based on what these people were telling her, she feared for his family's safety. She had previously met Dexter once, and had seen the Indian around, but didn't know the crude talking woman or the other guy and boy.

Not so shy either, Rhonda thought, maybe she should speak her mind to set the record straight where she stood on things; not that they had asked her opinion yet. She realized she was low in the pecking order, working this meager little job in the basement, but all things considered, she was just as important as anyone now. They were apparently in a fight for their lives. That alone put them on even footing. She was as good as anyone here, and it was about time they realized it.

"We've hidden in here long enough and we're really ready to leave. Henry is right. We should go home. Our families are probably worried about us."

Jay bit, "When did your families expect you back?"

"Yesterday," replied Rhonda.

"Don't you find it strange, Hon, that somebody hasn't come looking for you before now?" asked Fran, unable to stay out of the conversation.

"Maybe they have tried to reach us. The power has been out?"

"We have cell phones, Darling, and if you haven't noticed, they are out too. If you hubby were that worried because he couldn't get through to either, he would have come up here or called the authorities, don't you think?"

Rhonda was almost embarrassed to admit it, but she didn't have a cell phone. They had canceled it, trying to trim their budget. Times were hard. She bit the bullet and confessed, "We don't have a cell phone right now and he couldn't just pack up the children, driveway up here. I'm sure he's trying to find out what's going on at the resort."

"I hate to be the bearer of bad news," added Jay, "But Mira and I, then Chrissie and her bunch were probably the last ones to arrive last night."

"Tell me, Sugar. You and Henry are supposed to unload trucks and put away the stock. Have you seen any more trucks?"

She shook her head, no.

"Let's face it," added Dexter. "We were at maximum occupancy. There were plenty of opportunities for concerned citizens with the number of tourists we have here, people wondering why their loved ones hadn't called or why they couldn't reach them."

"Everybody is dead then, like you said," whined Henry.

"We never said anyone was dead," corrected Joe. "We're just not sure where they have gone or better stated, where they have been taken."

"Kiss my grits, Joe. Cut the 'BS'. Don't try to make the boy think they might have gone on an extended vacation. Poof, they disappeared. You can't pretty it up. More than ever, y'all done convinced me it is bigger than just us. Our world has bit the big one, an ending fit for the cinema or a best-selling book."

She was right. No one wanted to say it. Saying it made it all too real. You can't take back words once you speak them. Admitting something as catastrophic as this was just a hard pill to swallow. The evidence was mounting and difficult to ignore. They would have to make their way out of these mountains to confirm it sooner or later, one way or the other. Their only chance hinged on the premise that the sunlight would ward off whatever it was out there. On that thought, a second flashlight went dead. That left them with two and one kerosene lantern.

Joe decided to conserve the two remaining flashlights and now they only had the light provided by the single lantern. Everyone huddled around it, not confident that the root cellar alone offered a safety buffer, even though Rhonda and Henry had previously survived in the darkness here. The lone flickering flame ironically represented their mere glimmer of hope. The next challenge was judging when daylight arrived. That was when they would make their break for the great outdoors. With no watches and in the darkness of the cellar, this would not be easy. He'd have to depend on his biologic clock, and it was badly skewed out of kilter right now.

Joe's ancestors never had the luxury of the white man's invention. The sun, the moon and the stars told them all they needed to know. But then again, the time of day was not as crucial to them as the changing of the seasons. There was really no need to fret over the concept of hours, minutes, and seconds. If one was hungry, it must be mealtime. If it was dark, it must be bedtime. If it was daylight, it must be time to rise. Inside this tomb the sun, the moon and the stars offered little assistance. He thought about what Jay had said, why did some of the batteries fail while others did not? To be specific, why did only the flashlight batteries continue to work? "Jay, have you thought any more on the battery question?"

"The battery question," responded Jay.

"Why are the flashlight batteries unaffected?"

"Why are the flashlight batteries not impacted by it," repeated Jay. "What makes them so special?"

"Potassium hydroxide," spoke up Henry. "They're used once then discarded after they are spent. They are convenient and cost less.

Primary batteries have a higher capacity and initial voltage than rechargeable batteries, and a sloping discharge curve. Potassium hydroxide is used in many household goods, bleach, drain cleaners and soaps for example."

"Henry, what makes you such an expert on batteries, "asked Dexter.

"I love chemistry, plus I did a paper on it in school. Primary batteries hold a constant capacity over a wide range of current drains and continue to function in sub-zero temperatures. They come in a variety of sizes, including AA, AAA, C, D and 9Volt, and they require no special disposal, making them environmentally friendly."

"We have ourselves a regular Mister Wizard," said Fran.

"Lithium, on the other hand, is the lightest of metals and it floats on water. It also has the greatest electrochemical potential which makes it one of the most reactive of metals. These properties give Lithium the potential to achieve extremely high energy and power densities. It permits an exceptionally long useful life and small cell packages. Lithium offers high energy density, double that of premium alkaline batteries, high cell voltage and a flat charge characteristic. It has high energy density that is double that of the high-in alkaline batteries."

"Thank you, Mister Consumer Report," scoffed Fran. "What have we learned here, kiddies?"

Jay answered first. "Potassium hydroxide jumps out at me, this whole alkaline thing. Henry mentioned various household items too. Possibly there is a correlation. The safe, the cooler and this root cellar, what do they have in common besides almost being airtight?"

"You can rule out the airtight part. If that were a fact, this thing would have invaded all these areas anytime the door had been opened," said Joe.

"Possibly the lights kept our foe at bay," said Jay. "Those who were trapped in the dark didn't open the doors. They were found still locked away safe and sound. It's got to be something else, something we're missing."

Fran began cackling like a deranged hen laying the mother of all eggs. "Alkaline, son of a gun, it's afraid of bleach!"

"I don't follow you," said Jay.

"Once a month we clean certain areas of the resort with a concentrated bleach disinfectant. Bless my soul. The vault, all the walk-in coolers-freezers and this here root cellar are on my list. We clean the outside and inside of the doors, all floors that do not come in direct contact with food or high dollar guests' items when it comes to the safe. We pulled our monthly cleaning day before yesterday, just before this happened. We do this for all public restrooms and the pool area too. The rest of the time we utilize a very low non bleach concentrate, like any place in the resort."

Dexter reached over and gave her a sloppy wet kiss and then a hug. The others broke out in wild cheers. Even little Dwayne hooped and hollered, unsure why he was doing it. Joe wondered if other survivors could be hiding in the public restrooms or the pool area, but then he just as quickly dismissed it as being unlikely. While those poor souls might have been safe inside any of those areas, curiosity would have gotten the best of them, and they would have eventually ventured outside with no flashlights as a safety net.

"Where can we get our hands on some bleach," asked Joe.

"I keep it in small quantities in the janitor closets, each floor, but those have already been diluted, cut for everyday use."

"It's here," said Rhonda.

"In here," replied Jay, looking around the converted root cellar.

"No, not in here, but it's stored in five-gallon containers in the basement. We just unloaded a new delivery. It's locked up on the opposite side of the basement, away from any food, in a hazardous chemical storage cabinet."

15

Jay had to admit the kid must know his stuff, but then again, he didn't have the means to do a fact check. Bleach, a deterrent, seemed almost farfetched, but then again, this entire phenomenon had tested his sanity and belief in natural occurrences, those explainable and rational. Toss these concepts out the window based on what he had experienced over the past few hours. People were gone, fact, and his wife was among the missing.

He did his best to play the scenario out in his head. Assumption, both light and bleach, or the potassium hydroxide to be more precise, wards off the evil that has attempted to consume them. That may keep them alive, but how do they destroy it and the bigger question, how do they find and rescue those that have been taken? Can they even be brought back? He choked on those dreaded thoughts. This thing, whatever it is, appears to be anywhere and everywhere, all around them, just within the fringes of the darkness. How do you eliminate such an enemy? Can it be eliminated? The bigger question, where did IT come from and will IT return to its origin, a time of its choosing or ours? The old man had said it had happened another time many years ago.

Jay thought about Fran's various movie spins. He played them out in his head just for the hell of it, a method of deduction so to speak. Was it of alien origin? UFOs had been around publicly since that Roswell incident, probably much longer. Had it been leading up to this final conquest of earth? There was no proof that this extended beyond the boundaries of the resort unless you bought in to the premise of no contact or investigation from the outside world. No truck deliveries or police or even unities people checking in posed a compelling argument.

Worm holes, black holes, portals to another dimension, could any of these hold water? Sure, they could. If you don't have a leg to stand on anything is possible. Haskell Johnson and Joe Ironhorse had described what they had experienced and witnessed in this very basement as a wormhole. The unseen force pulled them like a gigantic vacuum. Worm holes don't possess intelligence, do they?

The enemy had the ability to counteract them, lure them and even use mind control or at least distort ones thinking. Surely a worm hole couldn't do this. But what the hell do I know about worm holes.

Demons, evil or restless spirits, entities from the beyond or witchcraft, could any of these be in play? It makes for good television, as do the others. At least there have been cases of possessions and exorcisms, but those were isolated to individuals, not hundreds of people. People didn't just vanish. Could this be a tug of war between good and evil, God and Satan, the second coming as Indian Joe had described? No, those thoughts had been planted in his mind. Then that brings me back to square one. Whatever this was displayed intelligence. This thing has a specific need, a purpose, an agenda, a hunger, and if it has fears, it can be destroyed. Can we destroy it? That was the million-dollar question.

"Hey fat boy, this thing hasn't sucked you back into wonderland, has it?" Fran poked her finger at Jay's chest.

"My damn name is Jay Myers. I would appreciate it if you would refrain from using your crude nick names. You really wouldn't embrace the one I have in mind for you, I assure you that."

"Feisty, I like that in you, Jay. So where did you wander off to a few minutes ago?"

"I was just trying to think through things, wrap my brain around what we might be up against and if we can derail it."

"I'll bite. Did you solve our little unsolved mystery? Can we kill it?"

"To be honest, I don't know. Light and bleach doesn't exactly sound like the weapons of mass destruction, do they? This sounds more like a child's fairy tale, something made up or told children just before bedtime."

"Fairy tales don't usually wipe out a butt load of people. I'm on pins and needles, waiting for our happy ending. Where's Prince Charming when you need him? I'm no quitter, but I wouldn't give you a plug nickel for our chances of coming out of this mess in one piece. Spill it to me straight. Do you think we can kick this thing's butt or not?"

Joe intervened. "We will stay our original course. Our intent is to escape this basement and to reach the daylight. We're not equipped to do battle with an unknown assailant. Its destruction is not on the table. I must make that perfectly clear. What if we're off on our assumptions? We cannot afford to anger our adversary."

"I agree with Joe," spoke up Dexter. "We can't fight this thing. Leave that to the experts."

Fran fumed at this approach. "Fellers, you don't get. You boys are holding out, thinking somebody is going to toss you a life preserver. For all we know there is no military or anybody else out there. We might be the experts, I'm just saying. I vote we go on offense, not defense. I know my stuff when it comes to bleach. Let me take a shot at this hungry varmint."

"Fran, I admire your convictions," said Joe, "but the truth is we should take baby steps first."

"Truth," shouted Fran. "You can't handle the truth." She looked over at Jay and whispered, "I always wanted to say that. It's from one of my favorite moves, *A Few Good Men, Jack Nicholson* as *Colonel Nathan R. Jessep.*"

"Fran don't get so melodramatic on us," warned Dexter.

"Then don't act like such a bunch of wussies. Locate your backbones, boys. This is no longer hide and seek we're playing here. It knows where we are. Tag, we're it now, our turn to do a little seeking."

"I side with Fran," said Jay. "We've got to go on offense. I'm tired of running."

Rhonda and Henry glanced at one another, as if to say, whose side do we choose? Without muttering a word, they both stepped behind Fran and Jay, nodded, showing their support.

"Majority says we fight," smiled Fran, arms crossed defiantly.

"I must remind you that I am the senior ranking official at the resort right now," warned Joe, attempting to take charge of the situation.

"Guess what," said Fran, hands now on her hips, "I quit. You don't hold diddly squat over my head now."

"Me too," chimed in Rhonda.

"I didn't like this job any way," added Henry.

"I think it's a mean bully," spoke up Dwayne.

Fran eyed Dexter. Where did his loyalty fall? He better choose wisely, or I'll cut him off permanently. She quickly received her answer.

"Joe, maybe they're right. This could be our last stand, but I say, so be it. I would rather we do this as a group, what you say?"

"This is what happened to my people in the first place. We trusted the white man."

"Don't look at me when you say that," smiled Henry.

"White people," corrected Fran. "Women have been liberated, remember."

"There is no future in arguing with buffalo dung. I believe all of you are full of it, but I'm in. I hope you people understand the ramifications if we move forward."

"Ramifications," said Fran, "It's pretty simple. We prove to this thing why WE are the superior race. It's picked the wrong playground or dinner table."

"I once read and have always remembered this quote," said Joe. *'When you walk to the edge of all the light you have and take that first step into the darkness of the unknown, you must believe that one of two things will happen. There will be something solid for you to stand upon or you will be taught to fly.'*

"And I say the unseen enemy is always the scariest, and nothing is scarier than that enemy you can't name," said Jay. "It's always the most fearsome. Enough talk, it's time to do as Fran has suggested. Let's go kick the shadow hugger's butt."

"First, we need the bleach and then a way to administer it," said Joe.

"Why don't we just bath in it," asked Dexter.

"Smart move, it would peel the flesh right off your bones," replied Fran. "Lantern is getting low as is the extra can of fuel, time to fish or cut bait."

16

Joe concurred, quickly pointing out to them the uncertainties. No one could predict how much battery life remained in the flashlights. Without light as their lifeline, they were fair game. Once outside the protection of the root cellar they must move swiftly to access the cabinet where the bleach was confined. Furthermore, they must devise a plan for when they reached the cabinet. Fran had suggested they dip precut and prepared strips of cloth into the bleach and affix them to various locations on their clothing, taking care not to expose their skin to direct contact with the potent chemical. She contended that having the fumes emit from their bodies might deter any attacks, even without the protection of lighting. This was of course an unproven theory.

Spray bottles should be stored nearby. These could be filled with bleach and sprayed about to clear the path and keep the thing at bay. A call had to be made to decide whether they should make their brake for the outside while they were out, gambling that morning had arrived. The consensus of the majority, no one wanted to return to the root cellar, only as a last resort. Joe pointed out to them that if their plan failed, returning probably wouldn't be an option anyway. No lights and if the bleach didn't work, game over.

There would be just enough Kerosene to refill the lantern one last time. Once filled they'd be on the move utilizing it and the flashlights, everyone staying within the protective field of light. Jay had argued for a smaller team of maybe three, the rest remaining put, but this had been shot down. Splitting up was just too unthinkable. No one wanted to be left behind. This meant they had to bring the little feller along, as Fran called him. She tried to reason how chaps and animals can be too unpredictable.

Once out of the root cellar Joe estimated their little jaunt should take less than thirty seconds. Allow a couple of minutes to access the bleach containers then soak the cloth steamers and attach them. Then they would fill the spray bottles. Working in teams this could be accomplished simultaneously. If the bleach worked, they would open the dock door and make haste their escape to the wonderful outdoors. If dawn had not arrived, they would hopefully utilize the bleach to ward off any attacks. It sounded simple enough.

"I think we should have a little prayer before we do this," suggested Rhonda.

"Hon, I admire your thinking. Having the Lord backing us up is always a good idea. Joe, you might want to call in any favors from some of those friendly Indian spirits too.

"Like I said previously, one God fits all."

Bowing their heads, Rhonda offered up the prayer. She delivered an inspiring little passage. It ended in a round of amen's. It was now or never. The lantern had been refueled. The three remaining flashlights had been tested. Rhonda and Joe would take the lead, both manning a flashlight. Jay would follow with the backup flashlight, switched off unless needed. Dwayne would be by his side. Next would be Fran, weapon on ready and Henry with Dexter bringing up the rear with the lantern. The plan, move as one, everyone staying inside the field of light. To ensure this, all except for Joe and Rhonda, everyone else would keep a firm hand on the person directly ahead of them. If one stopped, they all stopped. This would prevent any breaks or gaps too.

Joe eased open the door. He hesitated, senses on alert. He didn't feel the presence of the thing, no pull, no charged air, just the musky smells of the basement. Lights on, they were on the move, briskly yet cautiously. The basement's windowless confines gave no hint if daylight had arrived. Rhonda led them toward the cabinet's location, still not in sight of the flashlight's beams. Halfway across the basement, Rhonda's flashlight flickered and then went out. She whacked it a couple of times, but it remained off. She tossed it to the side. Jay switched on his and passed it to her.

Joe had the cabinet in sight. Seconds later they were there, standing in front of it. Jay grabbed the handle and pulled up. Nothing happened. He pushed down on it and then jerked it upward a second time. He froze. It was locked. He looked at Rhonda. She shrugged.

"You don't have the key?"

"No, it was always unlocked for us. I guess Mister Pinckney unlocked it ahead of time."

"Step aside, Sugar," said Fran, aiming her pistol and firing, the double doors flying open upon discharge.

"Jeez," yelled Jay. "Flammable liquids could have been inside too." Fran just smiled and motioned for them to retrieve the bleach.

Flashlight number two flickered, the one Jay had just handed Rhonda. Henry looked for spray bottles but found none. Now what, he wondered. Dwayne broke away to the right. Henry shouted to Joe, and he whipped his light around, keeping it on the boy. He stopped and smiled, tugging on something. Joe returned a warm smile. The boy had located one of those large insect or weed sprayers, a back mounted harness version. Henry snatched it up and herded Dwayne back to the others.

The bleach almost took their breath away as they dipped the cloth, making sure a free end remained bleach free. Four of them were affixed to each person. Locations varied dependent on the type of clothing they wore. Unfortunately, where it did touch their clothing, it penetrated it. Jay already had a burning sensation near his ankle, as did Dexter on his left side just before his belt line. Rhonda's second flashlight flickered again and went dark. Jay hurried them to finish with the personal protection, while he filled the large spray unit. By the smell it had been previously used for getting rid of insects in the basement.

The air pressure changed. It became electrically charged. With the limited remaining light, the thing was making its move. Dexter wasn't confident that the bleach was working. He still waited his turn. He would be the last to receive the dipped cloth stringers. He held the lantern up high to keep everyone inside the protective glow. A fleeting thought, he wished he were back inside the refrigerated unit. Tugs came from the outer reaches. Dexter panicked. He envisioned ravenous creatures moving about in the shadows, hideous things with long talons and mouths filled with sharp canines. He yanked his head one way then in the other direction attempting to catch any glimpse of the assailants.

Dwayne all but climbed underneath Jay, wanting no part of the bogeymen. Rhonda lost grip on her container of bleach spilling the contents to the floor. It formed a large puddle underneath her feet. The fumes burned her eyes, bringing her to tears, blurring her vision. Joe ignored the threat, meticulously filling the sprayer after handing his flashlight to Henry. He already had the bleach laced cloth affixed to his body. Joe blocked out the pain where it had begun to saturate his shirt sleeve contacting flesh.

Fran had taken time to soak her bullets in the concentrate hoping it would work like silver bullets fired at a werewolf. She likened it to holly water, poison for their nemesis. She aimed her gun about, hoping for just one shot at this thing. The remaining flashlight and lantern were losing the battle against the darkness, not offering a large enough safety zone to encompass the seven struggling to avoid the shadows. Dexter scrunched closer, encouraging somebody to hurry up and do him with the bleach. Most had become disoriented, fighting off the attacks to their subconscious. The unseen's mind control was emboldened by the dwindling light.

Jay realized too late that they had underestimated the creature of darkness. They had focused on warding it off with light and the bleach. Perhaps these were effective to a point, however, they had failed to recognize this thing had other means for getting what it wanted. Most had already experienced the mind over matter onslaught, so why had they excluded this from their planning session? It struck Jay like a lightning bolt. IT had somehow blocked the premise from their thoughts. Its intent, flush them from the root cellar.

Dexter had to reach the front of the line to acquire his share of bleach. He handed Henry the lantern, having reached a feverish pitch, but before he could move closer, unseen forces snatched him backwards. He was launched like a person recoiling on a bungee cord. His backside had become exposed to the shadows and now he was gone. Henry screamed, shocked by what he had just witnessed. First Seth Ledbetter and now more vividly, Dexter Parnell had vanished into the darkness. The others had not seen what he had just seen.

Joe noticed first that Dexter was gone, tipped off by Henry now possessing the lantern. He quickly sealed the sprayer's canister and began pumping the plunger to build up pressure, all the while fighting off spiritual visions bombarding his mind. Fran, as did the others, realized what had happened. She began cursing at the top of her lungs. She fired a couple of shots into the darkness, screaming more obscenities. Rhonda wanted to cover Dwayne's ears but dared not release the only flashlight. She splashed about in the bleach, some already penetrating her ragged old shoes.

Pressure achieved. Joe circled the perimeter spraying bleach into the darkness. The potency of the spray had begun to take their breath away, several already hacking and coughing. This didn't deter him from spraying more, a man on a mission. It appeared to be achieving the desired results. The thing seemed to be retreating. At least the tugging had ceased. Pressure had returned to normal. They had to somehow make it to the loading dock door. Chaos ensued. Joe had to restore order, while still fending off his personal demons. He could only imagine the horrible and misleading images invading the others' heads. Joe Ironhorse mustered up all the strength he had and barked, "Block it out. We're beating it back. We must reach the door. Flashlight in front, lantern in back, and close rank.

Rhonda positioned herself by Joe, clutching the flashlight. Joe had the sprayer strapped to his back. Fran and little Dwayne followed. Fran had her right hand on Rhonda's shoulders, her left gripping the gun. Dwayne had his face buried in Fran's back, hands clutching her shirttail. Henry had composed himself and now held the lantern high, bringing up the rear, his opposite hand pressed against Dwayne's neck. They inched toward the dock door, Joe releasing spurts of spray every ten seconds or so, hopefully clearing a path. Eventually they reached the dock door, as one, no more losses. The next challenge, the door was operated electrically. Obviously, that wasn't going to be an option. Joe tugged on a dangling rope with one purpose, to open the door manually. The door didn't budge. Jay joined him, both pulling with all their might. Still the door held firm.

Jay broke the silence. "That thing pulled the same stunt in the lobby. Somehow it possesses the ability to control even the manual operations when the power is out."

"Then there's no way out," said Joe, his spirit almost broken.

"Hells bells," fumed Fran, "I reckon we could go back up on the roof and catch the sun rays there. At least we would know if the light scared this thing away or not."

"I can't say I want to make that trip back up those stairs," said Jay. "There must be other options."

"The man door and this dock door are the only two entrances to the basement," confirmed Joe, having already tried the man door too. He sprayed the perimeter again, the nozzle set on mist instead of stream.

"We can go up to the lobby. Plenty of daylight should come through the windows there. All we need to do is break a window and we're outta here."

"All right, stay close, we're heading to the stairwell," barked Joe.

While the bleach was doing its job, the presence could be felt on the outer fringes, waiting for any opportunity to snatch up more prey. The remaining six traveled in two's, inches apart. Dwayne now paired with Fran, pressing his face hard against Rhonda's backside, still leading the way with Joe. Jay and Henry brought up the rear, Jay manning the lantern. He no longer carried his modified cue stick, seeing no use in such primitive weapons against what he couldn't see or kill.

The stairwell door came into view, the beam of the remaining flashlight just now highlighting it. Rhonda sighed at its sight. She just wanted out of this basement. She desperately needed to know that her husband and the children were safe. Jay still dreaded the climb. He thought about Fran's name for him and agreed his fat ass wasn't cut out for these Olympic style feats. He was on his last legs and was glad they had opted for the lobby instead of the roof. Henry nervously scanned the darkness; fearful he might be next to be gobbled up. Joe paused in front of the door and grabbed the handle and thumb latch. The door didn't open. He tried a second time, yanking the door. Nothing happened. He tried a third time. The door must be locked but after closer observation he realized there was no locking mechanism. The opposite side of the door had a push bar, designed for easy access and an escape route from the stairwell.

"I told you," whispered Jay, "this thing doesn't want us to leave the basement. Darkness is its friend. This is the one place at the resort that darkness will prevail, its nest."

"Now what," asked Fran.

All sense of wisdom eluded Joe Ironhorse. He said nothing. He yanked the door again, then again with the same results. They were trapped in the basement. The dinner bell had signaled they were next on the menu. They had been herded here like mindless cattle to the slaughter.

"Hey Joe, talk to us," said Fran, now shaking him by the arm.

Dwayne began boohooing, clutching, and twisting Rhonda's blouse tail. She pried his hands free and turned, tried to console him, thinking about her children as she did. Her mind was bombarded by horrific thoughts, visions so terrible she fought back screaming out loud. She really needed to be out of this basement prison and back home, now, not later. Henry became almost spastic, jerking about as if undergoing a convulsion. Fear affects each person differently. Faced with the uncertainty of surviving this ordeal, Henry had reached his brink. Jay ignored him, only vaguely aware of the boy's perilous situation, more focused on the Indian and the door. He held the lantern as high as he could to literally shed light on their predicament. The group was breaking down, succumbing to distorted signals invading their brains, all by cold and calculated design.

Joe continued his tug of war with the stairwell door. Fran babbled nonsense in his ear. He blocked out the foreign gibberish, focused on but one task, to open that door. Fran, frustrated by him ignoring her, fired her weapon into the air. The thunderous gunshot got everyone's attention, silencing them. Dwayne covered his ears and fell to his knees. Henry all but leapt into Jay's arms. Rhonda's visions burst like a birthday balloon. Wild eyed, she stared at Fran, still aiming her gun above her head, ready to take a second shot if necessary.

"Why did you do that," inquired Joe.

Fran stuck the barrel against Joe's hawkish nose and asked slowly and deliberately, "What in Sam Hill are we going to do now?"

Joe clutched the barrel and forced it away. "Don't you ever pull a stunt like that again, Fran," he warned her.

"Or what, Injun Joe, are you going to scalp me?"

"A Navaho's doesn't scalp people. If truth be known, it was the white man who started this practice, scalping innocent Indians."

Jay handed Henry the lantern, and then wedged himself between them. "Both of you stop this bickering. This is what it wants from us, divide, and conquer. Can't you see? We're being dismantled from the inside. We're being primed for the picking."

Fran blinked uncontrollably, deciphering his words, staring, almost as if she didn't know who he was. Her actions indicated to Jay that he wasn't sure he had gotten through to her. Arguing with a pistol packing mama wasn't the soundest decisions. Fran slowly holstered the pistol in her waistband, never breaking the stare down with Jay.

"You got something to say, so say it, fat…Jay."

"It's inside your head. Ignore the craziness."

Fran still didn't understand what she had done. She had no recollection of firing the gun or pointing it at Joe. Jay caught her up to speed, sensing she was not aware of these significant facts. She denied them, saying it wasn't possible. She would never point a gun at someone, not unless she intended to use it. Jay wasn't sure she wouldn't have pulled the trigger. The creature was planting and cultivating the seeds, preparing its harvest.

The circle of six huddled near the stairwell entrance, unclear what they should do now. Their tiny machine had broken down. Life and death situations bring the best and worst out of people. Currently this gaggle of wantabe survivors represented the worst scenario in survival techniques. They were in the middle of a full-blown group panic attack. Jay was possibly the only one thinking straight, and not because he hadn't already experienced his moments. To compound their problems, the lantern went out, its last drop of fuel spent.

17

The six, literally with their backs planted firmly against the wall, clung to the hope offered by the single Torch flashlight. Joe had arrived back among the living and was spraying a mist of bleach into the shadows. They were indeed in dire straits. Rhonda had the death grip on the flashlight. Whatever lurked in the shadows couldn't be held at bay indefinitely.

"We must head back to the root cellar," announced Joe.

"No, I can't go back in there," pleaded Rhonda.

"We are out of options, Hon." Fran reached over and touched Rhonda's hand attempting to reassure her things would be all right. Things were far from all right though and no amount of coddling was going to influence Rhonda otherwise.

"Think this through," warned Jay. "Once we're back in there, we are literally backed into a corner. We have one flashlight and a limited amount of bleach. The light must be on its last leg. We have no idea where the bleach threshold lies. At some point it will weaken to the extent it no longer works and then we're toast. The root cellar will not protect us then."

"Sugar, what chance do we have out here? This crazy thing is all around us chomping at the bits. This is worse than that movie, *Pitch Black*, where *Vin Diesel*, playing that hunk Riddick, and those folks were trapped on that planet with hellish night creatures. They were afraid of the light too. Let me tell you, when the lights went out, man oh man, they made mince meat of those poor souls."

"Fran, please spare us," said Jay.

"We're doomed," shouted Henry. "We're no match for this evil. Get real. We can't beat this thing. It can't be killed with the bleach. We don't even know if it can be destroyed by the light. We're already trapped whether we go back in that cellar or not. What difference does it really make? Pick your poison."

"Son, you're talking nonsense," warned Fran. "We're not quitters. That's not the American way. The good guys always win in the end. Well, I reckon some of the newer movies tend to string us along and then let the last hero get killed, but that's rare."

"This is not one of your damn movies," yelled Henry. "If it was a movie, the nerdy kid always gets it. Look around you. I'm the only one that fits that description. You see, I'm pre-selected. This thing is saving me for something special. I don't want to be the poster boy waiting my turn for some grisly ending."

"Come on Henry, you're here for a reason. You're the hero. You came up with the bleach idea. You probably have tons of ideas yet untapped. We're depending on your smarts to help us." Jay felt like he was trying to talk a jumper off a ledge. He was. Without warning Jay leapt into the darkness and was gone. No screams, no gory ending. He had simply chosen his way to go out, his terms, over and done.

"Stupid kid," muttered Fran.

Rhonda had only known Henry Wilder for a very brief time, but he may as well be one of hers. She had a meltdown, slid to the floor, still holding onto the Torch. She didn't scream nor cry. She took the Dwayne route out, exited the real world and escaped by going into deep shock. Joe bent down and retrieved the light. It flickered. He slapped his hand against its side. Thankfully, it remained on.

"Daylights burning," announced Fran. "We better do something one way or the other. I say let's put this place ablaze."

"Set fire to the basement," questioned Jay.

"Pile it up and set it on fire. Let's give this thing a hot foot."

"Fran, what about the smoke in such a confined space," warned Joe.

"Honey, stop your fretting. This thing is going to kill you sooner or later, so a little smoke ain't nothing. If it gets too bad, we just hop back in that root cellar."

"And become a roast in the oven," he added.

"Might work," said Jay. "We could smolder it with bleach, make a fog. That's how they spray for pesky mosquitoes. Just maybe we can chase it out of the basement. Once it's gone, possibly it won't have any power over the doors."

"Where is this thing going to go if it is daylight outside? I vote let's send it back to hell where it belongs," yelled Fran, caught in the moment, ready for war.

"We have liabilities. It troubles me to use that term. The child and the woman could hamper this plan. Look at them," said Joe.

Trauma had indeed consumed both. Jay couldn't say he much blamed them either. Insanity was often an escape. He had certainly tittered on the edge over the past few hours. He did understand Joe's liability reference. The burden now rested on Joe's, Fran's, and his shoulders. This didn't offer much leeway as caregiver and sitter. Losing Chrissie, Dexter and then Henry had added additional stress to their situation.

Watching Henry basically commit suicide had been an eye opener. Jay suspected this hadn't been Henry Wilder's first venture down that road. The kid, by self definition, had probably been a target for bullies. Jay despised bullying. After all, look at him. The bullseye had always been painted on his back, even at an early age. That's why Fran's name calling had so personally offended and impacted him. While being called Fat Boy was a new name tag, he had been called much worse. He wondered if the creature was forcing him to rehash his life, but then he quickly discounted the premise. Jay Myers really didn't need any help. He had relived this nightmare more times than he cared to count.

Kids had always harassed him, calling him Fatso, Lard Ass, Humpty Dumpty, and even Fat Faggot. Their cruelty had dogged him forever. He was no more than five or six when his dad had told him to stand up to them, fight back. He demanded that of Jay, expected him to not take anything off them. Jay reluctantly attempted to honor his father's wishes, but quickly discovered that name calling was much less painful than a butt whipping. Well, maybe less painful physically, but the mental and verbal abuse was devastating on an entirely different level. He'd better shake this off before he immersed himself into a much darker place than just this basement.

Oddly, bullies came in all shapes and sizes, colors and backgrounds, genders and so forth, and now he faced an entirely new bully on the block, one he could not yet define. Darkness concealed this bully's identity. Rather fitting, Jay thought. How ironic though, to have survived bullies for a lifetime and now to be done in by a bully he couldn't even see. He should name this force something other than IT. Steven King had used that name in his novel, IT, to label the clown-spider thing that terrified and snatched up the kids in Derry. Although this thing rivaled that creature and the story line, Jay figured he could come up with something more appropriate, a name worthy of being the menace responsible for wiping mankind off the face of the earth. Jay was drawing blanks, nothing creative coming to mind. A thing like this deserved a worthy title. And to think, Joe was worried about Dwayne and Rhonda. Escaping the real world at all costs under these circumstances was noted. Henry Wilder had taken the easiest and wisest of all routes. Why prolong the inevitable? Geeks and nerds were primed for the picking. He should know.

"Hey Joe, just thinking, what's a good Navaho name for this creature of the darkness?'

"Son, have you done lost it too?" asked Fran.

"I just think we should name our foe something fitting. Just humor me, please."

"We're hanging on here by the seat of our britches, one flashlight and bleach spray, and you want us to take time to name the monster. You've got to be getting me."

"Ignore her, Joe. I'm serious here."

Fran fingered her pistol, feeling just a tad too serious also. She didn't like seeing her allies go crazy crackers one by one. "Humor him. Do it and let's get this over with, Joe."

Joe nodded. "Navajo original stories begin with a First World of Darkness. From this Dark World the Dine began a journey of emergence into the world of the present. The creatures of the First World are thought of as the Mist People that had no definite form, but were to change men, beasts, birds, and reptiles of this world."

"Whoa, Joe," interrupted Fran. "I didn't call for a history lesson. Just give him a name for the beast."

"*Nihodilhil* was the name given the First World of Darkness."

Jay shook his head no. "That one doesn't exactly roll off your tongue. Do you have anything else, something easier to remember and say?"

"The Celtic lord of darkness was named *Elathan.*"

"We may be cooking now, got any more?"

"Erebus was a Greek demon who guards the darkness around Hell. In Iran, the demon of darkness was *Mush.*"

Fran fumed, waving the gun about. "You're an Indian, Joe. What the hell do you know about all those other folks over yonder?"

Jay nodded. "Mush, fitting, I think. I like it. From this point on I proclaim our foe is hereby named Mush. I can remember that one."

"Okay, fellers, fun time is over. Mush it is, but it sounds like oatmeal or cream of wheat to me. Yankees would call grits mush. Are we ready to build that bonfire now? I'm done with us standing around here with our thumbs stuck up our butts. We're either going to do this or cry uncle. I'm not the crying type in case you haven't noticed."

Joe sprayed another dose of bleach. Using their single beam of light, they inched about trying to locate anything that would burn. Mush toyed with them, invisible tentacles lashing out at their souls. Joe wasn't convinced this smokescreen was a safe bet. It could transform them into toasted human marshmallows. Their pile of flammable materials grew. It resembled a primitive sacrificial bonfire. They had placed Rhonda and Dwayne on the floor facing back to back. Joe had sprayed a light mist on their clothing. If the bleach burned them, they didn't let on to the fact.

Two buckets of bleach had been retrieved. The spray canister would be replenished and then the remainder would be used to smolder the fire. One-gallon bottles of Canola oil and a box of Canola spray cans had been located to fuel the fire. A lighter had been found in a desk drawer along with a pack of Camels. Fran couldn't resist. She fired up one. She had quit the nasty habit twenty-seven months ago, going cold turkey, but now it didn't seem so hazardous to her health by comparison. She chuckled, blowing a smoke ring, knowing that the resort had gone smoke free. They were about to fire up the big one right here in the basement.

Fran thought about Dexter one last time. The cigarette would have to do, a sad replacement for what could have been. She took a second and inventoried her ammo. She had one last clip, excluding the partial one in her pistol. Bullets were about as useful as tossing rocks at ole Mush, but still, the gun felt good in her hand, along with the bullets coated in bleach. She thought about *Dirty Harry Callahan* and mumbled, '*Come on Mush, make my day.*' Oh yeah, she thought, *Clint Eastwood* would take care of ole Mister Mush. If this script worked out the way she hoped, she might be the next big bad mama in the movies. Wouldn't that be a hoot? Maybe one of these laced bullets would hit its mark and bring down the Mighty Mush Monster.

Joe Ironhorse gave the signal, time to light this puppy and see what happens. A couple of fire extinguishers had been located and stationed nearby just in case. Intentionally setting a fire in the basement with no escape route or ventilation could potentially be a deadly scenario. None of them shied away from the possibility, facing facts that with Mush waiting its turn, what did it really matter? Jay Meyers stood next to Rhonda and Dwayne, neither showing any signs of rejoining them. In a twisted sort of way, Jay envied them. He held the flashlight, aiming it at the mountain of combustible items. This would either drive Mush from the basement or not, or kill them in the process, smoke and/or fire doing them in. Maybe it would just anger Mush and that would be that.

Fran Woodward stood, arms crossed, legs spread apart and smiling. She could hardly wait to see what happened to ole Mush when they put things in motion. Torch the son of a gun, she thought. Let's drive Mush straight back to the bowels of hell. Her only regret, she wanted a shot at Mush, hoping the thing would be forced to materialize, if indeed it could take solid form. Fran existed in movie land where anything was possible and where creatures eventually showed their true identity. Sadly, this wasn't a movie playing to a theater's audience. To Fran, that didn't matter. She envisioned the ending, one where they would come out on top.

Their last lifeline went black. The Torch flashlight's battery had gone dead. Jay pounded on its side, but nothing happened. The darkness consumed them. Jay couldn't see Joe or Fran standing less than a couple of feet away. He placed his hand on Rhonda's head, just to make sure he wasn't alone. The flash to his left signaled Joe was still there. He had lit the rag and quickly tossed it on the pile. The debris didn't catch fire. The rag burned but was going out. Jay's heart leapt to his throat. This couldn't be, shouldn't be happening, thought Jay.

"Give me that damn lighter," Fran yelled into the darkness, blindly moving to where Joe should be standing.

She saw it flick back on, making out Joe as he moved toward the pile, the rag all but smoldering out. Joe leaned down and attempted lighting various objects. Finally, a couple of them caught fire and the bonfire roared to life. Joe let out a warrior yell. Fran joined in, hollering like a wild banshee. Even Jay let out a yell too. The fire illuminated the basement. Odd, shaped shadows danced on the surrounding walls. Fran whirled around, checking out the perimeter as if expecting to see Mush. Not a creature was stirring, so goes the Christmas passage. Little Dwayne began blinking his eyes rapidly, the light and the heat from the ever-growing bonfire was bringing him around. Rhonda showed no signs of coming out of her shock.

The bleach that had been strategically placed on the bonfire began burning their eyes. Smoke was curling around the ceiling and was reaching them now. This forced them to back pedal away from the fire. Jay had to drag Rhonda along. Fran assisted Dwayne. Joe waited patiently for some sign that Mush had exited the basement. He seemed oblivious to the smoke. The Indian had reached some spiritual plateau as best Jay could tell. A rumbling from behind caught their attention. The elevator had activated. There was no indication of power being restored anywhere else. The door opened. Mush was making a play, had other plans for them. No one was taking the bait. To Jay, the elevator represented a large rat trap. He didn't smell the cheese just yet. That could change if the smoke continued to fill the basement. They had wanted a fog bank and they were certainly getting their money's worth. Apparently, Mush didn't appreciate their innovation. Lights blinked wildly from one end of the basement to the other.

It dawned on Jay. Mush had periodically restored the power, even the lights. It had the ability to restore lights where it wasn't. Could that equate to Mush not being here right now? Possibly the bleach scented smoke had driven it from the basement as they had hoped. Mush now wanted them out of the basement too. Jay was certain Mush wasn't trying to rescue them, wasn't offering them a lifeline. The entity obviously had something else in mind for them. Mush wanted them to take the elevator.

 Somewhere in the basement a phone was ringing. "Don't answer it," shouted Jay. "Mush is trying to split us up."

"Maybe it just wants to talk to us," replied Joe. "Or maybe it's someone from the outside finally getting through."

"Talks cheap and I'm not buying that the rescue rangers are on the line," spouted Fran. "But if the ole boy wants to cut a deal, I'm all ears."

"This thing isn't a person." Jay reminded them.

"Never said it was, but maybe it has had enough. We know it's smart. It could have picked up on our language listening to us. It could be learning from those it snatched. We could be one big experiment and now the lab work is over."

"Fran, I don't feel any compassion from this thing. Mush has an agenda. We're screwing with its agenda and Mush is simply attempting a work around."

"Should we enter the elevator," asked Joe. "Either that or we're going to have to put out this fire before the smoke leaves us no options."

"Are you crazy, Joe? That elevator does not represent our salvation. It's a trap. What we are doing here is working or the power wouldn't be back on."

"I'm with, Joe," added Fran. "This smoke is going to kill us if we stay here. It was a bad idea to set the fire."

"Then let's use the fire extinguishers and snuff it out," begged Jay. "Not the elevator."

"And then sit around here in the dark until your Mush Monster makes its move on us, I don't think so," replied Fran. "Any floor is better than down here. I say we take the offer."

"She's right. The lobby would offer us daylight. Other floors would offer the same. All we'd have to do it select a room and open the drapes."

"We don't have a flashlight," Jay reminded them.

"We have this," said Joe, holding the spray nozzle to the canister mounted on his back.

"What if it doesn't let us out of the elevator? Have either of you considered that possibility?"

Joe took a step toward the elevator. "What choice do we really have?"

The phone continued to ring.

"I'm answering it," announced Fran. "Douse me one more time with that bleach."

Joe pressed the lever on the nozzle. It squirted once and then sucked air. The canister was empty. "Well that pretty much spells it out for us, doesn't it? No flashlight and now we're out of bleach. It really doesn't matter if we stay or go. Once this bleach wears off us, we're goners."

Fran snatched up the phone and said, "Hello." She didn't say anything else, appeared to be listening.

"What do you hear," asked Jay.

She held out the phone, "It's for you, Fat Boy. I mean, Jay."

18

Jay licked his lips. Tears ran down his cheeks, the smoke taking its toll. "What the hell do you mean, it's for me?"

"The person on the other end asked to speak to Jay and you're the only Jay here." Fran coughed, the smoke getting the best of her.

"Person, what do mean by person?"

"It's what I said, person. She called you by name, Jay Myers specifically."

"SHE called ME by name?"

"Is this a man thing, pretending you didn't hear me? Are deaf and stupid?"

"Who is she?"

"Excuse me, who may I say is calling," asked Fran, between coughs. "She says her name is Mira."

Jay moved quickly and held out his hand for the phone. Fran plopped it into his open palm and stared at him, then coughed some more.

"Hello, this is Jay Myers."

"Jay, where have you been?"

"Mira, is this really you?"

"Don't play games with me, Jay. I'm tired of all these stupid games."

"Are you okay?"

139

"No, I'm not all right. I'm trapped and I have been for hours."

"Where are you?"

"I'm in out penthouse suite. Where else would I be, Jay?"

"I looked for you there when we first arrived. You weren't there then."

"I never saw you, Jay."

"Well, I yelled for you. I didn't exactly search the entire suite. I had to chase after our luggage." He began coughing now. "Have you seen anything strange?"

"Well, I'm not impressed with this place. I think the power has been off more than on. Did you locate our luggage?"

"Yes, it's in the basement. Just curious, how did you know to call me here in the basement?"

"You're in the basement? I called your cell phone number. I had to use the suite's phone. My cell is dead. Why are you in the basement? You've got some explaining to do, deserting me practically all night. I thought we were supposed to be working through our issues. Are you having second thoughts, Jay?"

Jay coughed some more, holding the phone away while he did. This person sure sounded like Mira. She certainly made perfectly good sense in her conversation. Could Mush pull off something as incredibly authentic as this? Who knew its capabilities? Maybe all of this was playing out in his head. No, Fran had called him to the phone. She had heard Mira too. What should he do?

"Are you there, Jay?"

"I'm still here."

“What’s so interesting in the basement?”

“Like I said, our luggage is here.”

“You’re telling me you have been gallivanting all night long and expect me to believe you’ve been searching for our luggage. How did you lose it in the first place?”

“Long story, but I have it now.”

“Are you coming up or should we just load everything back in the car and head home? If you don’t want to do this, I see no point in staying.”

“Give me a second.”

“Your wife is alive then,” inquired Joe, his voice cutting in and out due to the overwhelming smoke.

“She sure sounds alive if it is really her. Do me a favor, Joe. Talk to her.”

“What would I say to her?”

“It doesn’t matter. I just want a second opinion.”

“What? Was mine not good enough,” snapped Fran, rubbing her eyes, then spitting mucus on the floor.

Jay handed Joe the phone. “Hello, I’m Joe Ironhorse, resort facilities manager.”

“I certainly hope you’re on top of these power outages, Mister Ironhorse.”

“Mrs. Myers, have you seen anyone else?”

"To be honest, I haven't been able to get the door opened to this darn suite."

"Have you been in the dark the entire time?"

"Well, not exactly. We brought a few of those scented candles along. I had them in my carry bag. This was supposed to be a romantic weekend for us. I used them until this morning. The sunrise was quite breathtaking over the mountain ridge, not the sort of thing you want to witness alone. Just get the power back on, please, or we're checking out."

Joe handed the phone back to Jay. "So," he asked.

"She's not a happy camper. By the way, it is morning. She watched the sunrise. I think we should put out the fire and go up. It appears it's over. Mush is gone."

"Amen to that," added Fran, snatching up one of the fire extinguishers and blasting the fire just as all the lights came back on.

"Are the lights on in the suite, now?"

"Yes. Please thank Mister Ironhorse. Are you coming up or should I come down and help you pack the car?"

"Stay put. I'm coming there." Jay halted the call. "If she's okay, maybe others are too."

"We searched most of the rooms on the way to the roof," Joe reminded him.

"Yeah, and we found Dwayne. Rhonda and Henry were alive down here. There could be other pockets of people."

"Speaking of the other two, we need to get them out of this stinking hell hole," said Fran. "Let's load them up in the elevator, how about it? Fire is out."

Jay really wanted to believe this was over and that Mira was okay, but they had been tricked before. They had always paid a deadly premium. Something about the conversation just plain unnerved him. Mira was much too calm for them to have been separated this many hours, and for her to have been trapped in the suite the entire time. The lights were back on, and it was daylight outside. Wasn't this what they wanted? That's just it. Mush knew they wanted this outcome. Could this just be one more mind game? Fran and Joe had heard Mira on the phone too. So, what did that really prove?

Lost in the moment, it had not dawned on Jay what she had said. She had called his cell phone and it had connected to the basement phone. Red flag had he been rationally thinking.

"Are you going or staying," asked Fran, carrying Dwayne, and tugging Rhonda along.

The phone rang again. Jay reluctantly picked it up. "Hello, Mira?"

"Jay is that you? I need your help. Please, come help me. I'm trapped."

"Chrissie," said Jay. "Hey, it's Chrissie. She's alive. Where are you?"

"I'm not exactly sure. I've been in this pitch-black darkness forever, but I think I know where the others are. I've heard them."

"Chrissie, the phone, did you suddenly just find it?"

"Not until it started ringing," she replied. "I felt around until I located it."

"Who was calling, when you answered?"

"You, of course, silly, are you serious?"

Jay dropped the phone and wheeled around. "No," he screamed. "Get out of the elevator." It was too late. The door was already closing. Fran, Joe, Rhonda, and Dwayne were inside.

Jay skidded to a stop. He looked up at the digital display indicating they had already skirted past the lobby. Where was Mush taking them? Why didn't it just snatch them off the elevator? Jay figured that the bleach was still too strong in such a confined space. Even stranger, why were the lights still on? Could Mush be losing some of its powers? The elevator zoomed past floor after floor. It finally came to a stop at his penthouse suite. The roof, then the basement and now the penthouse, what was Mush really up to this time? Jay decided to try the stairwell door. The door pushed open freely. With lights illuminating the way, he began his climb. His body wasn't designed to climb this many flights of stairs. He pushed on, having no other choice. He had to reach the penthouse locate the others and solve the Mira mystery. Climbing all these stairs was going to be an agonizing process. At least they were well lit, for now.

Taking the steps at a snail's pace, he recapped the two phone conversations, attempting to decipher any clue of their real meaning. Mira was supposedly in the penthouse and Chrissie didn't know where she was. Jay figured the likelihood of it being either of them slim at best. Mush could sure mimic their voices, if it weren't as previously suspected, mind control. Mira was supposedly in the light of day while Chrissie was still in the darkness. This was ass backwards. Mira was in the light and the others had been whisked away to her destination. Chrissie was in the dark and still alive. These scenarios made absolutely no sense. What was he missing?

Jay pulled his shirt up to his nose. It still reeked of bleach. He held onto the rail as he ascended the stairs. Even if the lights went back out, he could follow the handrail to the penthouse. He was at the first level of the parking garage. The entrance and exit ramps were wide open, no doors obstructing them. All he had to do was walk outside. Why hadn't they thought about this before going to the basement? Stupid, he reminded himself, it hadn't been their choice to go the basement. He could locate his car and check it out, see if it would start. He might be able to drive out of here, go for help. That's it. Forget the penthouse. It's a trick anyway.

Jay pushed on the door bar. It didn't move. He pushed on the bar again, slamming his shoulder against the door. Nothing happened. Mush still controlled the game. It wasn't going to allow him to exit the stairs where he wanted to exit them. He was a lone cow and Mush wanted him to rejoin the herd. He slowly passed the other doors to the parking levels. All were locked tight. Next, he reached the lobby level and hesitated at the door. His mind screamed at him, going to the penthouse suite was nothing more than a trap. He could exit here, toss something through the glass doors and escape.

Jay pressed the bar on the stairwell exit door and nothing happened. Mush was blocking all the exits. Its intent was clear. Jay flopped down on the steps and looked what lay ahead. He just wasn't built for all this, the furthest thing from a marathon man. If he survived this ordeal, he should shed a few pounds, get himself in better shape. Who was he kidding? Greek god he'd wasn't and never would be. Chiseling this body into much of anything was a moot point. He and Mira certainly had their fair share of problems to work through but coming here to do it had been their worst mistake.

Amazingly, the lights remained on in the stairwell. Why didn't Mush just switch them off and take him here? Why was it so important for him to reach the penthouse suite? Or maybe Mush was going to play with him awhile and then gobble him up. Jay started to scream for Mush to end it now but thought better of it. He really didn't want to die or end up like the others if they had indeed been beamed elsewhere. He certainly didn't have the guts to end it all like Henry had. What was really the point in this madness?

Jay missed Fran's spin on things. She would have certainly had another movie reference in mind. He should consider going to more movies if he got out of this mess. What fun would that be without Mira? A guy alone in a movie theater spelled the 'Big L', loser. Jay glanced back up the endless steps, dreading the climb he knew he had to make. Then it dawned on him. He didn't have to go right to the penthouse. He could simply return to the basement and wait it out. If Mush was going to eventually take him anyway, why not do it on his terms, not its. There was no need old out of shape Jay climbing all those flights of stairs. Jay glanced back down the stairwell. Heck, why retrace those steps too. "I may as well stay here and wait it out." Settled, he would sit here on his 'lard ass' as Fran would put it and see what happened. He didn't have a lantern or flashlight. The bleach would wear off eventually. Here was as good place as any; last man standing, for what that was worth.

He thought about Jason, their son, off at med school. He was going to make a fine doctor someday. Jay felt a new surge, an urgency to live. He stood, surveyed his surroundings, and proclaimed loudly, "Mush, kiss my royal ass. You're gutless, ambushing people in the dark. Show your face, the real you, or do you just hide in the shadows because you're a coward?" Jay almost regretted the challenge as quickly as he had issued it. He held his breath, but nothing happened. He pushed the bar on the door again. It didn't budge. Mush was still in charge. Jay kicked the door just to make his point. That hurt like hell, he thought, feeling the pain in his toes to his teeth.

Jay grabbed the handrail for support feeling quite foolish about his actions and challenges. Stay here or go down fighting, that was the only question. Jay had never been a fighter. He was in virgin territory just pretending to be a crusader for the greater cause. Carrying the torch for mankind seemed extremely out of character, almost laughable. Hundreds of people were missing from the resort. Who was he to take on the villain? Still, the lights remained on. Could Mush have burned out, reached its quota, belly full, hunger quenched?

The scream sent Jay stumbling, grabbing at the air, almost yelling out loud. The blood curdling sound echoed in the stairwell, penetrating Jay to his bones. More frightening, he recognized the female's voice. It belonged to Mira, or a something that could imitate her likeness. One thing for sure, the scream emitted from up above, meaning he would have to climb the stairs if he wanted to know for sure. He really didn't but on the off chance it might be Mira, what choice did he have. A second scream, "Jay, help me, Jay, please help me." It sounded too 'put on' for his taste, but he could never forgive himself if he didn't resolve the unknown. Mush had him where he wanted him.

19

It would take more than a lifetime to understand life. Yet, we waste time in futile pursuits. We pretend that we have our whole life ahead of us, but it would probably take but a second to snuff out that precious life. Are we living life to the fullest? Are we prepared to accept death, to understand the meaning of life and death?

Jay trudged upward, forcing each step, already winded and sucking in the oxygen. Mountain climbing was reserved for those creatures best suited for such feats. These floors anchored by an endless supply of steps and stairways were the equivalent of any mountain he would have ever dared climb. At every other landing he paused to push the door bar with the same result. Nothing to do, onward and upward into the eye of the waiting storm. There was no escape.

At least the screams had ceased. They had stopped once he had planted his foot on the first step. Mira wasn't clairvoyant. Mystery, if any doubt, had been solved. Mush, here I come, ready or not. Four flights, time to rest, Jay leaned against the wall and looked skyward to the seemingly endless stairs. Hindsight, he should have taken that elevator. Mush could have held it for him if he had wanted him on board. Nope, Mush had something else in store for him. What made him so special? Was it because he had more meat on his bones?

Jay suddenly became aware that his bladder was about to burst. Obviously, he would not have access to the facilities, so he did something quite childlike. He unzipped and peed over the railing, his urine streaming many floors below. He smiled and then altered his stream one way and then the other. He reminisced how he and Craig Fielder, his old neighbor pal, used to write their names in the snow with their pee as kids. The running joke, Craig could pee his name better than he could write it on paper. He wondered whatever happened to Craig Fielder. Last he remembered, his buddy had volunteered for the Marines, directly after they graduated high school. Craig had wanted him to enlist too but he wasn't cut out for enlistment.

Jay thought he might have been a better man if he had given into Craig and joined. He just as quickly dismissed the thought. Bullied guys didn't stand a chance in that environment. He would have been a drill sergeants' dream come true, someone to punish relentlessly, the poster boy for abuse. Be all you can be, the challenge to transform him into a lean, mean, fighting machine. He remembered *John Candy* in the movie *Stripes*. Jay laughed, thinking about Fran and her movie references. Zipping up, he tackled the next couple of flights.

Jay's legs ached as did his back. This wasn't his cup of tea. He wondered how in the world those guys and gals competed in the Iron Man events, swimming, biking, and running. He wasn't morbidly obese by a long shot, but he doubted he could survive an episode of *Biggest Loser*. The title, biggest loser did sort of sum up his life though. Then he thought, look at me, I've gone further than most in this battle. Fat Boy is still here. "Oh great, so I have bragging rights, so what?" He could almost see the end of the tunnel, maybe four more flights to go. "Hey Mush, can you hear me? I'm practically at your doorstep now. What do you have in mind?" Of course, there was no answer. Jay was relieved and disappointed if that was possible.

An emergency phone located on the next landing began ringing. This couldn't be good, calling into an emergency phone in a stairwell. One flight of steps separated him and the persistent phone. He hesitated, hand on the rail. Did he really want to answer it? No one would call a stairwell; at least without an agenda in mind. Mush had his number. If the phone were working, maybe he could call out, check on Jason or call 911. Fat chance Mush would allow that. Besides, some of these phones were for in house use only. Debating the issues was getting him nowhere. He did possess the gift of procrastination and was quite accomplished at it, so Mira had always told him. Jay mustered up his reserves of energy and climbed the stairs. The phone continued to ring. He reached the call box and opened the door. It had no keypad, apparently intended to go to one emergency point in the resort. Jay took a deep breath, exhaled loudly, and then placed the phone to his ear. "All right, I'm here."

"Jay, where is here?"

"Chrissie let me guess. I called you again, right?"

"Of course, you did, Jay. Are you coming for me?"

"I have no idea."

"I know where they are. I think I can take you to them, all of them."

Jay rubbed the back of his neck, closed his eyes, and mustered up a response. "And where is this place?"

"You've got to get me out of here first, Jay."

"And where exactly are you, Chrissie?"

The phone went dead. Jay banged it against the box and then left it dangling by its cord. "Pointless crap, Mush," he yelled. "I climbed those stairs for this, you sick bastard."

Jay leaned his back against the wall and slid down it until he came to rest. Sitting there, he looked up at the remaining flights, dreading the climb. It wasn't the number of steps that concerned him but instead what waited for him in the penthouse. He compared his ordeal to being in one of those carnival fun houses, one with deadly consequences. This was insane. He knew he wasn't going to find anyone dead or alive. He just wasn't sure what role he played in the outcome or why he had been chosen the special one to play.

Thinking back to his childhood again, he had been one of those last kids picked when choosing sides. No one ever wanted him on their team. He was a bad investment if you really wanted to win whatever. In baseball he would be the kid that took three strikes swinging wildly at any pitches thrown. In football he was always the one on the line, placed there to block or at least get in the way of the offensive players. In hide and go seek he was always a seeker, never a hider. During dodge ball he was the obvious primary target. Forget basketball! No one ever passed the ball to him. Why would they? He couldn't dribble and he sure couldn't shoot.

It made perfectly good sense to him now; he had been the last one chosen to die or disappear. Mush hadn't thought him worthy of joining the others, or maybe there was just too much fat on the bone for its taste. Trying to spin something positive out of it, Jay sighed, "I'm alive, so why should I be whining about that?" Then it hit him. "Maybe I'm the only one missing and everyone else is okay. What a twist of fate that would be."

Jay heard a door open and then slam shut somewhere in the stairwell below him. He cocked his head. Someone or something was climbing the stairs several floors beneath him. The footfalls were heavy, but the gait was slow. Jay stood and peered over the side but could not detect the owner of ascending footfalls. He started to yell but thought better of it. He wasn't sure why he thought it was a bad idea. One thing for sure, he would know the identity in less than a minute by the sounds of it.

Jay backed into the corner, now seeing approaching shadows, two to be exact. He spotted the top of a head, then a second one. Two men came into view. The first gentleman was short, couldn't be more than five feet tall, thick glasses, jet black hair, obviously oriental. His feet and hands appeared out of place, much too large and out of proportion to the rest of his body. Except for those abnormalities, the man resembled a smaller version of *Arnold* from the *Happy Days* sitcom. The second gent must have stood well over six feet tall, very skinny, almost frail looking. *Ichabod Crane* of *Sleepy Hollow* came to mind. Fran would have been proud of his references to fictional characters. *Arnold* and *Echabod* froze in their tracks when they spotted him. Both back peddled two steps while they sized him up. Jay spoke first. "Hi, I'm Jay Myers, resort tourist and confused as hell." *Ichabod* chuckled nervously. *Arnold* didn't break a smile.

"Do either of you have a clue what's going on here?" They looked at one another and then returned an apprehensive gaze.

"Wade Newby," spoke up *Ichabod.*

"I'm Hiroshi Wantanabe. We are as confused as you."

Wade had a slight British accent. Hiroshi spoke perfect English. The two slowly ascended the remaining steps. Jay offered a handshake. Both obliged. He had expected the oriental looking guy to bow, but he didn't. It was bad stereotyping on Jay's part.

"Have either of you seen or experienced anything strange," asked Jay.

"Amusing," replied Wade, elbowing the little guy. "Let us in on the joke. What gives?"

"Okay, I'll cut to the chase. How have you two managed to survive while everyone else has vanished?"

"Survive, that sounds quite melodramatic, don't you think?" Hiroshi again exchanged glances with Wade. Jay could feel them scrutinizing him, almost as if they thought he was yanking their chain.

"Let me phrase this differently. Have either of you seen anyone while you made your way about?"

"The parking lot and lobby were empty when we arrived. The elevator was out of order. We decided to try the stairs."

"When did you arrive?"

Wade had a puzzled look on his face. "You're an inquisitive gent, aren't you? We arrived this morning, shortly after eight. We were ahead of schedule and hoped for an early check in."

"It's daylight?"

Wade looked over at Hiroshi and asked, "Mister Myers is something troubling you?"

"You're telling me the sun is shining and you just arrived."

"Mister Myers, perhaps you should have a seat and allow us to seek assistance for you."

"Perhaps you could explain to me how you entered this stairwell several floors above the lobby if you just arrived and the elevator was not working. That's quite a miraculous feat."

"Possibly you could define your jurisdiction in these matters, Mister Myers," replied Hiroshi. "You did say you were a guest of the resort, did you not?"

"What we have here is a virtual standoff," interjected Wade. "You seem troubled over our mere existence, Mister Myers."

"You can't tell me that you haven't noticed the obvious, no one is around. They've all vanished."

"I'm sure there is a logical explanation for staff not being on duty at this moment," answered Hiroshi.

"Did you see any people at all, in the hallways, restaurants, parking garage or anywhere?"

Wade responded, "Calm your self, please. We just arrived. I must apologize we have not conducted a thorough search of the resort. It is not something we typically do on vacation. You should really allow us to request assistance. Do you have any family we might hail?"

"Mira, my wife, is among the missing, as are many others. Chrissie and her husband and sister and brother-in-law, Fran, Dexter, Injun Joe, Henry, Rhonda, Junior Johnson, little Dwayne, and Mason the resort manager have vanished."

Hiroshi rubbed his chin. "You're quite the name dropper. When did you arrive?"

"I arrived last night with my wife. I met the others while we were fleeing from Mush."

"Mush, why that's porridge, isn't it? My Mum, bless her soul, fed me porridge as a mere lad in the UK. I was not very fond of mush."

"Mush isn't that the quant command those gents with sleighs shout out to their dogs in the great snowy wilderness," added Hiroshi.

Jay rubbed both hands in his eyes, growing weary of this exchange. "Guys, I'm trying to tell you that something has either killed or kidnapped every single person at the resort. It lurks in the darkness because it is afraid of the light. It also fears bleach."

Wade turned up his nose at the faint whiff. "I thought I detected the familiar scent of cleaning substance. So, you're warding off this creature of the night as one would use garlic to fend off vampires." Wade smiled at the mere thought of this gent and his odd, preconceived notions.

"Heed my warning. This is no laughing matter."

"Why, pray tell, are you cowering in this stairwell, Mister Myers? Are these mush monsters lurking in the shadows of some closet or under your bed?"

"The joke is on you two. You're trapped in here with me now and you are not wearing any protection."

"Trapped, protection" replied Wade.

"Humor me, try that door."

Hiroshi pushed the bar and the door clicked open. "Perhaps we should make haste our escape," he said as he stepped though the door, laughing as he exited.

Wade followed, looking back over his shoulder, "Would you be joining us, or should we send you that assistance?" He shrugged and stepped though the door, it closing behind him.

Something was all wrong about this, thought Jay. They had entered several floors above the lobby and had admitted the elevator was not operational. That was impossible. Either they were lying or…" Jay pressed the door bar. The door didn't open. He pressed it again, nothing. He slammed against the bar with his hip, nothing. He pounded on the door expecting the strangers to open it, but nothing happened. He had passed up an excellent opportunity to escape the stairwell or had he imagined the encounter.

The phone rang again. Jay eyed it, still dangling by its cord and off the hook. He was indeed going insane, or Mush had introduced new tactics to the game. "What are you up to, Porridge?" Jay laughed loudly at his sarcastic wit. "Mush, mush, on *Donner*, on *Blitzen,* dash away, dash away, dash away all."

20

Jay settled back down on the steps, absolutely no interest in moving another inch, game over as far as he was concerned. The phone, the mystery men and shouts from Mira were but mere illusions. He was no longer one to be baited. Jay had drawn his imaginary line in the sand. Mush could cross it or not. He really didn't care. He would wait here until help arrived, if help existed, or he would die or vanish along with the others if Mush decided to take him. There was a third choice, starvation. It made Jay hungry thinking about it.

Jay closed his eyes and leaned his head against the wall. Fatigue had taken its toll. Jay, a master of the power nap had plunged into Sleepy Town, dubbed that by his mother when she encouraged him to go to sleep and stop fighting the inevitable. He missed his mom. She had passed away three years ago of a deadly Staphylococcus infection contracted after outpatient surgery. She had put off a return visit to the doctor until it had become too late. He hadn't really known his father. He had died in an industrial accident in a textile mill when Jay was two years old.

Sleepy Town, why hadn't he traveled here before now? It was a pleasant escape. Eyes closed, Jay no longer feared the darkness and the menace he had named Mush. He drifted through good times, images of Mira, Jason, and him on a vacation to the Grand Canyon and Yellow Stone Park. Jason had been seven. Back then there were no issues between him and Mira. Life had been much simpler, no stress and no strain. They had hoped to regain some of that on this little getaway. Neither had envisioned miracles going into it. Both would have settled for baby steps in the right direction. Digressing, they stood on the wooden walkway waiting for the eruption of Old Faithful. Jay could almost feel the steamy heat, a sulfur smell burning his nostrils. Jason clapped and hollered when the old gal spewed her glory. Jay was choked up, just reliving it. No, he was literally choking, his nostrils burning. Coughing stirred him from Sleepy Town. He woke to complete darkness. The lights were out again, or were they? Could he be in the belly of beast?

A red glow from below, swirling smoke gave way to his location. He was still in the stairwell. The lights were indeed out. He didn't feel Mush's pull or presence. That was unexpected with darkness around him. He struggled to his feet, still hacking, and coughing. Jay peered over the railing. The fire in the basement had reignited, the stairwell serving as a chimney. For the hell of it he pushed on the door bar, but nothing happened. There was but one escape route, upwards. He could feel the heat from the fire pit below. The entire resort may already be in flames. If so, there would be no escape for him, only a temporary reprieve. Holding the rail, he pulled himself up the last two flights. Winded from the climb and smothered by the smoke, he heaved with every breath.

He felt around the door. There was no release bar. Struggling to comprehend the absence of one, it dawned on him that he was now at the entrance to the penthouse. It required a code to access it from the stairs. He located a keypad and ran his fingers over the ten digital keys. He wasn't sure if it worked with the power off. It really didn't matter. He couldn't remember the code. He beat on the door. If the others were inside, they could open it for him. No one did. Smoke burned his eyes. Perspiration dripped off the end of his nose. Heat funneled to its highest point where he stood. He could add death by fire as another possible ending. Code, what's the code? He searched for those magical numbers embedded in his brain somewhere. Death by fire was just too horrible to fathom. Why didn't Mush take him now? He'd welcome the action, wherever it might take him. Code, the stinking code, what's the code?

Mira, son of gun, she had written it down and given it to him before they had left home. What the hell did he do with it? My wallet, it's in my wallet on the back of a business card. Jay snatched his wallet from his back trouser pocket and began fumbling through its content, dropping credit cards, money, and his driver's license on the floor. He found the card, but it was too dark to see it.

The bright burst of flames soared from below. Using that to his advantage, he glimpsed the code on the card and punched it in, now hoping Mush hadn't thwarted his escape plan. The door clicked and opened. He pushed through it, closing it behind him. He wondered how long it would take the flames to consume the floors below him. It took him a second to adjust his eyes to the dark. The blinds were open to the balcony door. No morning sunshine shown though it. Those two interlopers on the stairs had lied, as had the Mira impersonator.

Mush had set him up as speculated from the get-go. Jay suspected those two he had encountered previously were engineered, fabricated entities to deceive him. Come to think of it, thought Jay, those two looked a little hooky, Wade Newby, a fictitious character from the pages of Sleepy Hollow and Hiroshi Watanabe, directly from an episode of Happy Days. They had not arrived at Big Blue Resort in dawn's early light as reported. That reference had been an obvious deception, intended to mislead him. Their grand entrance from a non-accessible floor had been the dead giveaway.

Okay, so now what, wondered Jay Meyers. I'm here in the penthouse suite, exactly where Mush had intended me to be. Where were the others? This night had already lasted a week. Jay, still standing at the doorway, allowed his eyes to adjust to his surroundings. He was ready for the nightmare to end and wasn't too particular on how it ended. Just get it over with.

Mira or a Mira Memorex voice had called out to him earlier supposedly from here. He started to yell for her and the others, but for whatever notion, he didn't. The penthouse consisted of a kitchen, den, and small dining area, two and half baths, three bedrooms and a wrap around balcony with scenic views. It wouldn't take long to complete a sweeping search. Yelling would probably be quicker, but his gut told him to just do the room to room. He sensed more surprises were in store. Oddly, he no longer feared what lay ahead. The blazing fire below would most likely take his life anyway. Burn or leap from the balcony. Both bad options. Jay presently stood in a laundry room that opened into the kitchen. He could use a drink, so he decided to check out the refrigerator first. Typically, it contained complimentary bottles of water, an amenity perk for owners. He opened the door and felt around inside until he located one. It was still cold. He unscrewed the cap and turned up the bottle. He bottomed it out, not realizing just how parched his throat had been.

Jay tossed the empty into a waste basket. It seemed trivial, but old habits die hard. At home he would have recycled it. They had designated bins for bottles and cans. He smiled, thinking about saving the world from the pollution caused by plastic and now this. He had a friend that was even more fanatical than him about plastic. She had authored a book entitled *Sullie Saves the Seas*, about a seagull and his bird friends who teach beach goers a valuable lesson about pollution. She spent time teaching the youngsters how to be more responsible. He wondered if Mush had gotten her too if this phenomenon had truly expanded worldwide. Mush, not plastic had destroyed the world.

Focus Jay, he had to remind himself. *Pollution and plastic are the least of my problems right now.* Mush lurked somewhere, ready to pounce and he still had to be concerned with the blazing fire below. How stupid had that been to set that bonfire in the basement? What had they been thinking? They hadn't. Could this have been the grand plan all along? Mush had planted the seed in their minds, a way to eventually herd them here or wherever. His brain was in overload. He needed to stop micro-analyzing every event, to tie a pretty ribbon around it and make it fit. There were no defined guidelines for what had been happening.

Jay made his way through the den and now faced what might behind doors one, two and three, the bedrooms. If Fran Woodward would have been here, she would have surely referred to the old game show, *Let's Make a Deal*. In tribute, Jay spoke out loud, "Hi, I'm *Monty Hall*. Jay Meyers, would you prefer reentering the stairwell and facing the flaming pits of hell or trade in that option for what's behind door number one?" The audience would be screaming stairwell and door number one simultaneously. He as the contestant would be giddy, fretting over his pending selection. The drama would build. Monty would entice him with other options, maybe with what's behind door number two or offer him cash to forfeit both options. The studio crowd would be going wild with anticipation. Without all the hoopla, it had lost its magical moment.

Door number one it is decided Jay. With the power off and the moon offering truly little illumination via the balcony doors, fumbling through the suite posed its fair share of obstacles. Door number one could offer the perfect ambush. Then again, Mush really required no hiding spot. Jay pulled his shirt up to his nose and took one last sniff. The odor of bleach still permeated from it. Garlic to a vampire, Wade Newby, the Brit clone had said. Sunlight also destroyed vampires. He sure hoped Mush was a hybrid vampire. Of course, he needed sunshine to prove that theory. Where was the sunrise when you needed it?

Jay's hand touched the doorknob. He contemplated his next move. Should he turn it slowly and cautiously open the door, or twist it and kick it open in one clean move? Either way it was going to be difficult to assess the room in the dark. He should have held onto that pool cue spear just in case more of Mush's clones were hiding and ready to pounce on him. Perhaps he should knock and announce he was entering. He'd not have the element of surprise but did that really amount to anything. He opted to turn the knob and guide the door open with his other hand.

As anticipated, he now stared into a dark cavity. Anyone or anything could be anyplace. He mentally counted to ten allowing his eyes to adjust. He could have counted to one hundred for what good that had done. "Is anyone in here?" Did he really want to know? "Mira, its Jay, are you okay?" That didn't prompt a response either.

Jay fingered his way along the closest wall until his knee banged against a table and his arm all but knocked a lamp to the floor. He scrambled to clutch the wobbly lamp with both hands, crumpling the shade. He thought he heard a noise but could hardly make out anything over his deep nasally breathing. Moving around the table, he continued his blind journey along the wall. This was insane. He had announced his arrival and stated his name. If anyone were in here and wanted to be found, they would have answered. He stumbled into some sort of chair and felt his way around it.

This wall hugging approach would take forever. "Okay, look, if anyone is in here, please speak now or forever hold your peace. I'm a friend and hopefully you're not a foe." Jay cocked his head and listened. He wasn't sure why cocking one's head improved one's hearing. He supposed it worked for those Robin Red Breast birds listening for worms under the ground. That song about the red, red robin, bob, bob, bobbing, invaded his head. He wasn't seeking worms and certainly didn't wish to hum that song the remainder of the duration. New strategy, he broke from the wall, hands held out in front, searching for the bed. His knees found it first, so much for that technique. He followed the bed until he could barely make out a doorway, the bathroom. A window in the bathroom helped silhouette the opening.

In a couple of steps, he reached the door facing. He could make out most of the bathroom. An enclosed shower remained the only mystery. Thankfully, there was no shower curtain, Images of the movie, *Psycho* danced in his head. Fran would have been proud once again. The shower enclosure had an opaque door, enough to distort the inside without any available light. Jay yanked it open. It was vacant. It didn't even offer a naked *Janet Leigh*.

One closet remained somewhere on the opposite bedroom wall. Oh man, closets were where most evil things lurked. Those with slats provided the perfect peep holes for voyeurs or wood be attackers. Jay inched his way along until he located it; slats, wouldn't you know. It was one of those tri-fold doors. It rattled to his touch. Enough suspense, he yanked it open. The clanging caught him off guard, causing his heart to skip a beat or two. Metal hangers rattled on the rod inside. No one leaped out. Bedroom number one had been cleared. The boogeyman must be elsewhere. One down and two to go. Surely if anyone were here, they would have already let their presence be known. I'm good at this, he reminded himself. I always play the part of the seeker. Thinking back, he didn't have such a great track record in finding the hiders. *Duh, that's why they choose me in the first place.*

Exiting, Jay located door number two, another guess bedroom. It should be a near replica of the first one. The master was the larger, plusher of the three. He would save that one until last, unless behind number two he uncovered hidden secrets. This time he changed tactics. He knocked on the door and placed his ear to it. Someone rapped a response. Jay almost soiled his pants. He fell backwards, bug eyed and didn't know how to react to what he had least expected.

21

Okay Jay, you've found someone or something. Now what? Standing in the dark, staring at the door, was sort of pointless. *Door number two or would you trade for what's behind door number three?* Enough of this foolishness, Jay reached for the doorknob. The knob turned, jiggled in his hand. He jerked his hand free as if being electrically shocked. Jay flexed his fingers and contemplated his next move. He had expected the door to open, but it hadn't. He rapped on the door twice. Two raps from the other side answered. He instigated the old seven note musical knock, *Shave, and a Haircut*, and received the appropriate response, *Two Bits*. He almost recited a knock-knock joke. It was now or never. He gripped the knob, turned, and eased the door open and inward. Darkness wasn't his friend. That was for sure.

The door opened until it bumped flush with the wall stop. Jay squinted, allowing his eyes to adjust once again. Something moved. He could make out a silhouette standing in the doorway. Whatever it was, it wasn't excessively big. "Who are you?"

In a whimpering voice came a response, "Dwayne."

It was the boy again. Of all possible choices, Jay had never expected to see the kid. "Hi, Dwayne, remember me, Jay. Is there anyone else in there with you, Dwayne?" Jay could barely make out Dwayne shaking his head no. Jay reached out and touched the boy on the shoulder just to make sure he was real. Dwayne flinched, a natural reaction. "Are you thirsty?"

He shook his head no, again. "I'm hungry."

"Sorry, we only have water in the frig. Come on out. I have one more bedroom to check."

"NO," he yelled, shrinking into the shadows.

"Dwayne, please come here." Jay stepped forward, but Dwayne retreated further. Jay didn't embrace all this stumbling around in the dark. The kid was terrified and understandably so. This ordeal was tough on adult minds, but this was the worst-case scenario for Jay. He really had no time to be a nursemaid once again. He would have rather found Fran's friendly face behind door number two.

"Dwayne, I know you are scared but I really do need you to come out of hiding." Dwayne didn't' reply and patience wasn't his best trait. "All right then. Stay there if you want to but I must check the other bedroom."

Dwayne shot past him, catching Jay by surprise. Jay twirled to try to keep pace. The boy had blocked bedroom number three, standing there with arms and legs spread apart, a kiddy roadblock.

"What is behind that door that terrifies you so, son?"

"The Mush-Monster lives in there."

"How do you know that? Have you seen it?"

"It told me to stay in the other room until you got here."

"It talked to you, Dwayne?"

"I'm not sure but it told me to stay until you got here. I did and you are here."

"What did it do with the others…Joe, Fran and Rhonda?"

"It took them away."

"Maybe they're inside that bedroom."

"NO! The Mush-Monster is in there."

"You say it talked to you. What did it look like?"

"I don't know."

"How did it talk to you, then?"

"I don't know."

Jay was getting nowhere. "Did you hear the voice in your head?"

"I don't know."

"Dwayne, I'm going to have to take a peek inside that bedroom."

"NO!" The boy was determined to keep him out.

Jay, as politely as possible, attempted to pry Dwayne from his post. It was easier said than accomplished in the dark. He managed to free one hand, but Dwayne repositioned it as Jay struggled to free the other one. The boy remained spread eagle between the door frame. A change in tactics was needed. Jay pulled the hand free and quickly grabbed the doorknob and kicked it open with Dwayne still locked in position blocking his way. In the blink of an eye Dwayne was sucked through the door, lost in the bedroom's darkness. He didn't so much have an opportunity to scream or anything. Jay could feel the power of the invisible vortex. Little Dwayne had warned him and had fended him off to the very end. Jay dared not reach inside the door and attempted to pull it closed, fearful he too would fall victim to the Mush-Monster. Just what sort of game was this thing playing?

Jay heard a familiar sound. The elevator had activated in the short hallway leading from the suite. It dinged, signaling the elevator was moving. It didn't matter. There was no way in hell he'd be taking a ride, not to that fire burning below. He couldn't see the door from where he stood but he heard it open, light pouring from the elevator's interior. He detected shadows. Someone or something had just exited it. The bedroom door behind him slammed shut, momentarily distracting him. The suite had transformed into a devilish funhouse.

Jay caught movement on the opposite side, heading toward the kitchen. He heard the refrigerator open and close. Jay swallowed deeply and then felt his way back to the kitchen, fighting off the urge to shout out to who might be in there. There's absolutely no end to this madness. Why wasn't it morning already? With his back against the wall, he reached the entranceway to the kitchen. Jay could sense movement just around the corner. He heard someone drinking from a bottle of water. That settled it. Mush would not be tossing back a bottle of water. What the hell did he really know about Mush's abilities and needs? No, this had to be a person or one of those fake persons. A fake person wouldn't require water, would they?

"Who goes there?"

"Well kiss my damn grits."

"Fran, is that you?"

"No, it's the *Creature from the Black Lagoon*. That was one stupid question even for you."

Jay stepped around the corner. He could barely make out a dark figure standing a few feet away. "Where are the others?"

"Poof, disappeared, right before my eyes. The elevator light went out as soon as the door closed. Injun Joe and that gal, Rhonda was gone just that quick too. The elevator plum stopped somewhere along the way. I just sat there and waited my turn. I guess it don't like a tough ole bird like me. It got the chap too."

"Dwayne was here."

"Was?"

"Mush practically snatched him out of my hands just before you arrived."

"So, he was with you?"

"Only for a few short minutes after I arrived," replied Jay.

"So how did you get up here?"

"The stairs."

"I'm impressed. You climbed all those stairs."

"Believe me, I'm feeling every single step. We probably don't have much time before this whole place goes up in flames. The basement reignited."

"Funny, I haven't smelled any smoke."

"Come to think of it, I haven't either."

"You don't have any candles, do you?"

"Maybe there are some accent pieces here."

"Well, let's see if we can find them and shed a little light on this subject."

"Fran, I don't get what this thing is up to. It's had its chances to take us. Why hasn't it?"

"I'm too tough and you're too high in fat content, I reckon."

"I wish I could believe it was that simple. This is too much, cat and mouse for me. Fran, what do you really think we're up against?"

"Armageddon, Hon, and we're down, but by golly we're not out just yet."

"Then we're doomed."

"Cinch up your pants. We're still kicking and breathing. This fight ain't over yet."

"Fran, you are real, aren't you? You're not another clone, are you?"

"You've met clones?"

"Two, in the stairwell."

"This boy has more tricks up its sleeve than you can shake a broom handle at. How'd you figure out they were make believe?"

"Long story, let' see if we can find some candles."

"Found me a three-armed candelabra over here with long skinny candles. Do you have any matches?"

"This is a nonsmoking suite."

"Then we're wasting our time with these candles."

The unit's phone rang. It was near where Fran was standing.

"Don't answer it," warned Jay.

"I reckon we've done played this game a time or two, haven't we? Let's see what your Mush-Monster has to say."

Whoa, she called it Mush-Monster. Little Dwayne is the one that just called it Mush-Monster. She's not Fran, gasped Jay. *I better just play along for awhile. I might learn something.*

"Jay, it's for you again. You're right popular around these parts for a tourist."

22

Why the Big Blue Resort, wondered Jay. What had prompted this event to occur in such a remote location in the Smokey Mountains, not once but twice now. If indeed it was isolated only here this time? He really had no way of knowing. Should he act on that assumption, that the world was on the brink and mankind's survival rested on his decisions and actions? Should he consider this his personal battle, live, or die, life goes on if he doesn't make it? Lesser of the two evils, do this for me first, he considered. Find Mira and the others, rescue them if possible and then reassess the situation.

The Mush-Monster had all sorts of tricks in its arsenal, a regular *Felix the Cat* with a bag of tricks. At first, everyone meeting with the dark had just vanished. Jay had been sold on the wormhole or vortex concept, people being sucked away into another dimension or to an undefined doom. In the beginning he had convinced himself that the power outages had been a result of some force field, disruptive phenomena, something unknown to man. That was before he realized that this thing could think, could strategize, could manipulate. It possessed unlimited capabilities. Jay held on believing this thing could be defeated. Light and bleach proved to be deterrents. He was still convinced light could hold the key to its eventual annihilation, or at least send it back to hell or wherever it had emerged. Mush-Monster was relentless though, show-boating its ability to control one's thoughts, use people like puppets to a certain degree.

The game changer had been its ability to mimic others. Not only had it successfully imitated people's voices over the phone, but it also produced clones, doppelgangers, replicates, or whatever you wanted to call them. It was pitting us against each other. Jay had been fooled convincingly by little Dwayne but not so by Fran. While Mush could utilize smoke and mirrors to portray people, it appeared to lack the ability to completely convert their personality and successfully pull off all vocabulary traits. Jay recapped his encounter with the two in the stairwell. Could these have been fabricated beings as he had first thought or was Mush just controlling the folks he had snatched?

Could be that little Dwayne and Fran were the real deals. Mush was just controlling them like a puppeteer. Jay had to somehow determine if Fran was authentic or not. He couldn't risk harming or destroying the original Fran Woodward.

"Are you going to take this call or what? It sounds urgent to me but then again, what the hell do I know? This whole place is screwed up, a regular *Alice in Wonderland* adventure. I've been expecting to spot that little white rabbit any minute or Mush-Monster yelling, off with our heads."

Jay attempted to scrutinize the woman shadowed by the darkness. She sounded too much like Fran, but how could he be certain? That reference to Mush-Monster shouldn't be part of her dialogue as had been used by Dwayne. He wished he could see her face, look into her eyes and then maybe, just maybe, he could decide. That was it. Mush didn't want him to see her up close and personal. He had not been able to see little Dwayne's facial features either come to think of it. Fran had suggested they find candles, but Mush had known they would be unsuccessful in creating a light source. This had just been a ploy by his foe to convince him of her authenticity. Jay now doubted the fires below existed. Why would Mush create the perfect environment that could destroy it or chase it away? It had been mere illusions.

"I'm not your secretary, Fat Boy. Do you want to take this or not?"

Jay had asked Fran not to call him that name and she hadn't again until now. Nope, this wasn't Fran or not the Fran he had grown to know. Yes, she was rude and crude, but she wouldn't deliberately insult anyone, especially if she had been requested not to do it. The questions at hand, could Fran harm him, would she harm him? He certainly didn't want to hurt her if she was the real deal.

Jay followed her voice and vague outline on the opposite side of the room. She handed him the phone, the keypad permeating a slight glow. He was tempted to hold it up to Fran's face but didn't want to play his hand just yet. He wondered if Mush-Monster could read his

thoughts or only plant seeds of deception in his mind. If it was a
mind reader, then the jig was up already.

"Hello, this is Jay Meyers. What can I do for you?"

"Jay, I thought you were coming for me."

"Not an easy task, not knowing where you are being held, Chrissie."
It had used both Chrissie and Mira to play on his emotions. Mira had
been the bait for him to reach the penthouse, but he still didn't know
Chrissie's location. Possibly this was the purpose for this phone
contact. Yet another piece of the puzzle was missing. Why hadn't
Mira or Chrissie's likeness, in the flesh, been used? Surely either of
them, especially Mira, would have influenced his actions more.
There had to be a logical reason, one Jay wasn't prepared to dwell on
right now. "If I tell you where I think I am, will you come to me,
Jay, save me from the Mush-Monster?"

*Here we go again, Mush-Monster. Chrissie disappeared long before
we ever came up with the reference to Mush. Joe had been
responsible for that name while we were in the basement. She had
vanished on her way to the roof. I'll play along.*

"Chrissie, I want to help you. I want to help all of us. Tell me where
you are. What can I do?"

"I think it's a large room, one of those where they hold meetings. I
can't move. I'm not sure why I can't, but I can't."

"How did you manage to reach the phone then?" *There are just too
many contradictions, flaws in these story lines.*

"I'm not sure. The phone was ringing. Somehow, I knew it would be
you, but Fran was on the line. Are the others there too?"

Jay saw it pointless to tell her he hadn't called. He continued to play
along. "And you're not alone, right?"

171

"Others are here. That is correct. I think your wife is nearby. Please, you must help us before it is too late."

Jay turned to Fran. "The resort has some sort of conference center; which floor?"

"It's one floor above the lobby. No one ever searched there. That must be where Mush-Monster is holding everyone."

"Yeah, Mush-Monster, right. It has them all in one tidy little place. The fire in the basement, it must be close by now," Jay lied, knowing there was no fire and Fran suggesting it before he had even asked her.

"Mush-Monster could have been playing tricks on you. This place should have already been up in smoke by now if it was real."

The illusion of the fire had served its purpose and was no longer needed, thought Jay. "I hate going back down those stairs, again."

"We could take the damn elevator," insisted Fran.

"Chrissie, hold on. We think we know where you and the others are. We'll get there as quickly as possible."

"Please hurry." The phone went dead.

"Let's go get them," Fran announced. "I'm pissed and ready for a fight."

"We need a plan first. Plus, I don't like the thoughts of feeling our way in the dark, do you?"

"I have cat eyes, perfect night vision," laughed Fran. "I can be your guide cat."

Right, thought Jay, you don't want exposure to the light, do you? If you're not Fran, then the light might destroy you. If you are Fran possessed, then exposure to the light might relinquish the control. I get it.

"You don't think this is just a set-up, Fran?"

"You heard Chrissie like I did. She sounded genuine to me. She was scared as hell, that's for sure."

"What if that wasn't really Chrissie. This thing has played tricks in our heads many times so far."

"Don't we owe it to her and us to make sure? I'd hate to think we had a chance to save all these folks and did nothing. Can you live with that? What if your wife's down there too?"

"I'm tiring of these wild goose chases."

"Look at it this way, it could be like that tale about the boy who cried wolf. The one time we don't run to the rescue could be time that counts."

"Could be an ambush is all I 'm saying. We need to keep that in play."

"I got your back, don't be such a worry wart. If ole Mush-Monster wanted us, don't you think that the old boy would have gotten us already? Something keeps it from getting us like the others. Maybe we're special. We could have immunity that wards it off. We ooze something that makes us not taste so good."

"What did you say earlier, too old, and tough, and high in fat content?"

"I don't reckon I care why, just as long as I'm still kicking and above dirt."

"But we do need to know. It could be the key to licking this thing."

"You think about this stuff too much. Take names, and kick butt, that's what we need to do."

"Why don't we just wait for daylight? It can't be long now. That was our original plan."

"I'll play what if with you. What if daylight gets here and daybreak chases it off or destroys it? That's not so bad, only if it doesn't take all those folks with it."

"The bleach, the light, it's almost like dealing with a vampire."

"Then let's go defang this booger."

Fran was always gung-ho, no argument there, but this Fran was just too insistent for Jay's taste. Gut instinct told him Mush had lost some of its punch and was using other tactics. Jay just wished his adversary would show his face if it had a face. Maybe the vortex or wormhole likeness was as good as it gets.

"I'm willing to wait it out and place my bet on the sunshine."

"You can't do that," yelled Fran, more frantic than ever.

"Why not?"

"We must save Dexter and the others."

"Chrissie never mentioned Dexter."

"She mentioned others, so I figured Dexter must be one of them."

"Don't you see? Mush is getting desperate, even sloppy. It's having a difficult time with us, finishing us off. Maybe its fuel is running low, no one left to eat but us."

"Who cares why? We can put this off. We must go now."

"Stupid me," exclaimed Jay.

"Now you're talking."

Jay reached into his pocket and retrieved his key chain. He shined the penlight he had forgotten he had directly into Fran's face.

Fran covered her eyes and screamed, a blood curdling one at that. Jay almost expected a vampire reaction, her going up in a blaze of flames, but she didn't. She collapsed to the floor, recoiling into a fetal position. He steadied his aim, maintained the beam directly at her face, attempting to exorcise the demon from within her. He wasn't sure if it was working or just wishful thinking. Her screams eased to mere whimpers and then nothing. She lay motionless. I've killed her, thought Jay. He nudged her with his foot, nothing.

Jay kneeled beside her, the pen light keeping her in check just in case she was playing possum. She remained perfectly still. Jay removed the cylindrical pen light from his key chain, placing his keys in his pocket. He gripped the penlight between his teeth, forcing his tongue against the activation button on the end, careful to keep it directed at Fran's face. He used his hands to pry Fran's hands from her face. It wasn't easy peeling them away from her face. She wasn't dead.

Jay struggled, but finally managed to flip her on her back. Straddling her, he penned her arms under his legs. He removed the light from his mouth and focused it on her eyes. With his free hand he placed fingers inside her eye sockets and forced her eyelids open. At first, they appeared glassed over, convulsive and then they changed. She blinked uncontrollably, her eyes focusing and gaining clarity. Sitting on her chest, Jay could feel her lungs filling with air. She began gasping, not unlike a diver rushing to the surface after running out of air. Jay found himself holding on for dear life, riding a bucking bronco.

"Get the hell off me, you damn pervert," yelled Fran. "If you wanted some of this you could have asked."

Jay held his position. He moved the light from one eye and then to the other. She blinked and squinted. "Take that light out of my face before I shove it up your…"

"Fran, is that really you?"

"Well kiss my grits, who the hell do you think I am?"

"Are you still up for gong after the Mush-Monster?"

"Is that what you're calling it now? I wish you would make up your dang mind. Where is Injun Joe and that little chap and the woman we found in the root cellar?"

"It is you?"

"Either get off me or we're going to have to share a smoke, Lover Boy."

"I like that better than Fat Boy." Jay rolled to one side but kept the flashlight aimed at her face.

"What's with the friggin light in my eyes?"

"You were under Mush's control."

"That dirty bastard, what will it do next?"

Jay caught Fran up to speed on what had transpired since he had seen her, and the others enter the elevator. She had no recollection of leaving the basement and had no idea what had happened to the others. She still had her gun, a frightening thing for Jay to discover now. Mush could have made her shoot him, but that hadn't been what it had in mind for him. He was supposed to go to that meeting room. He intended to do just that, but on his terms. Fran had compared it to the gunfight at the the *O.K. Corral*, the famous historical site in Tombstone, Arizona, where *Wyatt Earp, Doc Holliday, Virgil, and Morgan Earp fought the Clantons and*

McLaurys. She had mentioned the movie *Tombstone.* She was back, indeed.

"I missed your little movie magic analogies, Fran. Welcome back."

"A mind is a terrible thing to lose, so says that old commercial that made its point loud and clear. Are we going after this mind controlling freak or what?"

"We still aren't exactly sure what Mush is and how to fight it."

"I say we go to that conference room and find out."

"The other you said that too."

"But this me has a whole different outcome in mind."

"Fran, I'm not sure we can destroy whatever this thing is."

"Jay, we're still here for a reason. It could be that we're the sword of justice, God's tool to do in the evil doer.

"You sound like some kind of Avenging Angel."

"Revengeful Angel, maybe," she laughed. "I'm tired of this thing kicking our butts and playing with us like a bunch of toys."

"You might just be on to something."

"Kicking butts," she replied.

"No, it's playing with us like a kid would with a new toy. Think about it. It makes us afraid of the dark."

"Snatching people up and into the thin air will do that for sure."

"Then, it plants ideas, images in our head, distorts our sense of rationalizing. It makes us think we have weapons to fend it off, the light and the bleach. Maybe these are just part of the game."

"You're going off in la-la land on me. I'm not sure I follow you."

"Let me see if I can explain. As I kid, I had all these little figurines, plastic characters. I acted out scenes with them, not unlike a movie plot. I'd have the good guys against the bad guys, often mimicking some of my favorite TV or movie scenes. My bad guys would always be coming up with different ways to beat the good guys. Of course, I had control over both, so I wasn't about to allow the bad guys to win. I did allow them to inflict causalities among my good guys. I placed my good guys in one perilous adventure after the next. In the end, I allowed them to defeat evil."

Jay paused and looked at Fran, hoping this was clicking with her. She sort of nodded her head but Jay could sense she wasn't exactly convinced yet. He continued.

"Mush or whatever you want to call it, keeps evolving the plot. Now we're interacting with voices on the phone, people we know. Those two characters on the stairwell were placed there to test me. They might have been real or maybe they weren't. I was put in another decision-making situation, don't you see? Then this, you and that boy, Dwayne, interacting with me, and I wasn't sure whether you were real or not. We've been led in circles, to the roof, to the basement, in elevators, to this penthouse and now we're being prompted to go to that conference room. Don't you get it? It's playing with us and enjoying every single minute. We are its toys, and it continues to twist the plot, having us work through perilous scenarios."

"Why did it make everybody disappear then?"

"New toys, gathering them up in its toy box and deciding which ones to play with first," explained Jay.

"I'll bite, Mister Genius, why didn't it gather us up too?"

"How do we know it didn't?"

 "I think we would have remembered something like that, being put in its toy chest."

"Why, you don't remember you from just a few minutes ago. Don't you get it? We're being controlled. We have been all along. We didn't die because it didn't want us to die yet. It's picked its heroes from the pack. We're them, the perfect pair of underdogs. Look at us and I don't mean this to be an insult, but you, an old brimstone and spitfire lady and me, not the stereotype for the handsome young virile protagonist."

"Sadly, you're right. I would have never picked us in a movie to go up against the monster. Those roles would have been reserved for new young pups, in love and having the audience cheering them on."

"Seriously, think about what I'm saying. It gave Joe and Junior Johnson a shot at being the leaders, but for whatever reason it eventually discarded them. The resort manager was even tossed in the mix."

"I get it. That gal, Chrissie, it tried to make her your love interest. You and she were getting sort of close leaning heavily on one another your wife and her husband out of the picture."

"I'm not sure about that."

"It used Dexter to string me along too, to toy with my emotions and sexual needs. Then just like that he's out of the picture."

"Don't get any ideas, Fran. I don't see you and me…"

 Fran laughed. "Hey Bubba, anything is possible. If you're right, we're not controlling the movie plot." She puckered up and tossed him a sarcastic air kiss.

"Does any of this make sense or am I just delusional?"

"I'm not sure what's the real us and what's not based on what you're throwing at me. Do you think we get to save the world in the end?"

"I suppose that depends on just how much flexibility we have in determining our destiny. With my toys, I picked the winners, and the bad guys always came up short."

"My vote, we take charge of this little storyline. Nobody makes Fran Woodward do what she doesn't want to do. And you, Jay Meyers, deserve a happy ending. Let's go find your wife."

"Why settle for peanuts? Let's go rescue all of them and set the tone for future play. Let's do it in style. We're taking the elevator."

"The elevator it is. It's either going to stop us or not, take us or not. I'm ready to take my medicine, good or bad. We'll see how far we can take this. We're coming for you, Mush. Are you up for it? If you're not, you can just kiss my royal grits."

"You can kiss my bowl of grits too, with a little shrimp blended in for good measure," chimed in Jay.

Jay allowed Fran to do the honors. She pressed the elevator door button. It swooshed open. They stepped inside. She pressed the floor that would either take them to where the conference room was located or where Mush wanted them to go. They were prepared for either scenario or the consequences it may pose.

24

The elevator rumbled to life. Under normal circumstances this could have been any ride to a selected floor. Nothing seemed unusual. All the bells and whistles were operating as one would expect. Jay wondered if his assumptions were dead on or wishful pipe dreams. Just as quickly, he wondered if Mush was planting the doubt in his head. How much of this did they really control? Toys have no minds of their own. Mere toy soldiers or other action figures are not humans and depend on the kid playing with them to manipulate what they do. Could they fight such manipulation?

To put Fran's spin on this, it resembled a movie plot or a sitcom episode. Survivors rallied against an unknown foe. Good always conquered evil, didn't it? Not necessarily, thought Jay. Unlike movies of old, Hollywood had twisted today's outcomes. Rocky didn't defeat Apollo in that very first movie. No one could kill Jason, Michael Myers, Freddie Kruger or that Alien creature. Look at how many sequels had been made in those franchises. It wasn't possible to kill evil because evil was part of the balance. It evened the scales with good. One couldn't exist without the other.

Evil could only be deflected, slowed down, deterred to fight another day. The Bible was filled with such encounters. Battles were won by both sides, but the war raged on to be taken up by others. Jay would settle for any win right now, no matter how small the setback to the evil doer. Just allow him to find his wife alive and bring her back. He needed that happy ending. Someone else could carry the torch for the ongoing war. He thought, how selfish. There are hundreds missing in the resort alone. What about the others, Joe, Junior, Dexter, Chrissie, all of them? He had committed to saving everyone, so he would stay true to his convictions. He just hoped Mira was one of the lucky ones if luck played into this.

Jay wasn't sure how far he and Fran could take this fight. Fran was fearless and he no longer feared what Mush represented. Together they would take it to this thing, unless it decided their fate, like he mastered the toys of his childhood. Jay wished for the might of his former comrades, Indian Joe, Haskell Junior Johnson and even Dexter. None were warriors but each fought the good fight to the bitter end, or at least until Mush had corrupted their brains.

He wasn't fooling anyone, especially himself. These men were just that, men, nothing more. He had met them just hours before and had witnessed them stumble through the many challenges as had he. Were they stronger for it? Probably not. They were merely trapped in this living hell and nothing more. Anyone could have taken their place and done just as well. They were not special, gifted or in possession of any superhuman powers, but for a brief period they had been his friends and fellow combatants. They had shared trials and tribulations. Their vulnerabilities had been exposed one by one. No, there would be no strength in their numbers but sometimes you just wanted to finish it with those with whom you had started the journey.

The elevator stopped at the designated floor; the one Fran had pressed. Mush wanted the same thing that they wanted apparently. It really wasn't all that surprising. Jay looked over a Fran and nodded just before the door whooshed open. She nodded back, her left hand gripping the pistol. They instinctively flinched, not expecting to be greeted time the door opened. To their utter shock, three figures stood shoulder to shoulder blocking their exit.

Joe Ironhorse, Haskell Junior Johnson, and Dexter Parnell stood there larger than life. This was just too uncanny, thought Jay. If he would have known he could wish them back, he would have probably wished for an entire regiment to support them. Fran was just as shocked. Neither had expected to see any friendly faces.

"You better give them the test," advised Fran. "You know, make sure it's really them and not a make-believe bunch. Remember the *Body Snatchers*."

"What are you babbling about, woman," asked Dexter.

"Humor us for a minute," said Jay, retrieving his penlight. He aimed the light in Dexter's eyes first. He squinted a bit but other than that displayed no adverse effect. He repeated this maneuver in Junior then Joe's eyes. None of them floundered like Fran had done.

"Guess you're the real deals."

"Who were you expecting," asked Junior.

"Can any of you tell me where you were before appearing here?"

All of them shrugged.

Fran spoke her mind. "Haskell, you've been gone the longest. You don't remember anything."

"Yeah, he's right, Junior, you vanished before we went to the roof," added Joe.

"I swear. I don't have a clue. If I was somewhere else, I don't know where that someplace else might have been."

"Do any of you know why you're here now," asked Jay.

"To help you, I think," answered Dexter.

"Here's the deal and even Fran wasn't aware of this. On the elevator ride down, I had wished the three of you were still here to help us and poof, here you are."

"You're yanking my chain, aren't you," asked Fran.

"More toys are in play," replied Jay.

"Why didn't you wish for your wife instead?"

"I would have Fran if I had known what I know now."

"Then why not wish for her now? Wish the lot of them back while you're at it and save us the trouble of going through this whatever we think we are tasked with doing."

Jay figured what the hell and did. He scanned the perimeter, but nothing happened.

"You notice anything peculiar," asked Fran.

"The lights," replied Jay.

"The lights," repeated Fran, "They're on and brighter than ever. This thing isn't afraid of the dark, is it?"

"Darkness just added an element of surprise, forbidding, one of man's fears. Mush tossed it into the mix to confuse us and scare us."

"That certainly worked like a charm," added Fran. "I guess you were right about the bleach too, then."

"It was a hokey concept, don't you think?"

"You mean we doused ourselves with it for no good reason," questioned Joe.

"It sowed another seed to throw us off," said Jay. "It even used Henry to cultivate the misconception. Mush has been changing the game, making us believe what it wanted us to believe. Giving us hope then yanking out the rug. It's been playing us and then reacting to our reactions."

"Well, if that's the way it is then what really convinces you we can lick this thing, whatever the hell it is," asked Dexter.

"It's childlike behavior," answered Jay.

"I see nothing childlike about killing all these people at the resort," rebutted Dexter.

"I don't believe they're dead. If I'm right, they're in its toy box."

"I've got to side with Dexter, this is a load of bull crap," added Junior.

"The lights are back on, maybe it's gone," said Dexter.

"If that's the case, the phones should be working," stated Joe.

Jay retrieved his cell phone from his pocket, dead. He held it up for the others to see. Joe checked his with the same results. Dexter snatched up a nearby house phone, no cigar and offered an explanation, "It fried the batteries and phone system, so what? That doesn't prove anything. I say we don't wait for help to reach us, let's walk out of here."

"We can't exit from this floor, but we can go down one to the lobby," advised Junior.

"Suit yourselves, but I'm heading to the conference room," said Jay.

Fran confirmed she was with Jay to the bitter end. Dexter and Junior questioned her loyalty to the resort, taking sides with a tourist. Jay almost regretted wishing their return. As a child he often played out this scene with his toys, having those turning on the leaders, questioning their intent. The movies followed the same plot. It had to play out. Jay didn't try to sway them. Grown men made their own decisions.

"Where's the conference center, Fran?"

"Follow me."

"Fran, don't do this," begged Dexter, just as Joe fell in line behind her, chanting, "Onward Christian soldiers."

Junior looked over at Dexter, feeling him out. Dexter looked away, wanting no part of this little scheme. He wished he would have remained in the cooler. He hadn't signed up to be a Christian soldier or any soldier as far as that goes. He was a chef, not someone with military experience and certainly not willing to battle this creature of darkness. Supposedly this thing had snatched him away once to origins unknown. He had no memory, and that was probably a blessing in disguise.

The illuminated atmosphere was a welcome sight, thought Jay, much less ominous. Still, he sensed this was far from over. For once in his life, he wished he were wrong. Speaking of wrong, what if his suspicions were unfounded? He could be marching them directly into the jaws of death. Why was it critical that they reach this conference room? The same urgency had been placed on their rooftop excursion, as had been on their journey to the basement and penthouse. This had been one farce after the other with causalities along the way. Reunited we stand, maybe.

Leadership roles had certainly changed throughout this ordeal. Jay again found himself sitting in the catbird's seat, a spot where he had no desire to be. He had a predetermined destination, a mission, but absolutely no plan when he arrived there. Time was running out to develop one. He held true to his conviction that this charade was being orchestrated by a child or something child like, naïve to the factors involved. The lack of a method to the madness convinced him of this fact. Jay was now faced with where he would take that assumption and how he could parlay it into a rescue or escape. Would the phantom entity negotiate or even understand the process of give and take?

He could use some insight from the kid, Dwayne. Jay was too far removed from his childhood shenanigans. He did remember how he and his pals would trade one toy for another. He also recalled how he had been burned by this process. A mere twelve-year-old, he had accumulated a stash of more than five hundred comic books, many extremely collectable in today's world. Darrell, one of his friends, had a weight bench set. Jay had never been the athletic type, as one can still see, but he had yearned to be a better male specimen, one with actual muscles. A stronger Jay could fend off the bullies.

Darrell had convinced him with little trouble to trade his comic book collection for the weigh bench set. Jay had figured why not; he had read the comics countless times; had paid no more than ten cents for most of them. It sounded like a fair swap. He could always buy newer releases of the comic books. With the barbells he could develop muscles, sledgehammers for arms and then just dare someone to mess with him. So how did that go? He stuck with his weightlifting program for every bit of two weeks before the daily ritual faded to every other day, then once a week and eventually the bench became a catch all for toys and clothes. Pumping iron just wasn't for him. It did firm up his biceps, but he still got his butt kicked by the playground bully.

Jay wasn't sure whatever happened to the comic book collection. Darrell never mentioned it again. Shortly after they graduated high school, Darrell enlisted in the marines and was killed in Viet Nam three weeks after he arrived there. Some of the Superman, Batman and X-Men issues would have brought a small fortune now. Jay still had no muscles or a body to die for, the mirror never lies. He had been blessed to have met Mira, who didn't care that he was not the best catch in the sea. Heck, he was the type most gals would have tossed back in the water if hooked.

"There it is. That's our conference room," said Fran, disrupting his journey down memory. "What's the game plan?"

Jay just stared back at the others with that deer in the headlights look he predominantly displayed. Some leader he was. Junior stood with his arms crossed. Joe rubbed his hands through his hair, unsure about their decision to be here. Dexter stood several feet behind them, not wanting to be part of this fiasco. He was only here practicing safety in numbers. Jay remained speechless, thinking how stupid this had been.

25

"I admit it. I'm not good at this," sighed Jay. "I say we go inside and check it out and improvise where needed."

"That's no damn plan," yelled Dexter. "It's plain suicidal."

"We followed you here for that," chimed in Junior.

"They do have a valid point," agreed Fran.

Jay threw his hands in the air. "I'm sorry. I'm winging it. I've been jerked around for hours and some of you have been dealing with this longer. I don't know what to do. There I said it. I do believe our adversary is doing its fair share of winging it too. I don't think Mush really knows what to do with us either, improvising as we toss out new curves."

"There you go again, babbling nonsense," raged Dexter.

"Why don't you go back into hiding inside your cooler until this is over," snapped Jay.

"Boys, this isn't the schoolyard, so cut your crap," spoke up Fran. "Let's face it. None of us know a hill of beans about what's going and that's the honest truth. Dexter, if you want to be in charge then get your ass frisky and hop to it. If not, shut your trap."

Jay appreciated Fran stepping in. He would have appreciated it even more if she would have taken charge of the group and the situation. She didn't. He was it, like it or not. "Does anyone feel its presence?"

All shook their heads no, except for Dexter. "See, it's gone. Screw this, we should just go too."

"Has anyone felt lately like it has tried to enter their head? You know, made you see or think stuff you thought was sort of weird."

The 'no's' have it. Dexter just rolled his eyes, growing tired of twenty questions. He flopped down in a chair and cursed under his breath. Fran encouraged Jay to continue.

"I'm not agreeing with Dexter, that it is gone, but just maybe it isn't as strong as it once was, or it could be resting, tired of all this," said Joe.

"The dark resting, now that really makes a lot of sense," spouted Dexter.

Jay stuck to his convictions. "I'm going in. The rest of you can remain here."

"Like hell, Sweetie Pie, I'm going in there with you."

Joe stepped forward. "I as well."

"Ah what the hell," added Haskell Junior Johnson. "This is good a time as ever for us to the bottom of it."

Dexter didn't move, nor volunteer. He held his ground. The lights in the hallway behind them shut off within a few feet from where they waited outside the conference room.

"I would call that an invitation," suggested Joe. "Our host still has some life in it."

"I say it is poor wiring, Joe, Mister Facility Manager," smarted off Dexter, still holding his position in the chair.

The sucking sound began. That vacuum vortex anomaly had emerged just behind them. Dexter sprung to his feet, twirling in midair quite acrobatically to face the noise. The darkness was blurred and moving, reaching out to him. Dexter backed up until running into Junior.

"I guess that settles that," said Fran. "The conference room it is, and I reckon you're coming with us too, aren't you Hon?" She added a smirky smile and wink for his ex-lover, Dexter.

"I don't think it wants to kill us," announced Jay. "I don't think it can."

"Did you just pull these revelations out of your ass," asked Dexter, still eyeing what he couldn't really see in the shadows behind them.

"You might say that. I guess it's time I play my hand." With that, Jay stepped through the conference room threshold and vanished into thin air. He was there then he wasn't. This time darkness played no part in it.

"Well kiss my royal grits," said Fran. "That was just like one of those time machine portals, bless his heart." With that and without any warning, Fran followed. She vanished as soon as she broke the door's plain. Joe was right behind her.

"Junior, don't do this," warned Dexter, grabbing him by the arm. "Let's wait here."

Junior pulled his arm free and followed. Dexter stood alone. The noisy darkness behind had crept closer. He could feel its pull. Choices, be sucked into the dark or vanish into the light straight ahead. Neither sounded very appealing to Dexter. Safety in numbers prevailed. He ran through the door and immediately stumbled over a leather swivel chair. He tumbled to the floor, swatting at the air, fending off what, he didn't have a clue. Dexter sprung to his feet and quickly assessed his situation. He stood in the conference room alone. It looked perfectly normal. The others were nowhere in sight. The creeping darkness was now just outside the door. Dexter yelled for the others and then screamed for his life as he was pulled into the darkness feet first and airborne. His final thoughts, he had blown a second chance and hoped for another.

Jay covered his eyes blinded by light brighter than anything he had ever experienced. He couldn't make out the interior of the conference room. He was suspended in nothingness. Jay patted his foot just to validate he was standing on solid turf. Squinting, he tried to look about, but his eyes couldn't penetrate the brightness. This was some contrast from what they had been previously battling. It defied explanation. He held out his hands hoping to touch something or somebody, but his fingers wiggled in open air. He called out the names of the others but received no response. Jay thought he heard laughter, but he wasn't sure. Possibly the sounds were in his head. He decided to backtrack. Without turning, he slowly retraced his steps all the while holding his arms straight out and parallel to his torso. It reminded him of being a child, pretending to be an airplane flying. He bumped something and the something grabbed hold of him. Jay dropped his arms and attempted to pull free but whatever had him would have none of it and tightened the grip on his shirt.

"Please tell me this is you, Jay."

"Fran," responded Jay.

"In the flesh if you could see me. We have a train going. Junior has all but bugged up my butt and he says Injun Joe is bringing it up as the caboose."

"Dexter," asked Jay.

"No Dexter, he didn't join us."

"Can any of you see anything?"

"Three blind mice back here, "answered Fran. "What's up with that dark crap and now this? It reminds me of that movie *Poltergeist*, them saying to that little girl at first to stay away from the light, and then they tell her to go to the light. I wonder which one we should be doing."

"We're immersed. You make the call," replied Jay. "Can we back out of here and return to the corridor?"

"Joe said there is something behind him, spongier than a wall, but solid just the same. This is not the way I remember this conference room, and I should know, I've helped clean this puppy too many times to count."

"Mush wanted us here for a reason."

"That thing has been sending us to every corner of this place all night. I've just about had it with all this foolishness." Fran belted out a yell and an assortment of off-color language.

"Fran, are you okay?"

"Hell no, I'm not okay. I fell like I just stuck my finger in a light bulb socket. That hurt like a son of gun. Now I'm just plain pissed off."

"Mush retaliated. It didn't appreciate your candor, apparently," whispered Jay.

"Well, it can kiss more than my grits, then." She screamed again. This time her voice seemed to fade in the distance.

"Fran," yelled Jay.

"I'm over here, somewhere on my can. That little jolt sent me flying."

"Mush understands us or at least it speaks our lingo, Fran. If it understands, then we should be able to communicate with it. Maybe we can even reason with it."

"Well, I got me a few things I want to tell the sneaky bastard."

"First of all, I would tone it down if I were you," warned Jay.

"Well, you're not me, are you? I speak my mind; always have and always will."

"Joe, Junior, are you both still there?"

Both confirmed to Jay that they were. "I'm staying low profile. I don't won't to rile it," said Junior.

"I believe I preferred dealing with this thing when it stayed in the shadows," added Joe.

"Mister Mush, Sir," Jay addressed the entity. "Can we come to some sort of compromise? You obviously want something from us, and we simply wish our freedom and the release of those others you have taken. Surely, we can discuss this civilly."

Jay was lifted off his feet and turned slightly as if being held by an unseen hand and examined. Seconds later he was lowered and released. Okay, maybe we're getting somewhere, he thought. Something touched his thigh, almost groping his crotch. It was Fran, using his leg to pull up and stand. She had crawled back following his voice.

"We're in the belly of the beast," she whispered.

"Now the Lord had prepared a great fish to swallow up Jonah. And Jonah was in the belly of the fish three days and three," recited Joe.

"Maybe not exactly the belly, but I do believe we have found its lair," replied Jay.

"Belly, lair, I don't like it," whispered Junior.

Jay pressed his luck and asked, "We call you Mush as it relates to darkness. Who, what are you and where did you come from if you would be so kind to answer us? What do you want of us?"

"What the hell was that?" asked Fran, reacting to the sound that seemed to envelope them.

"I swear it sounded like somebody laughing," stated Junior.

"Almost too mechanical if you ask me," said Jay.

The laughter and it did have that distinction, erupted again. It could have been almost childlike if not for the deep tone. The bright light continued to impair their vision.

"Ouch," hollered Junior. "Something pinched me on my right arm and then brushed my face."

"It is with me now," announced Joe. "Where are you taking me?' Joe's murmuring passed above them. He was being lifted and carried past their location. His voice faded into the distance.

Jay, Fran, and Junior were knotted close interlocking arms at the elbows. One could not be snatched without the others knowing it, or it might have to take all three. Seconds, then minutes passed, and nothing happened, not as much as a peep from Mush. Quite some time had expired. The three had slid to the floor in a sitting position still locked as one. Jay had made several more attempts to contact and reason with their foe, but all remained quiet. He nudged Fran.

"Do you still have your gun?"

"I do."

"Fire it in the air."

"Fire it in the air! What kind of nonsense is that?"

"I want you to get its attention."

"Whoa," said Junior, "Let's think about this. What if it thinks we're trying to attack it?"

"Trust me, Fran's gun can't harm it. Mush would have disarmed her or worse if it felt threatened or intimidated. Shoot, Fran. Aim skyward but angle the shot away from us."

She did. It was a deafening blast. An endless echo ensued. Their surrounding exploded in moans and screaming voices, hundreds of them by the sounds of it. Jay had not expected that. It had the feel of being at a sporting event.

"They're all here," Jay announced. "The missing people are here. Mira is here."

"How can you be so sure," asked Junior.

"Are you deaf or plain stupid, Junior? You heard them. Those were the voices of a hell of a lot of people," said Fran.

Junior asked, "What makes you think they were our people? They might not even be people at all, just more of these things. You may have put them into a feeding frenzy, boy."

"Fire it again, Fran. This time aim in the opposite direction," Jay informed her.

"This is a bad idea, I'm telling you."

Fran fired round two. The chorus of voices responded, moans, screams, wild yells.

Jay had stood, prompting Fran and Junior to do the same. "Stick close, we're going to find them."

"We're operating in the blind in case you haven't noticed," cautioned Junior.

"Not anymore, that's why I had Fran fire that second shot, so I can home in on them."

"What if we walk off some sort of cliff or something? We're not in the actual conference room, remember," cautioned Junior Haskell.

"Maybe, maybe not," replied Jay.

Fran giggled. "You think we're in some sort of alternate universe, don't you, possibly a parallel dimension?"

"Oh boy, now you two are going sci-fi on me, aren't you?"

Fran slapped Junior. "Hey crap for brains, would you rather we went paranormal?"

Junior wasn't buying this approach. "Tell me one thing before we go on this wild goose chase. Why didn't your Mush creature react to those gunshots? It must have heard them."

"Not reacting in our presence doesn't mean it hasn't reacted," replied Jay.

"I wish you would stop talking in gibberish."

"Junior, I'm just saying it is here. It never left us. It's been observing us, waiting for us to make the next move."

"How can you be so sure? We can't see our hand in front of our face."

"Telepathy, it's been communicating with me."

"You sure those are not just imaginary voices inside your head, boy. Wait a minute, why are you just now telling us?"

Fran answered. "It swore him to secrecy, didn't it, Jay?"

"Sort of. Enough of this right now, Fran, place your hands on my shoulders and you do the same on Fran's, Junior. We're moving out."

26

The way Jay Meyers perceived this, the others had been returned to him with one purpose in mind, to seek the truth. He wasn't sure if he could pull off any kind of rescue, but he intended to meet this thing face to face. Take it on if necessary. The Mush Monster was at least giving him a fighting chance. What other reason would it have had for returning the others? Jay sensed the script was being written on the fly, the author as unclear of the ending as them. These granted do-overs and offered opportunities to play out the different scenarios. Eventually there would be but one outcome, the final chapter. Who would come out on top, the good toys, or the bad ones?

In his heart he now believed the others were still alive. He had heard people, lots of them. They were here close by, and he was going to find them. He held out hope that Mira would be among them. He thought about Chrissie Waldrop and wondered why she had not been tossed back into the mix. She had been part of the original group too. Maybe Mush considered that she added no value to his plot, was too weak, not a convincing foot soldier. Look at me, he thought. I'm anything but a man of combat. Don't shortchange yourself, he reminded himself. I have outlasted all of them. I've done so because for whatever reason, Mush chose me to be the unlikely hero, the challenger, the oddity in the mix.

Can a loser like me come out on top? Something about me intrigues Mush. I will not squander this opportunity. Leaders are those who strive to do the right thing, have a purpose, a vision, a goal. Leaders fight for a cause. I fit the mold, if not physically, emotionally. Leaders are not perfect. They must overcome challenges and that I have done. The protagonist in any plot must fight personal demons and undergo transformation along the way. I have certainly encountered these traits and obstacles. This will not be over until I say it is over. You're getting mighty cocky Mister Myers. You're not quite a legend yet. Sometimes you must die to reach legendary status. I'm ready for whatever Mush has to bring.

This story will evolve to a conclusion sooner or later. Mush will grow tired of playing with its new toys. When that time arrives, will Mush simply discard us and place us in its toy box, or return us to where it found us? It's my job to lobby for our return, restored order and as the military promises, no man, woman, or child left behind. Who are you, Jay Myers? What have you become? You're no GI Joe by a long shot and Rambo is out of the question. Why do I think I can pull this off, answer me you stupid slug?

I can play make believe too, Cowboys and Indians, soldiers, Superman battling Lex Luther. I've done it all my life, imagined what if I had super strength, x-ray vision, the ability to become invisible, or fly. I would settle for anyone of those powers right now. Hey Mush, can you grant me one of them to even the playing field? It's me against you when it comes right down to it, isn't it? That's why you've allowed me to survive all the challenges. I earned the right to be here. Grow up Meyers. You're becoming a legend in your own mind. If it would have wanted me, it would have taken me, just that simple.

Okay, so what now, Mister Leader, Sir? I can't see a darn thing in this excruciating blinding light, but I'm leading the others along, thinking I'm the self-appointed Seeing Eye Dog. They believe in me. Well, maybe the verdict is split. Haskell Junior Johnson hasn't drunk the Kool-Aid yet. Fran Woodward is in my corner though. That and a cup of coffee get me what? A blind hog can find the acorn occasionally. I certainly have that blind thing going for me. Fran has pointed out I'm hoggish in appearance, but I'm sure she meant that in her loving sort of way. Lard ass to the rescue, or fat boy as she likes to call me. I'm one slab of ham, that's for sure. I have a matching set of hog jowls to prove it. See, that's what I don't like about me. I've always had this knack for putting me down. Low self esteem oozes from my pores like a ruptured water line.

Mira has always scolded me for exhibiting a lack of confidence. She should see me now. I'm Mister Gung-ho, take no prisoners, fearless, never let them see me sweat, and as Fran would put it, kick butt, and take names. I hope this charade can fool Mush. Something tells me even it knows me like a book. Possibly that's why I'm still here. The underdog gets a chance to save the day. More than likely, I have one rude awakening ahead. Mush is giving me enough rope to hang myself. Just before I snatch that golden ring, it will yank the rug out from under me and bring me crashing back to earth, inflated ego no more.

Leaders have too much time to reflect. I should be using my time more wisely, like scheming a plan to conquer the enemy. Obviously, I'm not really leadership material, but I've played one in the make-believe circuit oh so many times as kid. I survived my childhood by living in a fantasy world. Back in the day I could create my perfect little world, one where bullies didn't exist, and I got the girl in the end. Well, I didn't like girls back then. My dog was my best friend as the saying goes. We were the dynamic duo when it came to slaying dragons. With him by my trusty side we could take on the world. Boy how I could use old Champ about now.

My brain is running in circles. I'm digressing too much into my pathetic past. Is that my fault or Mush's plan? Could it be picking my brain, preparing to utilize my memories against me? Whatever so be it. I should probably have Fran fire another shot and find out how close we are to the others. This will freak out Junior when we do. I think he may be more of a wimp than I am, and I didn't think that was possible for anyone. I've come a long way baby. Carrying the torch for this little band of misfits speak volumes. Mira can be proud of me.

Jay returned to reality having completed his mental assessment. It was time to put his thoughts into action.

"Fran, let's pause for a second. Take another crack at it, fire at will. Let's see how close we are."

"Come on man, you're messing up with all this shooting. I'm telling you; it's going to think it's under attack."

"Chill, Haskell, if it wanted us dead, we'd be dead already Shoot, Fran!"

She did and the chorus responded, awfully close now, catching Jay off guard. He almost felt as if he was in a stadium environment. Someone or something poked him in the chest quite aggressively, rocking him off balance. If not for Fran perched behind him, he may have landed on his duff. Jay righted himself and swatted at the air, attempting to contact the intruder. His hands simply swished thought empty air. One thing was certain, Mush was back, if it had ever left in the first place.

"We're here. What's your point, Mush? Are you going to deny us finishing this? You know, you remind me of the school yard bully. Is the dark and light just a way to protect you? Are you afraid of us without your little security blanket?"

"There you go again," whispered Junior. "You're taking things too far. Please stop antagonizing this thing."

"Pay him no never mind, Jay. Sometimes the best way to deal with the schoolyard bully is to kick sand back in his face. Hey, you, like I told you before, I'm done taking your mush madness!" Fran braced for another doss, but it didn't happen. "Show yourself. You can't be that ugly."

The light began flickering around them, resembling a series of miniature thunderstorms. Between the flashes, Jay could almost glimpse the surrounding landscape and it in no way looked like a conference room or any part of the resort he had seen so far. Sadly, he had not been able to make out any people. This disturbed Jay dramatically, shaking his newfound confidence to its core.

"Fire another shot, Fran."

She pulled the trigger. Jay heard the distinctive click. A succession of clicks followed.

"Out of ammo," exclaimed Fran.

"I thought you had more clips," inquired Jay.

"I did, but don't ask me what happened to them."

They continued to be bombarded by the strobe light phenomena. Their eyes blinked spasmodically, attempting to take in the strange scenery. Slowly but surely, they were adapting to the borage. Just as quickly as it had begun, it stopped. Now they were immersed in red light, void of any other colors. Jay thought instantly of the red planet, Mars. Ground, sky, and an endless horizon were all red, void of any shapes or forms, including the people they had been seeking. The red had replaced the bright light that had replaced the dark. Why was it that Mush's world was so one dimensional?

"Now what, ole self-appointed faithful leader," smarted off Junior. "Where are the survivors? Better still, where the are we?"

"It's like playing hide and go seek," commented Fran.

"Exactly," said Jay, thinking of his childhood seeker experiences.

"Pick your direction. It all looks the same to me," said Junior. "You wasted all those bullets for this?"

"Stop sounding like Dexter, Hon. It's unbecoming."

Jay yelled out for anyone within shouting distance but there was no response. He called out the names of Mira, Chrissie, Joe but not so much as an echo. Mush had tricked them again, brought them here, but why? Then it clicked.

"You son of a bitch, I get it."

"Get what," asked Fran.

"This, the voices, the lightshow, none of it is real. It's just more mind games."

"It looks pretty damn real to me," said Junior.

"Humor me again, please. Both of you concentrate. Think about how you remember the resort's conference room is supposed to look."

"How about you," asked Fran.

"I don't recall ever seeing it so I can't envision it. Just concentrate and remember it as it exists."

Fran squinted. Junior closed his, but nothing happened.

"Think about an event you remember, something larger than life, an occasion that means something or impacted you."

"Cleaned up after too many of them, they sort of run together."

"Please give it a try, Fran."

The reddish surroundings began to flicker, diminish, and pulsate. Jay's head swirled. He was dizzy from the shifting scene transforming before his eyes. It was working though. The almost transparent images took on a life of their own. Tables, chairs, a stage was beginning to appear. The red gave way to a multitude of colors.

The scene unraveled as if trying to tune in a weak television signal. Then boom, they were in the conference room. Nothing looked out of the ordinary for such a gathering place.

"I'll be," said Junior.

"Double damned," added Fran. "How did we do this? How'd you know?"

Jay wasn't quite ready to divulge his thoughts. Doing so exposed his weaknesses and fears. He owed them some sort of explanation though. Little white lies among strangers or recent acquaintances weren't that deceitful, were they?

"Gambling on a hunch," he finally said. "It's played on our minds in an array of ways. I thought this might be the latest. You two helped prove my suspicions."

"Now what," asked Fran.

"Now we head back to the basement."

Junior was livid. "That's just plain crazy. I'm not going back down there. That's where it wanted us to go. Have you forgotten that?"

"But it also warned us not to go to the basement at first. Bad things happened associated with the basement. It purposely kept us away until it was ready for us to be there."

"I agree with Junior on this one. Why in the hell would we go back down there? We almost burned slap up in that mausoleum."

"Because this time it is our choice and not Mush's, don't you see. It has led us around by our noses to one place then the next, all the while scaring us. The basement is still our key to an escape."

"What about the others," asked Fran, "You were on your high horse to rescue them."

"I was dead wrong on my assumption. We can't rescue them. Mush will never allow that."

"Are you now saying they're dead?"

"Junior, I don't know what they are, or where they are, but I suspect they've been used up, spent and can no longer be reclaimed as one of us."

Junior was fit to be tied. "You're as bad as this thing, leading us on all these wild goose chases. Why should we believe you, let alone follow you to that basement?"

"I can't blame you for feeling like that."

"So, we're really all that's left in this apocalyptic hell?"

"I can't say that for sure, Fran. It brought some of you back, didn't It?"

"This gets confusing by the minute," she replied.

Junior experienced one of this ah ha moments and said, "Wait a minute, Fran, don't you find it queer that he has been untouched through all this. How do we know you're not this Mush thing? Maybe you're the one that's not real. Maybe you've being playing us for fools. That's why you want us back in the basement. You've just been claiming to be a tourist."

"Touché," responded Jay. "Actually, we own the penthouse suite."

"That's your story. Fran, you sure you don't have any more bullets. I'd sure love to see you fire one at him to see if he is real or not."

"I wouldn't do if I did. You're talking foolish talk, Junior. Jay has done nothing but try to do the right thing by us."

"That's your version. He brought us here and we lost Joe a second time. We lost Dexter a second time. He said he lost the kid again too. We're next. He's never been taken at all. Don't you find that just a little strange? I know you and you know me, but we have never met this character before tonight. He claims he has this lost wife, Mira. Hell, we never saw her. She might not even be real."

"Look, you do what you want to do. I'm going to the basement and then I'm getting out of here."

"We've been to the basement and there wasn't a way out, or have you forgotten that tiny detail? It's dark as pitch and we don't have any flashlights."

"Dog crap for brains, unless you haven't taken notice, the power is back on," added Fran.

"Yeah, for how long this time; until it traps us in the basement again."

"It doesn't require the dark any longer. That phase is over. This isn't a debate and I'm not asking your permission, Junior. I'm going to the basemen and I'm taking the elevator."

"See, he's trying to trick us, Fran. He never wanted to ride the elevator before, why now? Stay away from that basement. It's a death trap. Don't get back on that elevator."

"I tell you what, Junior, if you have a better plan, I'll stick it out with you, but you need to crap or get off the pot, time's wasting."

He didn't answer. He just shifted his eyes to the floor, hands shoved in his pants pockets. Jay walked toward the conference room exit doors. Fran patted Junior on the shoulder as she passed. Junior didn't follow.

28

Jay stood at the elevator door and control panel, wondering if he had made a sound decision. The basement had been the root of all evil ever since he and Mira had arrived. And what, he was playing a hunch that somehow this trip there would be different. Haskell Junior Johnson had forced a compelling argument, so why had he been so stubborn in his conviction to go back down there? Self proclaimed leaders faced awkward and often difficult decisions while in the grip of battle. He had now tasted the not so fruitful benefits of being the man in charge. He stared at the recall button, mustering the courage to press it.

The doors opened before he had an opportunity to press the button. Mush had decided to take charge again. Jay resented the interference. This had been his decision, not Mush's. He could feel Fran's stare, waiting for him to do something. If he entered that door, he would relinquish ownership of the game back to Mush. He wasn't prepared to that. This was supposed to be his call. Supposed to be, but had Mush merely planted another seed inside his head? Maybe Mush really wanted them to return to the basement or was this Mush's way to fake him out?

It was now or never. Using Fran's terms, crap or get off the pot. Taking a deep breath, he stepped through the doorway. Fran followed. Before the door closed behind them, Jay pressed the penthouse suite button instead, attempting to double fake out Mush. The doors closed. The elevator headed toward the basement instead. This was still Jay's game to win or lose. He didn't embrace being trapped in that basement a second time. He couldn't believe Fran had remained quiet this long. Maybe she sensed the executioner approached.

He watched as the floors clicked off. His stomach retched. He could feel bile building up in his throat. Puking now would show weakness. He swallowed the acidic eruption and prepared to meet his maker, vowing he would go down swinging. To his utter surprise, the elevator stopped on the lobby level. The door swooshed open. Fran started to step off, but Jay held his arm across her chest and lightly nudged her back. This was not their floor. Mush didn't want them in the basement for whatever reason. That was perfectly clear now. Jay still had choices and maintained control of his destiny. He pressed the basement button this time. Nothing happened. The door remained open.

We could take the stairs, thought Jay. What if they exited the elevator and Mush denied them access to the stairs? It had pulled this trick often, denying entry and exit to various doors, including a clear escape to the outside. The door remained open. Jay pounded the various buttons with his closed fist. Under normal conditions they'd be zooming to an assortment of destinations, but the elevator remained locked in position. From the corner of his eye, he could tell Fran was growing antsy. His patience was hanging by a frazzled thread too. What could he do? Mush wanted them off the elevator. Was he supposed to merely roll over and obey? He had to make it to the basement. It somehow held the key.

Fran finally broke the silence. "Guess we're not driving this thing, are we?"

Jay shook his head no.

"I reckon we either stand our ground or get off then? Which is it?"

Jay shook his head no, and then half ass shrugged.

"The parking garage levels stand between us and getting there. If you're damned sure that's where we should go, then we could use the stairs."

"No good," replied Jay. "Mush is counting on us exiting the elevator. It won't allow us to use the stairs either."

 "Why are we here in the lobby? Isn't this where you started your part of the adventure?"

"I think this is the lesser of two evils, given the basement as our chosen option."

"If that's the case, why did it even allow us to use the elevator? It could have blocked us from leaving where we were."

"Fran, you hold the elevator and make sure this door doesn't close. I'll check the stairwell door and signal you if I can access it."

"Dumb question I know, but why do we need to stand guard at the elevator if it's not allowing us to use it?"

"Humor a deranged man, Fran." She smiled and moved into the elevator's doorway to prevent the door from shutting.

The stairwell entrance was located just around the corner from the elevator. Jay took a deep breath then dashed for it. He closed his eyes and then pulled the handle. The door opened. He couldn't believe it. Had he outsmarted Mush? He yelled for Fran to join him, and then waited with his body wedged between the door and doorframe. A few seconds passed and no Fran. The thought hit him. Mush wanted to separate us. Mush had snatched Fran again. How had he been so careless? Finally, he heard approaching footsteps on the tile. They were too loud to just be Fran. He could make out two distinct shadows before they rounded the corner.

"Look what the cats done drug in," announced Fran.

Jay couldn't believe his eyes. It was Mira, his wife. "How did you know who she was, Fran? You've never met her?"

"She told me, silly. That gal asked me if I had seen Jay Meyers."

Jay ran to her, clutching her in an affectionate bear hug. He had never been happier in his entire life. He had given up all hope of ever seeing Mira again and now, here she was, alive and well. "Where have you been?"

"I have no idea. I'm not even sure how I got here."

"Never mind, we can figure that out later. We're heading to the basement." Jay turned and pulled on the door. It didn't move. He yanked it again. The door held firm. "You bastard, you tricked me."

"I thought you said the door was unlocked?"

"It was, Fran, I swear. Mush lured me away from it with Mira."

"Would you prefer I leave?"

"I didn't mean it like that, Mira."

Fran asked, "No elevator or stairs, so how do we make it to the basement now?"

Mira just stood there dumbfounded, too far removed from their current situation to understand the rhetoric. Jay recognized she was a mere shell of her former self. She lacked her usual exuberance, almost seemed too lethargic. How could he really blame her? Her ordeal could have been tenfold worse than theirs. Mira had been held captive somewhere if captive was the appropriate analogy.

"My brain is fried. I've exhausted my options. I played a hunch and lost."

"Why don't we find a way to crash through the lobby doors, if they're still locked like you found them earlier? We're on the ground level. The parking and basement are below us."

The door bumped behind him and opened. Jay turned, expecting, hell, he didn't know what he expected. Standing with the door held open was Dexter Parnell, huffing and puffing, wringing wet, but a sight for sore eyes just the same.

"Did you miss me, Hon? And just where the hell have you been?"

"Too spooky up there alone," he answered. "I thought you might be headed to the basement. I heard voices on this level, familiar voices and took my chances, opened the door to check it out."

"And it opened with no problem," asked Jay.

"Yeah, I just pressed the push bar."

"What are you up to, Mush," whispered Jay.

"Who's the lady?"

"Meet Jay's wife, Mira."

"Where'd you find her?"

"She found us," answered Jay.

"Does she know where the rest of them are?"

 "Afraid not, she has no memory of what happened and where she has been. She just sort of keeps blinking out on us."

"Bomber, so why are you in the lobby?"

"Detour, Dexter, but just a short one, let's head down."

"Not to the basement again, why not go check the lobby doors and get out of here?"

"Mush has them locked down," Jay sort of lied. He hadn't checked them this visit but suspected there had been no reprieve. He didn't really care, possessed in making it to the basement. He pushed past Dexter, holding the door, with Mira in tow. Fran followed and Dexter dropped in behind them. The lights remained on. Jay opened the door leading into the basement. There was no sign of a fire, nor smell of smoke. The blazing fire had been a brain plant as suspected. The single truck bay door and man door were the only exits, just as before, so what made this visit different? He probed his brain. Surely, he had an explanation for returning, a purpose, or some sort of grand scheme. Blanks, he drew nothing but blanks.

"All right, let's have it," said Dexter. "Other than the power on and lighting our way, now what, surely you have some sort of plan, don't you? And what happened to Junior?"

"Junior decided not to join us. The power is on because Mush has decided such. That truck door should operator now, right?"

"All right then, let's give that door another try." She walked over and pressed the OPEN button. It didn't as much grunt. She tried the man door too, same.

"Something has been bothering me," said Jay. "Mush took us to the lobby. It also made sure we couldn't use either the elevator or stairwell to get here. You just so happened along, and the door opened easily. Why you? Why then, just a minute later? That seems just too odd, Dexter."

"It beats me, it just opened. You should thank me. You're here where you apparently wanted to be."

"Why did you really return to the basement, Dexter?"

"It was freaking me out to be by myself."

"You're the same guy hiding in that cooler, by yourself and kept saying you wished you were back there. Solitude never bothered you before."

"We've been through a lot. It has a way of sprouting new perspectives."

"No, this is all wrong. You're not Dexter. If you are, Mush is controlling you. Our host is covertly using you to control the situation."

"That's crazy. You're crazy."

"No denying it, I'm totally bonkers. Who wouldn't be after dealing with this, but you're not Dexter? That's a fact. You disappeared and now you have reappeared. Why should I believe anything that comes from your mouth?"

"Tell him, Fran, he has lost it."

"Who hasn't? You must admit, ole pal, that it does sort of make sense. You've been quite the flip flopper from the get-go. Friends, meet Mush," announced Jay.

Dexter pointed his finger at Jay. "You're just plain loony. Keep your distance." The lights flickered but didn't go out.

Jay looked at the ceiling, and then back at Dexter. "You're losing your grip aren't you, Mush?"

"You think I did that."

"In your anger, I do. It shows weakness. You're floundering, aren't you? That's why you had to take human form."

Dexter threw his hands into the air and almost instantly the elevator instrument panel began lighting up like a Christmas tree. The door opened and then closed, repeated the actions, over and over. The phone began ringing. Smoke detectors alarmed without probable cause.

"This is like in *Poltergeist*," shouted Fran.

Jay rushed Dexter, tackling him and it was quite impressive, considering he had never played any serious football. He yelled for Fran to find something to restrain him. She snatched up a roll of duct tape. Mira just stood there, mesmerized by the antics, offering no assistance.

29

Jay stood beside Fran and Mira, assessing Dexter Parnell's duct taped incarceration. His hands were taped together behind his back. His ankles were secured with tape, legs stretched out directly in front of him. Their captive was in a sitting position on the floor. Jay had taken the liberty to tape his mouth shut too. He conveyed no remorse for his actions, convinced that the individual before him was either Mush in the flesh or Dexter Parnell possessed and controlled by the Mush Monster. Fran hadn't hesitated in hog tying him, as she called it. Mira remained neutral and despondent but watched as the saga unfolded.

Duct taping Dexter had killed some time and should have offered Jay an opportunity to formulate a plan, at least a purpose for returning to the basement. He had not utilized his time wisely unfortunately and had no explanation for putting them in this precarious position a second time. So far neither Fran nor Mira had pushed the issue. This was indeed a sad set of affairs, tying up one's own, but until he could decipher the truth, he really had no other choice.

Fran shifted her position and stepped into Jay's line of view. Here it came, he surmised. She was about to ask him about his intentions. He scrambled for an answer, anticipating her question, something viable and believable. He still wasn't sure why the urge had struck him, but he knew this was the key to the mystery or at least their escape. How could that be if he couldn't solve the puzzle? The pieces were here. They had to be. Jay just needed to piece them together. He hated jig saw puzzles and had never been good at them.

"Duct tape, not just a man's tool," smiled Fran, happy about her handy work. "You think ole Dexter is really the thing that has been messing with us the whole time?"

Jay scratched his ear and eyed Dexter, "I don't suppose I can be a hundred percent sure but there were too many anomalies to suit me."

"Figure on this one, how about it? If Dexter is our culprit, and I'm not saying he's not, what makes you think hog tying him is going to keep him from having his way with us? I don't really think Mush needs use of his limbs and vocal cords to do whatever the hell it wants to do. I mean, we've been dealing with stuff of supernatural proportions, and I say that comes out of his brain and not out of his appendages."

Jay hated to admit that what Fran had said did make sense. He still wasn't convinced this had been the wrong thing to do. Sometimes a leader must make difficult and unpopular decisions. Sometimes they're the wrong ones but often they're dead on. One must take the necessary precautions to prevent the big train wreck.

"Just thinking, what if it had gained control of Dexter's body and now it up and decides to use one of us instead? Let's just say it goes inside of you next. Mira and I will be screwed royally. One man will be tied up and the other one will be the monster. I don't like those odds, not one little bit."

"Do you want to set him free and take that chance?"

"I'm just talking out loud, figuring on what might go wrong if we've bound an innocent feller or if it snatches another body. *Body Snatchers*, tell me you saw the original movie or at least one of the remakes."

"Fran, movies are not real life."

"Hold them horses, what about the *Amityville Horror* or the *Entity*, those were based on factual occurrences, unexplained and unsolved mysteries. Hell Jay, we could have one of those unfolding before our very eyes."

Jay should be thankful that the momentary diversion had fended off any questions from Fran on a plan to either conquer the evil or pave way their escape. He had a temporary reprieve. He held Mira in his arms for now, drawing comfort from her being here. Sure, they still had a long way to go in reconciling their problems, but events like these were supposed to make you stronger, draw you closer to one another.

"Jay, are you going to just act like a lump on or log or answer me. Am I going to have to duct tape you too?"

The lights blinked like strobes. The phone was ringing again. Dexter shook his head and attempted to use his eyes to convince them he wasn't doing it. They weren't buying it, or at least Jay wasn't. Mira broke away from Jay and answered the phone. Fran and Jay watched as she responded to the mystery caller with a series of Yes and No answers. Her movements were jerky, almost too robotic. One could expect those mannerisms from a person in shock, figured Jay, trying to justify her antics.

Fran spoke first after she placed the phone back down. "Who was it, Hon?"

"I don't know."

"What did the caller want?" asked Jay.

"For us to die, and we will if we stay in the basement. We must go to the lobby. The doors are open there. We are offered our freedom. This is over. We have passed the test."

"Test, we've been tested for what, by whom," asked Jay.

"We must go to the lobby, now." Mira began walking toward the elevator.

Dexter was screaming a muffled yell through the duct tape and thrashing about like someone having an epileptic seizure. He slammed the back of his head against the wall and his bound feet against the floor. The man had really lost it this time, thought Jay, confirming that they had done the right thing. He rushed to thwart Mira's attempt to enter the elevator; the doors already open waiting her arrival. Jay stepped in front of his zombie wife and gently grasped her by both arms. "Mira, honey, listen to me, the voice on that telephone was our enemy, Mush. It wants us back in that lobby. Mush thrives on chaos, deceit, and manipulation."

Mira stared at him with cold empty eyes. Jay wasn't sure she had even heard him. He softly instructed her to come with him and attempted to redirect her. She stood fast, anchored to her position. Jay tugged a little harder. Her rigidity rejected his influence. Jay repositioned his hands on her shoulders and again tried to turn her. She blinked, resembling someone awakening from a deep drug induced sleep. Mira looked into his eyes and smiled. Jay returned the smile; thankful Mira was snapping out of it.

Mira then placed her hands-on Jay's forearms, his hands still resting on her shoulders. Before he could speak a few words of encouragement she clamped down on his flesh with a vice like grip. Pain rippled down Jay's arms. Her eyes were no longer the pools of dark brown. Instead, Jay thought he now stared into those of a dangerous predator, great white shark coming to mind, black and callous, evil, and forbidding. At that moment, Jay knew he was being held firmly in the clutches of Mush. Dexter had been trying to warn them that he wasn't the threat. Mira was.

"Fight it, Mira. Don't allow it to control you," he pleaded with her.

The grip held firm. Mira took a step forward, steering Jay towards the elevator. Fran realized what was happening and rushed to Jay's aid. She attempted to pry one of Mira's hands free, but it wouldn't budge. This little gal possessed amazing strength, thought Fran. Jay looked at Fran, terror blazing in his eyes. Fran recognized the concern and tried to wedge her fingers between Mira's. She managed to free one finger and worked on the next only to see the first finger reattach its grip. Fran was getting nowhere, fast. Dexter helplessly mumbled through his duct tape and jerked about, attempting to signal to the others to free him so he could help them. Caught up in the moment, neither so much as gave him a courtesy glance. The duct tape did its thing, offering him no hope of escaping. He watched helplessly as Fran and Jay grappled with the female that wasn't. Mira took another step, pushing Jay to the elevator while dragging Fran along. Fran became more assertive in her efforts and slapped Mira across the face, attempting to jar her from her trance.

"What are you doing? Don't hit my wife like that, please."

"Does the little woman always manhandle you like this? Get real. She's a demon, possessed by the shadow monster." Fran searched for something she could cold cock this gal with and spotted a broom propped up in the corner. She could use that wooden handle like a baseball bat and knock it out of the park. She sprinted to retrieve it.

Jay saw what she intended to do and yelled, "Don't do it, Fran. She's not herself. You won't be hitting it. You'll be hitting her."

Fran hesitated, taking in what Jay had just said, and then she did the only thing she could do and nailed Mira with a full blow across the top of her noggin. Blood trickled from an open gash to confirm this gal was Jay's wife in the flesh. She almost immediately regretted her little maneuver, almost. The next blow caught Mira in the ribcage. The sound left no doubt that Fran had cracked a few of the gal's ribs. This time Mira turned her head slightly and smiled at Fran, a creepy little demonic smile directly from a scene in the *Exorcist*. She even resembled Linda Blair's character, thought Fran. She expected to see green puke spew from her mouth next.

"She's zombie-fied and can't feel a thing," shouted Fran.

"Just stop beating on her. You could kill her."

"Then what the hell do you want me to do, watch her carry your butt into that elevator and back to the land of the lost? Sorry, I can't do that. You're misguided by what you want her to be. You're not seeing the forest for the trees, old buddy." With that Fran whacked her across her forearms. Miraculously, her arms went limp, freeing Jay.

"This is a damn nightmare," yelled Jay. "It can't be happening. Mira, please, fight it, don't give up. I love you."

"This is why you're my favorite, Jay Meyers. Love can conquer all. You never have to say you're sorry, correct? I so enjoy your melodramatic moments. I adore your persistence and belief in good conquering evil. Good guys always wear white, right? You, the unlikely hero, so priceless and fresh, maintain hope to the bitter end. Stay in the shadows away from the bullies. Maybe they will not notice you and pick on someone else. Ah, but when there is no one else around, you are in the spotlight and you do not cherish being in the spotlight, or do you?"

Jay and Fran were captivated, almost hypnotically by Mira's words, Mush's words. Even Dexter had ceased his struggling to listen to what Mush-Mira had to say. The game had changed again with the introduction of actual dialogue, utilizing Mira as a spiritual medium or conduit for communication. Jay had wanted to talk it out and now he had his opportunity.

Fran stepped in. "What have you done with the others? Are they alive?"

"Fran Woodward, the she warrior, you are my second most favorite character. I almost dismissed you earlier, but I must admit, you add something to the mix, you with Jay Meyers. I had to bring you back for a well-deserved encore. You two are the perfect blend, the reincarnated odd couple, new and improved version of course. Your blend of styles adds a refreshing twist, keeping me on the edge of my seat."

"Is this some sort of mass alien abduction you got going for you? You do talk like you might be one of them space fellers from another planet straight out of a science fiction movie."

Mira clapped her hands. "*Close Encounters of the Third Kind*, how quaint. I so enjoy your analogies and references to the cinema."

"Are you from another plant," asked Jay.

"How many times have this been blamed on UFO's, strange lights in the sky, stealing away earthlings for experimental purposes, all so priceless. The human mind is such a terrific kaleidoscope. One's imagination has endless possibilities."

"You still haven't answered her question."

"People go missing all the time, a long series of unsolved mysteries. Children end up on milk cartons or their faces on posters, stapled and displayed across the vast landscape. Your friend Junior has gone poof again. Odd, don't you think? The fear of serial killers and pedophiles has grown by leaps and bounds, epic proportions, some of them even apprehended and held responsible for the atrocities. Still, so many go unaccounted for, love ones' lives destroyed, not knowing what really happened. That is so sad but part of playing the game as you have so dubbed this special occasion. Or is this a war, the final battle, mankind's destruction, the Armageddon, and Apocalypse rolled into one? Inquiring minds do wish to know. Double your pleasure, double your fun; isn't that the way of the commercial? By the way, you really should free your friend, so he can participate in these reindeer games. Duct tape, with it, a man can fix anything, or in this case, a woman. I do apologize, Fran Woodward. You are an equal. You've come a long way, baby." Mira chuckled, and it was not a familiar laugh to Jay's ears.

"So, you're not going to tell us, then, you alien bastard," fumed Fran. "And what the hell did you do to Junior, this time?"

"That's for me to know and you to find out. Hide and seek, now that's your game, isn't it, Jay Meyers? Hide from the fat boy and always pick him last. That so devastated you, didn't it, to be picked last or never picked at all? How humiliating peers can make one feel. Ah, but one must have peers first. No one ever treated you as their equal, did they, Jay Meyers?"

Jay remained quiet, too rattled by the rhetoric, hitting too close to home to suit him. Mira spouting this nonstop rhetoric had him in a tailspin. He had almost withdrawn, his worst childhood experiences resurfacing.

"Are you a spirit, a ghost or some lost soul," asked Fran.

"Ah, the second most selected explanation for the unknown, Casper, the unfriendly ghost, those things that go bump in the night. Spooks and goblins haunting the houses and cemeteries. Restless souls unable to find their way to the hereafter, and instead they choose to terrorize those among the living. Too often they don't realize that they have departed this world. The million-dollar question: when the haunting begins, who are you going to call, *The Ghost Busters* or *Ghost Hunters*?"

Jay finally spoke up, "Why all this dark stuff? Is that where you reside, in the dark? Do you fear the light?"

Mush-Mira tossed back her head and laughed loudly. The blood had already dried on her scalp, some visible on her forehead. "Darkness cannot drive out darkness. Only light can do that. Hate cannot drive out hate. Only love can do that. You can't study the darkness by flooding it with light. We can easily forgive a child who is afraid of the dark, but the real tragedy of life is when men are afraid of the light. Into the darkness they go, the wise and the lovely. Darkness always had its part to play. Without it, how would we know when we walked into the light? It's only when its ambitions become too grandiose that it must be opposed, disciplined, sometimes, if necessary, brought down for a time. Then it will rise again, as it must. There is darkness inside all of us, though mine is more dangerous than most. Still, we all have it, that part of our soul that is irreparably damaged by the very trials and tribulations of life. We are what we are because of it, or perhaps despite of it. Some use it as a shield to hide behind. Others usen it as an excuse to do unconscionable things. But truly, the darkness is simply a piece of the whole, neither good nor evil unless you make it so. Death doesn't exist. It never did. It never will. But we've drawn so many pictures of it, so many years trying to pin it down, to comprehend it, thinking of it as an entity, strangely alive and greedy. All it is, however, is a stopped watch, a loss, an end, darkness, nothing more."

"This is just gibberish. I've read or heard many of those quotes you've jumbled into one. You have no originality. Can you not speak for yourself and dismiss all these riddles and nonsense? *Fear can only grow in darkness. Once we face fear with light, we win.*"

"I see you are astute in embellishing mankind's' quotes too. Accurately stated it goes like this, *Fear can only grow in darkness. Once I face fear with light, I win.* You must not plagiarize, Jay Myers. It is not the American way. Now China, on the other hand, has no scruples, and will steal shamelessly, patents posing no obstacles, mere scribbling of nothingness on parchment. They will win the trade war and bring the land of the free to its knees. Tough love, lessons learned, you cannot spend more than you take in, simple math, only fools choose to ignore it and the conservative values."

"So, you're into politics too?"

"I am all about everything, little to do about nothing. Jay Myers, I do so adore you. You have successfully emerged from your shell these precious hours. We should embrace this feat and together celebrate your coming out party, a man to no longer be taken lightly, forcefully stumbling onward, challenging that what he does not understand and no longer fears. Sadly, you should have discovered this, Jay Meyers, in your youth, and you could have nipped it in the bud, those ghastly encounters with the bullies of your day. Nip it, nip it, nip it. Barney is such a hoot, isn't he. Unfortunately, this isn't Mayberry, is it Fran Woodward. You can surely appreciate my television references. You do have the gift and that makes you special and dear to my heart also."

Fran had de-duct-taped Dexter Parnell. Both temporarily kept their distance from the Mush-Mira thing, unsure where this might be heading, but obviously sensing the ball was not in their court. Jay glared at the face of Mira Meyers, wondering if she would return to him or forever be lost. He held out little hope for any of them escaping. Talk was cheap and this conversation would end sooner or later, and with it, what would come next?

30

Jay methodically replayed the events since arriving at The Big Blue Resort, trying to piece something together that would explain this extraordinary phenomenon. He hoped by doing so he could devise a counter action to free them from Mush's clutches. He had one thing on his side. This, whatever it was, apparently liked him or his character representation. He had to use that to his advantage at all cost and stall for time, if indeed time played a factor now. He fretted about Mira's injuries, even though she seemed oblivious of them. Perhaps, being in her comatose or possessed state was a blessing in disguise. Fran had certainly delivered several severe blows, so the likelihood for substantial injury seemed inevitable.

Were they the only remaining four beings on earth, wondered Jay, or were Mush's references to Armageddon and the Apocalypse meant to mislead them? Why would it use these terms unless there was some merit in it doing so? Surely, he could not be that special to be singled out as one of the few survivors. Jay wondered if there was some basis for two men and two women. Surely it could not be for reproductive purposes, repopulation of the planet. He and Mira's relationship were strained at best, and they weren't the most fertile of the land. Jay wasn't sure Fran could offer up a child, given the mileage on her body. Dexter wasn't prime beef either. Nope, their existence could be discounted for any sexual purposes for sure. He almost laughed out loud, thinking Fran would probably take exception to that argument, given some of her previous comments.

What was this obsession with dark and light? It had played on their fears, spooking them about creatures lurking in the shadows, the boogeyman so to speak. Jay decided to pose the question. "You can't be destroyed by the light, can you, or the bleach?"

Mush-Mira laughed at the mere mention. "Without hope, all is lost, don't you agree? Isn't it deliciously sinister to give the audience what it wants, those scary images of an enemy yet
identified? People thrive on fear and love to be terrified of something. What better than a force that can't be seen and resides on

the fringes of one's imagination? You must admit, the lurking menace in the darkness added plenty of gotcha moments. Those images of wormholes and vortexes were quite effective."

"You're one sick bastard," yelled Dexter.

"Dexter Parnell, chef extraordinaire, the one cowering in an icebox with no regard for those for whom you were responsible. Whatever happened to the master chef always goes down with the kitchen? And so indecisive, you're in, you're out, let's do it, let's don't, you lead, and I'll follow, or was that every man and woman for themselves? How thoughtless, the way you treated your daytime friend, nighttime lover, Fran Woodward."

"Cut him some slack," spoke up Fran.

"Fran Woodward of Annie get your gun fame, let's not be too naïve. You wanted more and Dexter Parnell always delivered less. Oh, how I anguished, allowing Dexter Parnell to have more chances than a cat has lives. This man is no woman's man. Sorry Fran Woodward, nor is he a man's man. Allow me to provide a hook to hang your hat, Fran Woodward, something even you can understand. If auditioning for a theatrical performance, Dexter Parnell would be a shoe in *for Doctor Zachary Smith* of *Lost in Space* fame. Have no fear, Smith is here. Dexter Parnell is quite untrustworthy when the rubber meets the road or possibly more accurately articulated, when the pasta hits the wall. Did you know his claim to be a master chef is a mere farce? His credentials are, can we say, a bit of a stretch. His previous experience was one who dished out hash at a middle of nowhere rest stop, a diner-gas and go. One can fabricate the most believable work history on Resumes Are Us software. Confession is good for the soul, Dexter Parnell. So, cough up the goods or forever hold your peace, so thank you God."

"Doctor Smith, I couldn't have pegged you better," said Fran. "What did I ever see in you?"

"Dominatrix my dear, you have always strived for that top position, haven't you Fran Woodward. Your way or the highway! Dexter

Parnell served as the best vehicle for you to hone your skills, perfect your techniques and quench your thirst."

"Can't you see? This thing is just trying to turn us against one another, drive a wedge between us, another trick in its arsenal. I for one am tired of this bull. Why don't you just finish us off? Save the suspense for someone who really gives a damn."

"Bravo, another classic performance, indeed, Jay Myers" applauded Mush-Mira.

"I've listened to this long enough," announced Jay. "Let's talk brass tacks, if you can really provide honest and direct answers instead of hiding behind the curtain like the masterful Wizard of OZ."

"And who do I have here before me, the resurrected Cowardly Lion? Growl like you mean it, fat boy."

"First, just exactly what are you?"

"What am I? Just what exactly am I? You put so much importance on taglines and titles, gender, and race, real or is it Memorex? What do you wish me to be? What eases your ego? What makes me more acceptable? How much imagery can you really stand? Let's recap. You have accused me of being a space alien, a spirit, and the walking dead, searching for my final resting place while making your lives miserable in the meantime. Could I be the legendary Sasquatch? Are you searching for Bigfoot, maybe? I'm cuddly enough to be the Easter Bunny and just cunning enough to pass for the Tooth Fairy? I could be a hybrid of both with just enough Santa mixed in to deliver the goods. Ooh, I have it. I am Satan, or maybe the offspring of the Devil, Son of Lucifer. That would explain my evil intent, wouldn't it? I've got it. Jay Meyers, you are dreaming. Wake up and it is no more. Possibly you are participating in Fran's dream, or Mira's."

"I should have expected as much from you, no straight answers. Are you afraid to tell us what you really are? Does it make you more vulnerable?"

"Ooh, now you're trying to psyche me out. I like it, challenge me to the truth. *Frankly, you can't handle the truth.* That's one of my favorite lines, yours too, isn't it, Fran Woodward?"

"How badly hurt is my wife? What would happen if you exited her body?"

"Excellent questions, you have given this some thought, haven't you? Should we give it a test spin and see? Just what if my presence is the only thing keeping Mira Meyers among the living? Aren't we just tingly all over anticipating the outcome? You really buy into these fictional portrayals of possession, don't you? Mere movie magic, aren't they, Fran Woodward? Why does one have to partake of the inside of the body experience to assume total body control? Have you not heard of telepathy? I seem to recall you have been accusing me of mind control numerous times. Mind over matter, does it really matter in the big scheme of things? I am her. She is me and we are family."

Jay couldn't get over the fact that this garbage was spitting out of his wife's mouth. Nothing about it sounded like Mira except her voice. Her facial expressions were exaggerated, almost as if she were overreaching her part. Her arms hung limp by her sides, the bruising hideously black and blue from where Fran had whacked her with the broom handle. He feared she had suffered broken or fractured bones in both. There was no doubt Fran had cracked some of her ribs and most likely she had a concussion. The puppet speaking on behalf of Mush showed no obvious signs of pain or discomfort.

"Can you at least share with us your origin? Is it of our world, another planet, maybe beyond our solar system or something purely supernatural?"

"Why is it you think so small, Jay Meyers? Maybe I am the beginning, the middle, and the end of all there is. I could be your universe, your reason for existence, even your God. Without me, there is no you. Consider that."

"Why are you doing this to us? What do you get from it?"

"Give and take, take, and give, what does it really matter? Think how fortunate you are, Jay Meyers. Consider an insect's life cycle. Mortality, it runs you down sooner or later. Do you believe your time to die has been predetermined at your birth? You can't alter the future or change the past. Live for the present, baby, as if it's your last day. Do you have a last wish, Jay Meyers?"

"Does this mean you're about to commute our death sentences?"

"Negative vibes, never a positive way to end your day," laughed Mush-Mira.

Fran and Dexter exchanged looks. This was getting out of hand and tiresome. Fran liked it better when it stayed in the dark and didn't speak at all. All this nonsensical conversation had worn out its welcome. The thought hit her. What if she killed the host, would the parasite inside die too? She had already battered Mira Myers up pretty good, but she was still alive and breathing. Stop the breathing, snuff out the one depending on her to breath. It sounded logical. Jay wouldn't embrace this, but he would get over it, especially if it resulted in their freedom. She contemplated including Dexter in on her plan, then thought about Doctor Smith, the wimp and turncoat. Smith would always cash in any opportunity to better his standings with the villains. She had no doubt now that Dexter would probably follow that same blueprint to CYA.

Fran wished she still had her loaded pistol. One pop and she could test her theory. The broom handle didn't offer her the element of surprise. She doubted if either Jay or the puppeteer would allow her to close the gap and deliver the final blow. Listen to me, she realized, I sound like a hired assassin. She was considering murder, wasn't she? Not necessarily, if Mira was already a lost cause. She could be simply putting her out of her misery. After all, she had already attacked the gal once and hadn't considered the consequences then, why dwell on them, now.

Dexter, utilize him as a diversion, without him knowing why, that's what she had to do. She watched and waited, eying Jay and his once upon a time wife, biding her time and looking for an opening. The

Mira thing and Jay were almost nose to nose now. Jay was about to kiss her, it appeared. Fran struck. She nailed Dexter, full swing with the broom handle in his breadbasket. Dexter doubled over and collapsed to the floor, holding his mid section, breath knocked out of him and unable to talk. She concealed the broom to her blindside and ran toward Jay and Mira, screaming that Mush had just attacked Dexter. Jay took the bait. Mira didn't. Fran was tossed through the air by an invisible force, dislodging the broom from her clutches. She landed on a heap of crates, tumbling head over and heels, coming to a rest motionless. Jay wasn't sure what had happened to Dexter or Fran, or why, but it left no doubt in his mind that Mush-Mira had served some sort of warning.

"Why did you do that?

 "Disobedience must not go unpunished."

"Do you thrive on pain and chaos, or what?"

Mira never diverted her attention, staying focused on Jay, caring less if the others survived her or its wrath. "Pawns, merely pawns, dime a dozen and totally replaceable, I assure you, Jay Meyers. We have more important things to settle, you and I."

Jay, in his best cat like move, caressed both sides of Mush-Mira's face and laid a deep, sloppy, passionate kiss on her. She, it didn't fight or resist the kiss. Still holding her face in his hands, he backed out of the kiss, looked into her eyes, hoping to see any glimmer of his wife.

"Pain, chaos, pleasure and so forth, what's love got to do with it? Fran Woodward would have named that tune, if able, and the artist who sang it, *Tina Turner*."

"You felt nothing?"

"Coupling among species doesn't always result in romance, unique, but not always affective. I do respect your innovation, Jay Meyers, another one of your surprising qualities. But tell me, weren't yours and your wife's relationship strained? Is that not why you traveled to this destination?"

"How could you know something like that? I forgot. You can get inside our heads, our thoughts, make us see and do things against our will."

"I understand my characters, their traits, likes and dislikes, inner most thoughts and just what makes them tick. Would you expect anything less from me?"

"I've said it and I'll say it again. You're just a big kid and we're your toys. Isn't that true? You draw pleasure from playing out various scenes with us, just for your own entertainment. You have absolutely no respect for anything. You are indeed a real monster."

"Sticks and stones, ouch, but what you say does hold some merit. Life is but a cabaret, my friend."

"What are you, the cliché master? Can you not think or do for yourself?"

"On the contrary, Jay Meyers, I do what I wish, or should I say, you do what I wish. Your distractions are quite deceitful. Do not think they go unnoticed or unpunished. I do appreciate the creativity. You are quite the anomaly, but don't for a second confuse the independence as a sign of freewill or a door to your escape."

"Let me get this straight you damn control freak. You like playing with me and you adore that I have a mind of my own, but you're in no way willing to relinquish total control to me. Do you fear I am a threat or more an equal than you dare admit? Me against you, with no strings attached, what you say?"

"Jay Meyers, you dare challenge me?" A thunderous laugh ensued, rattling the basement. "This is simply delightful and yet another unexpected excursion. *And if you'd care to take a dare, I'll make a bet with you. Now you play a pretty good fiddle, boy, but give the devil his due. I bet a fiddle of gold against your soul, 'cos I think I'm better than you.*

"My name's Jay and it might be a sin, but I'll take your bet, you're gonna regret, 'cos I'm the best that's ever been. I know the lyrics. Charlie Daniels is one of my favorites. Maybe we should play a round of name that tune. I'd clean your clock."

"Tell me then, Jay Meyers, how does this little contest work? I will give you the honors."

"First answer me this. If I escape this resort, have you destroyed the remainder of the world? I must know or there is really no point in continuing, is there?"

"But that is the same old contest. What's the appeal in that? The carrot dangles for you to find out. Are you the last man standing? It sends shivers down your spine, doesn't it?"

Jay struggled with this thing talking through Mira. This was like their very worst fight ever. He attempted to block it out. "My game, my goal, my terms, why should this matter to you? Tell you what, why not we sweeten the pot? When I escape, you release the others, and you go away forever and leave us alone. Is that enough excitement for you?"

"What do I win when you fail?"

"You get me."

"Silly man, I already have you."

"The devil gets my soul, then."

"Your soul does not interest me. How about this? Jay Meyers continues to be Jay Meyers, freewill and determined. There are endless scenarios and plots and together we play them to an ending. You exist in my version of your hell."

"Whatever, it's your dime. By the way, please inflict no more harm to Mira, Fran, and Dexter. Just ignore them but allow them to referee. They determine the winner."

"I agree to two. I choose which one plays and which to sit out. As for the winner or loser, Jay Meyers escapes, or Jay Meyers remains with me forever."

"Pick."

"Dexter Parnell, he will be your challenger. We take this to the limit. My word is my bond. "

"Does this mean you free Mira?

"Indeed, I am Dexter Parnell, Dexter Parnell is me."

"What does this do for her? I mean, will she survive without you?"

"That rests entirely in your hands. How does one mend a broken body?"

"No deal unless you promise she lives."

"She's alive, she's alive! I would suggest seeking medical attention for her, but then, that would assume Jay Meyers wins."

"Let's even the playing field, unless you're afraid I can whip you."

"I am supposed to interpret that, how?"

"You play the role of mere mortal, Dexter against me. You can use no mind control, no illusions, no invisible barriers or forces and no super strength. It's Dexter and his fortitude against me and mine, the ultimate fantasy for you."

"Dexter Parnell verses Jay Meyers it is. Mira Meyers is giddy all over. I fear we will have but one referee, Fran Woodward. I'm not so sure your dear beloved will be up for the task." Mira collapsed to the floor and then Dexter tapped Jay on the shoulder. "Shall we begin?"

"Let me have a mere word with Fran to tell her what we are about to do. You can revive her, can't you?"

"Road hard and put up wet, but willing and able to mount the steed one more time, rise my dear." Fran did, groggy headed but moving.

Jay first positioned Mira, making her as comfortable as possible. She was breathing but barely. Jay stepped in front of Fran, his back to Dexter. "Fran, are you with me?"

"With you, it takes more than what this bastard has to take me down for the count."

"Mush is inside Dexter. He and I are about to do battle. If I can escape, we win, and everyone is rescued, and life is restored. You're the designated referee. You do remember the movie *Butch Cassidy and the Sundance Kid*, don't you?"

"One of my favorites," she grinned.

"Picture the knife fight with Butch and that monster outlaw. Go with it, okay."

"I'm all over it. Is this thing going to have all those supernatural powers?"

"Nope, not if Mush is agreeing to my terms and can be trusted."

"You should be able to take Dexter, then. Good luck. If not, tag me in, I can kick his ass."

"Here goes nothing."

31

"Let's get ready to rumble," yelled Dexter, a sparkle in his yes. "Join me in the center ring."

Jay walked toward Dexter, delivering an over handed right, glancing harmlessly off Dexter's cheek. Jay was no fighter and the blow had merely been a poor attempt at a surprise attack and not a show of superior strength. The thing called Dexter rubbed his cheek, feeling the slight sting. Pain, how exhilarating, it thought. Dexter balled up his right fist and held it up to his face, rotating it to the left and then the right. Jay took advantage and buried a fist into Dexter's belly, not having the same affect that Fran had delivered with the broom handle.

Jay quickly realized this may have been a bad idea; not because Dexter possessed an athletic body by any stretch of the imagination, but instead, because he didn't. Thinking too much while fighting deemed to be a bad idea as well. Dexter's fist struck a solid blow to Jay's chin sending him backwards and crashing to the floor. Fran watched, stifling a yell to cheer him on, trying to appear neutral in her referee role. She could have counted him out twice. He was hardly moving. Jay was no match, even for Dexter with Mush in tow.

"Fran Woodward, do you deem this fight over and declare me the winner?"

"We didn't really establish any rules or time limits, so how can I declare you winner by knock out? Am I supposed to count him out or what?" She was stalling, hoping Jay would come around, possibly catch a second wind.

He groaned, moved slightly. His rubbed his chin. Jay propped up on his elbows, eyes still blurry, but trying to shake it off. Things came into focus. He saw Dexter standing over him, less than four feet away. He sucked in a deep breath and slowly made it to one knee.

"Get up," Fran whispered.

"Shall we continue, then, Jay Meyers?" Dexter assisted him to his feet. "Surely, you do intend making this more of a contest. I had looked forward to an actual donnybrook. Please don't disappoint me by rolling over too easily."

Jay stood on wobbly legs. He could not win, and he knew it. He looked at Mush-Dexter and said, "I'm not sure what I was thinking when I called you out. I'm no fighter. I've always run from fights."

"This is your moment, an opportunity at redemption. Take one for the poor pathetic bullied race," said Dexter. "Surely, you stand for something, Jay Meyers. Make me proud. I believed and that is why you exist."

"I can't. That's not who I am. You hold onto false hope. Look at me. I'm no hero. I'm no leader. I'm an overweight middle-aged failure. It was foolish for me to think I could stand up to you and deliver mankind from the clutches of evil and total obliteration. I'm nobody. I've been good at being nobody all my life. New deal, keep me and I'll play out your little story lines with you. Just let the others go."

"You're tarnished goods, I'm afraid. You're no longer in A-1 mint condition, a collector's edition. How can I possibly view Jay Meyers as I once did? You are a flawed character, beyond repair. You, like so many others, are common, nothing special. You have ruined this for me. I had expected better. You showed true grit and promise."

"I beg you. Whatever the hell you are, do something good. Perhaps you will feel special, a new experience."

"Good versus Evil, what a novel idea. Deciphering right from wrong, how quant. Navigating with a moral compass, warm and fuzzy feelings oozing from my pores, makes for a feel-good moment and possibly a group hug. Jay Meyers, you are different indeed, a unique character among those flawed around you. Welcome back. My instincts are justified. You are the chosen one, the defender, doer of good deeds, consumed by doing the right thing. Now, take a breath. Contemplate how you will attempt to defeat Dexter Parnell in the flesh, one on one, no strings attached. Dig deep. Find inner strength. This battle is far from over. Certainly, Jay Meyers will not allow the baker man the upper hand."

"None of this makes any sense. How can you be one thing and then another?"

"I do not understand your question, Jay Meyers."

"I go back to the beginning once more. You lurked in the shadows like a coward and there you stole people shamelessly. You played on our fears. You gave us the impression that you were flawed, fearful of the light and then something as simple as a cleaning compound. You lied to us. You made us think we were seeing things, hearing, and seeing loved ones and friends. You controlled our lives, herding us through your maze. Why should I believe you intend to make this a fair fight?"

"Impressive, you have given this some thought, Jay Meyers. I encourage you to explore your analysis. It is all so human like. The world is never as it seems. Perfection does not exist. To survive and succeed, you must recognize this, adjust, and often make allowances. You did this courageously."

"What the hell are you babbling about, now?"

"Temper, temper, it is so unbecoming Jay Meyers and not one of your best character traits."

Jay embraced the stall tactics, figuring if he kept Mush talking, he delayed the inevitable. Maybe he could outwit Mush. Who was he fooling? This thing was not about to allow him to win, physically or intellectually. He slipped in a peek at Fran. She held her position, remained uncharacteristically quiet. This was probably a good thing given the situation. Mush seemed more focused on him and would most likely not tolerate a distraction. He just hoped she had caught his drift and would act when the time came; and it would come, sooner or later, no doubt.

"Speechless, Jay Meyers, then allow me to breakdown my analogy in terms even you should understand. Humans function on emotions, a flaw that can always be used to one's advantage if one intends to be victorious. The fear of the dark, a common phobia, and playing pranks on those who fear the darkness is common practice. You must overcome those fears to thrive in chaos. False premise, chemicals for instance, is merely illusion to lure one's prey and devour them at will. To quote untruths, mere ploys, there is no honor among thieves. As for hearing and seeing these things, Jay Meyers, you seek warmth in those who make you feel comfortable and safe, nothing more. I merely cultivate. Fair fights, Jay Meyers, never bring a knife to a gun fight, is that not another localism? I ask you once again, do we finish this, or do you vanish as those who have vanished before Jay Meyers?"

Things were spiraling out of control. Jay was no strategist. Out thinking his opponent seemed an impossible feat. Dexter Parnell stood before him, but he was not the Dexter Parnell, not in the whole. An entity, something supernatural or alien had possessed the man, controlled his thoughts, and while it made claims of mortal strength and capabilities, how could he really be sure? Furthermore, Mira lay crumbled in a heap, and she badly required medical attention. If he could not defeat this thing that challenged him, she would die. Everyone would die or simply vanish. Did mankind truly hinge on his actions, his ability to defeat evil? Can good always defeat evil? Was he good enough to defeat evil? What was true evil, anyway? Up until now he had never really thought about it or had faced it.

Why couldn't this just be that bad dream, the one you wake from and then forget? Jay couldn't rationalize a method to the madness. Just what was this thing and why did it feed on us? There seemed no rhyme and reason supporting Mush's existence. Revenge didn't seem to be a factor, nor did some urgency to conquer the world, dominate the universe. Nope, this entire fiasco felt too childlike in a way, and Jay clung to his belief that humans were mere toys, breakable ones at that, and this thing was learning to play with them. He couldn't shake the feeling. If Mush was indeed a child, then he should be able to spank his ass, send him to timeout, but there was more to it, wasn't there?

"A penny for your thoughts, Jay Meyers," spoke up Dexter.

"What, you're nor reading my every thought?"

"I am a mere mortal for the time being, as agreed, your terms, not mine, Jay Meyers."

"If I kill Dexter Parnell, will you cease to exist too?"

"Are you really prepared to commit murder to receive your answer? Your justice system does frond on such dastardly deeds, does it not?"

"Don't kill Dexter," pleaded Fran. "He's not the enemy. This thing is just using him. Make it cry uncle or pin it or something. Remember, I'm the designated referee. I decide the winner."

"Spoken like a true official, now shall we continue our little encounter, Jay Meyers?"

"One last question."

"Ask your question then."

"We were told that you had been here before, this very place, many years ago. Those who staffed the hotel then vanished and so did you. Why did you return?"

"A rewrite, unfinished business, I was in search of answers too and I found you, the ultimate answer to my prayers, Jay Meyers."

"Prayers! Give me a break. You are incapable of prayers."

Jay lunged toward the Dexter hybrid, hoping to catch Mush off guard. It with cat like dexterity, twirled, stepping sideways like some martial arts expert, causing Jay to merely stumble past. For good measure, Dexter backhanded Jay across his cheek, the slap jarring Jay's teeth and stunning him. Dexter couldn't possess such agility, so Mush wasn't being completely honest about its capabilities. Jay paused and rubbed his aching reddened cheek. The Dexter thing stood its ground and smiled.

"This is quite invigorating, Jay Meyers. I must commend you on your marvelous suggestion. Surely you will not allow this to be so one sided."

"Take him, Jay," encouraged Fran.

"I must warn you my dear Fran Woodward to not dishonor yourself by displaying bias. You must remain neutral to judge this contest fairly or I shall be forced to strip of your sworn duty."

"I don't remember the swearing part, but I will call the fight, win, or lose. You just refrain from using those superpowers or I will disqualify you for not abiding by the preset rules. Dexter is not a fighter either, so how about backing off and let him fend for himself."

"I assure you; I am not utilizing anything abnormal. I, as Dexter, possess the same strength and mechanics as does he. I am merely controlling them, channeling his strength and agility."

While distracted, Jay made another maneuver, grabbing Dexter from behind and placing him in a strangle hold. He hoped he could choke him into an unconscious state. Dexter began moving clockwise, gaining speed as he spun. Just like that, Jay was suspended off the floor, the centrifugal force sending his legs out straight and suspended in the air. He remembered how his dad used to spin him like this until he became drunk as a skunk. Déjà vu, the counter response was working, his head becoming woozy. Mush increased the speed of the spin, obviously not impacted by dizziness, yet more evidence that Dexter wasn't really Dexter and was a no-good cheater.

Airborne, Jay landed face down on the floor several feet away, his elbows and knees burning in sheer pain from the impact. His breath had been slightly knocked from his lungs. The room was rotating. He could not stand. For good measure, Dexter placed his foot in the center of Jay's upper back, striking a victory pose. Jay waited for Fran to conduct the customary count out. Instead, he heard an unfamiliar sound, something mechanical had been fired up, was roaring to life. Jay caught a whiff of diesel fuel.

32

Jay attempted to right himself, eager to zero in on the engine now sputtering to life. There sat Fran in the forklift's seat. All things electrical and mechanical were apparently working with Mush now pretending to be a human Dexter Parnell. The question at hand, what was Fran up to on that yellow front loader? She had raised the twin forks to a level of about five feet and was making a quick right turn. She wasn't targeting Dexter. Instead, she was moving away in the opposite direction. Had she misunderstood his instructions?

The Dexter Parnell thing took note but for all practical purposes appeared to remain in character. It hadn't thwarted whatever Fran was attempting to accomplish. Possibly, curiosity had gotten the best of Mush too. Fran floored the gas. Her speed increased three-fold. Jay spotted her destination. Full speed now, the dock door in the crosshairs. Taking full advantage of equipment now operating and Mush's distraction with the fight, she intended to ram through the truck bay door. And crash she did, the forks imbedding in the middle of the door and Fran ripping it free and crashing through carrying the door along for the ride. The welcome sunshine poured in, the same sunshine that had once been thought to spell Mush's doom. Dexter Parnell stood unfazed by the sudden burst of light. Lies, it had been a bunch of lies. Neither sun light nor bleach had ever been a valid threat. Jay would have made haste his escape if not for Mira. He could not leave her behind.

"Bravo," clapped Dexter. "Lesson learned. Dexter Parnell, the human, can be distracted but not deterred from his mission. With no referee, how shall we finish what we have started, Jay Meyers? Might this be to the death after all?"

"I'll ask again. With Dexter's death what becomes of you?"

"And with your death Jay Meyers what becomes of you? Is there an afterlife for either of us? Shall we solve the mystery and satisfy our curiosity?"

"Why is this so important to you? Why does there have to be a winner and a loser? There is no purpose that I can understand. Can't we simply coexist?"

"What would be the fun in that? Where is your sense of adventure, Jay Meyers?"

"I lost all my sense when you entered the picture. People vanishing took the wind out of my sails. Look there. That's my wife. If she doesn't receive medical attention she might die. What you say we shake hands and end this?" Jay took a step toward Dexter extending his hand. The Dexter thing didn't reciprocate.

"All God's creation's have an expiration date. You are no different, Jay Myers."

"What do you know of our God, or any God as far as that goes? Do you believe in God as the creator?"

"Dexter Parnell believes. He has been praying to your God, pleading as a matter of fact. Dexter Parnell wishes your God to strike me dead. Can your God do that, Jay Myers? Or is it mere fairytale and wishful thinking to believe in something as mighty as whatever you think I am or might not be?"

"Perhaps, we both do." Jay lunged forward burying the extended blade of the boxcutter deeply into Dexter's midsection.

The expression on Dexter's face was not one of pain, but rather a mixture of surprise, blended with a slight smile. "I've never experienced pain before. It is quite exhilarating, something I think your people call a rush." Blood trickled from the wound. Jay twisted the blade.

"Bringing a knife to a fair fight, Jay Meyers; you have indeed evolved and outdone yourself."

Jay didn't respond. Instead, he turned and aided his wife, leaving the boxcutter imbedded in Dexter's gut. Dexter remained standing, swaying a bit but he made no attempt to remove the blade. Jay could no longer hear the forklift's engine nor had Fran returned. He didn't blame her for not coming back. If not for Mira, he would have been hauling ass too. Mira groaned just a tad when he touched her shoulder, but she did not open her eyes. Her condition had worsened. Jay kept a watchful eye on Dexter still standing there and bleeding out on the floor. Dexter remained alert and observing him but said nothing. That disturbed Jay. Just what was the creature up to now? Could Mush be dying? Could it die? Mush had refused to answer that question.

The deal had been to fight this out to the very end with Mush remaining in Dexter's body. Could a monster be trusted to keep its word? Time would tell. The lights flickered. Should he interpret that as a sign of the creature's dwindling power, or was Mush exiting Dexter, reneging on the agreement? Jay needed to focus on the task at hand, exiting the building with Mira while the getting was good. Easier said than done, turning his back on his nemesis. Dexter 'Mush' Parnell remained silent but still alert. Fire burned in his eyes.

"Mira, I'm going to help you to your feet. Tell me if I hurt you." Jay grabbed her by her forearms. She screamed. Her eyes were open. She frantically looked about wildly. Jay released his grip. He had forgotten that Fran had broken her arms with the broom handle, an attempt to kill Mush when it was inside her.

"No pain, no gain, Jay Meyers," spoke up Mush still occupying Dexter Parnell.

"Kiss my big ole butt," yelled Jay, giving him a quick glance, blood still leaking from the boxcutter wound. "Why don't you just do us a favor and die?"

"How much blood must Dexter Parnell spill before this act is complete, Jay Meyers? I have no control over his bodily functions, not to that extent." Dexter touched the wound and then held his hand to his face. He suckled each finger, smacking his lips as he tasted the blood. "Metallic, interesting, isn't it?"

Kneeling by Mira, Jay's hand contacted a broom, probably the same one Fran had used. He clutched it, stood, and closed the distance in one swift move whacking Dexter squarely across the bridge of his nose. Dexter plummeted backwards, feet momentarily leaving the floor from the force of Jay's strike. Jay did not stop there. He whaled away at Dexter's head until his bloody face was no longer recognizable. Jay, realizing what he had just done, dropped the broom and then fell to his knees. He sobbed, the tears flowing as if they had been bottled up for a lifetime. He had committed murder, something he would have never been capable of doing until now. He had hit his breaking point and had done the unthinkable, killed a fellow man. No, this was no man, he attempted to remind himself. Dexter had to be sacrificed. Was Mush dead too? The body lay lifeless.

This was no time to dilly dally. On the off-chance Mush had somehow survived, he needed to get the hell out of here and locate medical attention for Mira if the world still existed out there. He must hold on to that hope. Insanity lurked in the shadows, but he was not ready to succumb to it quite yet. Jay was startled by movement from the corner of his eye. He twirled expecting the worst. Standing there and mustering up a smile was Mira or was it.

How had Mira gained consciousness that quickly and stood without assistance while possessing two broken arms? Jay risked another quick look at the crumpled Dexter Parnell before returning his attention to Mira. She smiled at him. Jay did not return a smile still unsure. Instead, he did the unthinkable. He squatted and removed the boxcutter from Dexter's lifeless body. The wet stickiness of blood smeared his fingers and palms. A deal was a deal, but how could he prove if this person standing before him was indeed his wife?

Mira's screams jolted him from his quandary. "Jay, please help me! What's happening? Who did this to me? It hurts! Please make it stop!"

"We agreed to a fair fight, Mush, with Dexter only. Are you true to your word?"

Crying openly, Mira responded, "Who are you talking to Jay and what is Mush?"

Think Jay, look for something, some sign to quench your suspicions. Wait, Mush always addresses me with both names, Jay Meyers. She only said Jay, not Jay Meyers. Still, how is she so suddenly alert? Life is not supposed to be this difficult. It never has been for me in the past. Okay, simple, do I love this woman? Yes. Can I trust her? Yes, but only if she is Mira. How can I really be sure? If Mush is inside her, does he have access to her memories? Of course, it does. Mush becomes that person. Can I really hang my hat on the fact that she addressed me only as Jay, and not Jay Meyers? Can I trust Mush's pattern? Can I trust him as being a feign of his word?

"Jay, why aren't you helping me? What's wrong?" Mira then unleashed another blood curdling scream. "Is that a dead person behind you? Jay, did you do that?"

Jay suddenly realized how this must look. There was Dexter Parnell, a bloody mess and here he stood holding an equally bloody boxcutter in his bloodied hands. Circumstantial evidence could be so misleading. How could he possibly defend the obvious crime scene Mira had discovered? He swallowed. His mouth suddenly felt as if an elephant had crapped inside it. Before he could muster up a response, her next words cut him like the boxcutter he still held firmly in his hand.

"Jay, did you do this to me?" Her arms still dangling by her sides, she stepped backwards a couple of steps.

Regardless to how this must look, Jay could not release the boxcutter. He replicated her move and took two steps forward, never breaking eye contact. Their trust and relationship had been questionable when they had arrived at the resort yesterday. They had high hopes of mending broken fences, but now, did she think he had agreed to come here just so he could murder her? How could he explain what he had done to Dexter Parnell? Exorcising a demon would never fly. Up until recently, he would have never bought into it either.

"Mira, this isn't how it looks. Trust me, please. You know I don't have a violent bone in my body. Look at me. You know me. I've never laid a hand on you in my life."

"Why are you holding that knife? Why is it bloodied? Who is that person on the floor? Are they dead?"

"Please try to remember anything. Just think about what happened after we arrived here yesterday."

Mira looked about frantically not recognizing the surroundings. "Where are we?"

"We're in the resort's basement."

"Why would we be down here, Jay? Did you bring me here? Why can't I move my arms? Why do they hurt so?"

"They're broken. I didn't bring you here. I promise."

"I don't know about this, Jay. Please don't come any closer. I've got to think and it's tough to think right now. I hurt like hell. What happened to that person over there?"

Oh man. I am screwed. This headed downhill fast if I tell Mira I killed Dexter Parnell. I did not think I would ever wish Mush back, but without its presence, how can I plea my case. I would not believe what has happened if I hadn't lived through it. This sort of stuff only happens in the movies or on the pages of novels, not in real life, not in my life. How can I explain this in terms that will be believable? The truth, just tell her the truth. She will either buy it or she won't. My guess is she won't. Why would she? What's my plan when she doesn't? I am not cut out for this, and now I'm now a natural born killer.

"It's complicated, Mira, especially when your memory loss is muddying my explanation."

"Complicated, just answer the questions, Jay. It's simple. Did you do this to me and to that person?'

"I never harmed you, Mira. My word is my bond."

"What about that body lying on the floor behind you?"

"I had to do what I did to protect everybody."

"What does that mean, Jay, to protect everybody? We're the only ones here."

Jay tightened his grip on the boxcutter, frustrated and baffled as to how he could justify his actions in terms she would understand and accept. He rubbed his forehead unaware that he was smearing it with Dexter's blood. Mira was aware and took another step backwards. She wasn't sure who this man was waving the knife about covered in a stranger's blood and her suffering from extensive injuries. There was something terribly wrong with this picture.

"We're all that's left. There's no one else here."

"That's the first thing you've said that sort of makes sense, Jay. I don't see anyone else here but you, me, and that person on the floor. It explains nothing."

"Work with me. I'm trying like hell to make you understand. Everybody in this resort has vanished. We're it. Strange forces have been in control. It was inside you earlier. Fran clobbered you with a broom handle. That's how your arms were broken and how you received that injury to your head."

"Fran…who is this Fran person, Jay? Is she the bloody mess at your feet?"

"No, Fran Woodward is the manager in charge of the staff that cleans the rooms here. The guy on the floor is Dexter Parnell, the resort's chef."

"Jay, you killed the resort's chef, why? Did you kill the Woodward woman too?"

"No, Fran drove a forklift through that bay door over there. I haven't seen here since."

"Was she escaping from you, Jay?"

"No, she was escaping from Mush."

"Mush? You're making no sense, Jay."

"Mush was inside you and Fran thought by killing you, she could kill it. I thought the same about Dexter."

"Then you did kill this man, Dexter?"

"He wasn't Dexter when I did. You must believe me."

Mira was one to always use her hands when she talked. She found it exceedingly difficult to focus with both hanging limply by her sides. It clouded her thinking, that, and the extreme pain. "Jay, there is nothing you are saying that is believable right now. I'm not even sure who you are or what you have become."

This is going about as well as I would have expected. Why would she believe any of this garbage? We lived a normal life until arriving here. Well, normal is an over statement. We came here because we were having marital problems. That hasn't exactly improved. Now she thinks I'm a deranged homicidal maniac, not exactly the perfect recipe to mend a broken heart, or broken arms and a bashed skull.

"We really do need to get out of here and find you some medical help."

"Jay, I think you're the one who needs medical help."

"Listen to me, Mira. I love you. I always have and always will. I know we have had some issues, but we can work through them. That's why we came here in the first place. I never expected to be in a battle for my life with forces I didn't understand. It happened and I can't undo it. I just hope there is a world outside these walls for us."

"World for us, those are mighty powerful words, Jay. Our world doesn't look too bright right now. Jay, you murdered a chef. I'm not convinced you didn't try to murder me. Words are not going to mend this mess."

"I know all of this is extremely difficult to take in, but I assure you, I am not the enemy." Jay slowly moved toward Mira. She had backed herself into a corner and had nowhere to go. He now stood less than two feet away. Eyeing the blade, she couldn't even hold up her hands to defend herself. Footfalls, they both turned.

"It's Fran," whispered Jay. "She'll back up what I have said."

The gunshot echoed through the basement.

33

The smoking barrel of the gun indicated justice had been served.

"Are you all right," asked Fran.

"Thank you, but why did you have to shoot?"

"I saw the blade. He looked like he was about to kill you dead. We couldn't have that, now, could we?"

"He's my husband, Jay Meyers."

"I know who he is, Mira, honey. We go way back. Well, at least we go back a day, but a lot has happened since I met your hubby. He was special to the very end, but we must right the wrong. It's the American way. I've certainly learned plenty; let me tell you that. We should probably get the hell out of here if you're up to it. I have my jeep outside."

"Is he…"

"Oh yeah, deader than hell, I'm a deadeye when it comes to firing this baby, Mira. I retrieved it from my vehicle. I have a concealed weapon license and this puppy came in handy, didn't it? It's tough to beat a good magnum. Ask ole *Dirty Harry*, one tough hombre he was, good ole *Harry Callahan*, make my day. *Clint Eastwood*, from *Rawhide* fame, played him."

"I don't understand any of this."

"What's to understand? You really need to watch more action movies. We're alive and well, fair and square. I'll do my best to fill you in later. Right now, I say we get the hell out of Dodge. Now that *Matt Dillon, the Marshall of Dodge City*, that's who the hell we needed here. He would have kicked butt and won it for the guys in white hats. *Gun Smoke* was one of the best westerns on the tube. We have a whole new frontier ahead out there. The world is at our fingertips. It's time we got us some breathing room, don't you think, Mira Meyers?"

"Mrs. Woodward, what should we do about them? He was my husband and I understand that guy over there was the resort chef."

"Ah mush, you can call me Fran. I say we make like horse hockey and vanish down the ole trail right now. In the words of *Scarlet O'Hara*, '*tomorrow will be another day*.' That's one of my favorite movies, *Gone with the Wind*. There was a lot of butt kicking in that one let me tell you. Scarlet, she let that hunky Rhett slip right through her fingertips. Not me, I always get my man."

"I like you, Fran Woodward."

"What's not to like, Mira Meyers. I am everyone's dream come true, or nightmare; depends on which side of the fence you find yourself. You're quite the character too. That's what I like about you. You're special. I saw that in you from the get-go. Your chariot awaits you, Princess. Let's go visit the kingdom below before darkness gets the best of us. Farewell Camelot and long live the king, *Elvis* that is. I surely did like ole swivel hips. He was one of my favorite characters. He was special too, right up to the bitter end. Some people just don't appreciate what they got until it's gone. Poof, in thin air, just like that."

Epilogue

I, Roderick Habersham, best selling author, always struggle when I am developing a new novel. It's a work in process. That should explain to you why the journey deviated so many times without the glint of a warning. Sometimes I can be indecisive when I am working the plot and evolving the characters. I hope my characters appreciated my anguish. I had originally chosen Jay Myers as the likely hero in my story. I allowed the Mush Monster to toss everything it had at him. I even allowed 'Fat Boy' to inch close to understanding the concept of the creature he faced, the analogy of a child playing with toys, me changing the manuscript this way and then that, unorthodox I do confess. Still, he proved to be just too weak to defeat the monster of his nightmares.

I considered Injun Joe briefly but made him too spiritual with an approach that became almost too logical to take on a creature that defied man's logic. Then there was Fran Woodward, a spitfire indeed, piss and vinegar, my words, not hers. She had the spunk to close the deal, even with her reckless redneck ways. I gave most of the characters a fighting chance, hopeful that one would rise to the occasion and solve the mystery behind the one dubbed Mush. A protagonist was tough to cultivate from the struggling and bumbling assembled cast. I did embrace the Mush Monster and it's ever evolving approach to making these people's lives a living hell. I concluded that evil in this case was just too powerful to allow it to be defeated. I allowed Fran to point out this fact, how in today's novels and movies the good guys don't always come out on top.

I so enjoy leaving my readers with an unexpected twist, something that they could have never possibly envisioned as the ending. Jay Myers carrying the torch dies when one least expects it and by the hands of his gun packing sidekick. And then there is always the dangling carrot, the cliff hanger. The readers still don't have a clue what the Mush Monster was and where it originated. Worsened their fears and frustration, Mush now possesses Fran Woodward. This opens the certainty of a sequel, book 2, the saga continues. Questions never answered. Was this merely isolated to the remote resort in the Smokey Mountains or was it a worldwide apocalyptic event? Inquiring minds wish to know. Only I can provide that ending totally dependent on the success and marketing of this novel. I hold the audience captive as did Mush. Only I decide when the game is over, and it is time to place my toys back in the toy box. No brag, just fact. Rise to the occasion readers if you want more. Sales determine if I finish this or move on to another unrelated book.

Who has the audacity to ring my doorbell at this time of the night? Do they not understand the significance of a fence and gate? I require privacy. I earned this right and demand that the autograph seekers abide by my wishes or endure my wrath. I could ignore the uninvited and unannounced visitor, or I could dress them down for their rude encroachment. Perhaps I should just dial 911 and report the breach, allow due process to run its course. I have no patience for this. Persistent, ringing the bell was not enough. Now you must pound on my front door. Very well, beware what you wish to accomplish. You'll not receive a friendly welcome at this hour.

"Might I ask what prompts you to knock on my door uninvited at this hour? You are trespassing on private property. Please evacuate my personal space. Be gone immediately."

"Excuse me Mister *Steven King* wantabe, sir, but what makes you think you're in charge of this dang spine tingler? I'm pulling rank on you with one of those *Twilight Zone* moments. I just loved those twists even better than yours. My friend Mira Myers here could use a hand, maybe two, thanks to you. Maybe it wasn't you after all. Poor gal has two flopping arms, cracked ribs and bump on her noggin, compliments of me, uh…us and she needs medical attention. By the way, allow me to introduce myself. I'm the real Boogeyman, your personal worst nightmare, the final ending to your absolute best novel to date."

"Fran Woodward, impossible, you're just the nemesis in my novel, created from my imagination, no more. What sort of sick joke is this?"

"And you, Mister Roderick Habersham, are but just one more of the playthings in my big ole toy box. Not to worry, let's just get this over with, how about it? Face the facts, son. You've been mushing with the wrong varmint and now it's you who's absent upon MY arrival. You're not that special after all, but fret not Hon, this will be painless. I'll make sure the last scene appears in your stupid little book, but it is simply pure fantasy. Fun times are ahead for one and all. Surely there's a keeper among you, a worthy protagonist I believe you call them. I reckon that's for me to find out. Roderick Habersham, come on down. I so loved the *Price is Right*. That *Bob Barker* was hunk, wasn't he?"

"Impossible, I created those characters and you."

"Surely you know better than that, Roderick Habersham. Plots, characters, twists, and tangled webs add to the suspense. Mira Myers, you had just a bit part in this and now your time has come and gone."

"You're not real. I created you."

"On the contrary, Roderick Habersham, it was I that was responsible for you, no collaboration intended I assure you."

"Fran Woodward was my character as were the others, including you, Mush Monster."

"Don't belittle yourself during your last seconds of existence, Roderick Habersham. Now stop being such a gawker through that peephole and open the door. Or let's just make it easy, I'll open it for you. Ready or not, here I come, Sweetie. The End Begins Now. You call me Mister Mush, origins unknown, just the way you and I like it. Oh yeah, and you can kiss my grits. Let the fun times commence, closing scene and credits rolling that is…Mush Monster portrayed by none other than Mush Monster. Now wasn't this a doggone hoot?"

About the Author T. Allen Winn

Winn began writing in 2003 while being cooped up in hotels during business travel. Completing a 650 page so called novel he became hooked. The homegrown Abbeville, South Carolina boy embraced the experience completing one novel and then leaping into the next one, fun and therapy at the time. That changed in 2011 when a chance encounter brought stranger and new neighbor Bob O'Brien to his Pawley's Island doorsteps. Bob did not realize the neighborhood home had been sold and apologized when Tom greeted him instead of the man he had expected to see. Book in hand, Bob had just published his first novel, The Toppled Pawn and explained the previous neighbor had shown interest in writing. Tom remarked he dabbled in writing to which Bob asked, do you have a manuscript? Tom replied 'ten'. Bob had just started Prose Press, a publishing company and suggested publishing one. You cannot make this stuff up.

T. Allen Winn's first novel, Road Rage joined the ranks of the published a few months later, and he owes a special thanks to Bob O'Brien for making this possible, publishing Winn's first seven books. Detective Trudy Wagner emerged as a main character in Road Rage prompting three more books in the series (North of the border, Tithes and Offerings and Trudy Wagner Southern Belle.) In 2016, T. Allen Winn established Buttermilk Books, his publishing company and has now published forty books. He and his wife reside on the South Carolina Grand Strand.

Ole 'T' does not write a specific genre. He writes what strikes his fancy. If you don't see something that fits your reading wheelhouse, tell him what you like, and he might just write it for you.

Books are available on Amazon or online where books are sold. Select books are available at Calabash Photography, Art and Curios in Calabash, S.C. Or *Message* T. Allen Winn on Facebook to arrange delivery of signed copies, or to schedule him to speak at an event or book club.

Fiction from T. Allen Winn
The Perfect Spook House
Dark Thirty
Lou Who
Raw Ride, a Wild West Zombie Apocalyptic Shoot'um Up
The Man Who Met the Mouse
Mister Twix Mystery, a Cat Scene Investigation
Come Here, Getouttahere, Tyler's Tail Wagging Tale
The Tenth Elemental
Last Stand on the Grand Strand
The Lord's Last Acres
Covert 19, 2020 A Devil of a Year
The Sot and The Savior
Outside the Clique
Guns and Ashes, Four Friends at a Fish Fry
Forced Family Fun, God Bless the Whiteside's
Throwback Christmas
Grandpire, A Boy, His Dog and His Vampire
Absent on Arrival

The Detective Trudy Wagner series
Road Rage
North of the Border
Tithes and Offerings
Trudy Wagner, Southern Belle, the Prequel to Road Rage

Bigfoot Trilogy
Book 1: Foot, Tree Knockers and Rock Throwers
Book 2: Another Foot, What Really Happened to D.B. Cooper
Book 3: Final Foot, Willow Creek

Non-Fiction from T. Allen Winn
Being Bentley, A Dog Like No Other
December's Darkest Day, While I Breathe, I Hope
The Hardwood Walker of Port Harrelson Road
Cuz, My Brother, Life is Good, God is Good

Memoirs
The Caregiver's Son, Outside the Window Looking In

Vol 1: Cornbread and Buttermilk
Vol 2: Don't Sit Naked in a Grits Tree
Pushed Into the Pull, Thank You Cuz
The Endless Mulligan, Short Shots from the Golf Whomper

Books with Co-Author Benji Greeson
About Abbeville, South Carolina Football
It's All About the 'A'
It's All About the Angels in the Backfield

Biographies
Clay Page, Somewhere In Between
Screw It, Let's Ride, The Legend Bub Lollis
The Horry County Pickers
Grits and Grace, A Life Not Lived